DEVIL'S KLOOF: THE COMPLETE ADVENTURES OF THE MAJOR, VOLUME 6

DEVIL'S KLOOF
The Complete
Adventures of the

Major

VOLUME 6

BY

L. PATRICK GREENE

ILLUSTRATED BY

WILLIAM M. ALLISON

COVER BY

WILLIAM REUSSWIG

ALTUS
PRESS

2024

TABLE OF CONTENTS

DEVIL'S KLOOF

CHAPTER I
Streets of Cape Town

A FIERCE southeast wind was blowing, warning the seasoned residents of Cape Town to seek the warmth and shelter of their homes. The white cloud, which all that day had been hovering like a white, damask cloth above Table Mountain, darkened and spilled itself down the steep slopes, fogging the valleys and making the town a place of howling desolation.

For a little while the winding streets were alive with a cosmopolitan horde of hurrying people, but soon they were deserted, left to the white police and their native helpers, to an occasional belated merrymaker and to those who preferred to work when the fogs swirl down and the street lights flicker.

Addison Street was even more deserted than the others. In its whole length there seemed to be but the two men who had met under a lamp light. One was a policeman; the other, a man in evening dress, wearing an opera hat rakishly tilted to one side.

1

"Evenin' officer," he drawled affectedly—and a monocle gleamed in his right eye. "Regular London particular, eh, what? And cold! My word! Thought this was supposed to be the bally tropics?"

He shivered and made a great show of swinging his arms in order to induce circulation.

The officer looked at him suspiciously.

"What are you doing out alone this time of night, Percy?" he asked.

"I am on my way to my hotel. And my name is not Percy; it's Aubrey St. John Major. But you may call me Major, dear old pal of my youth, if it pleases you."

"What's the name of your hotel, Willie?" the other asked stolidly, ignoring the opportunity offered him.

"The Mason—and my name is *not*—"

"Better get to it then," the policeman interrupted curtly. "Know the way?"

"Oh rather: Yes, quite! I proceed in the way I was going for a little way, then I take a side street—"

"Better keep off the side streets, tonight, Reggie, and go the long way home. It'll be shorter."

"My word!" exclaimed the man who called himself Major. "You're a very exasperating fellow. Of course I shall take the short cut to my hotel, and my name is *not* Reggie. It is—"

"I heard you the first time, Algy. And you be warned by one who knows—you keep to the main streets an' keep in the middle of 'em."

"But why, old thing?"

"New to the town ain't you? Just come out?"

"Well—er—yes. I think it would be correct to say I've just—er—come out."

THE POLICEMAN nodded. "Thought so. You look that way. Look as if only the other day you was hanging around stage doors, doing the lardy-dah! I wish you'd tell me something I've always wanted to know; why do chaps like you wear a window in one eye. If your eyesight's bad, why don't you wear specs?"

"That's a poser, dear old representative of the law. But you wouldn't expect a one legged man to wear two cork ones, would you? No! Of course not. So, having only one eye weak—"

"Thought it was your brain," the other growled.

He of the monocle appeared to consider this.

"Maybe you're right. On the other hand a monocle does improve the appearance, don't you think? Paints the lily, as it were; provides that final touch of—er—elegance, what? Oh, well—I must toddle along. But why must I keep to the middle of the street?"

"Because there's men in this town that 'ud cut your throat for a quid. You're just the kind they get fat on— damned fool dudes who ought to be tied to their mamma's apron strings. Good night."

He turned on his heel and clumped off down the street muttering something about, "Another damn fool remittance man who thinks he's still in London."

The monocled man beamed after him, an expression of boyish good humor on his smooth, clean-shaven face; then, whistling cheerfully, he continued on his way.

Presently he turned down a narrow alley leading off Addison Street, and here, by reason of the murky gloom, was forced to proceed at a slower pace.

He was conscious of some one ahead of him, could vaguely discern two shadowy shapes. Voices, muffled by the fog, sounded as if raised in argument. The voices sounded louder: a man's in threatening anger, a woman's tearful and entreating. The shapes presently materialized out of the yellow murk and "the Major," as he had already begun to be called—for this was early in his South African career—saw ahead of him a woman and a man. The woman was crouching back against the wall, cringing, looking up in fear at the stick the man raised threateningly above her head.

"Help!" she screamed as the stick was brought down with brutal force.

The stick was raised again, but before it could fall the Major rushed up and wrested it from the man's hand. Instantly, two other men rushed out from a doorway where they had been hiding and closed in on the Major, hitting out blindly, kicking, cursing. Their very eagerness to finish him quickly proved their undoing, for they got in each other's way and made it possible for the Major to shift his ground so that his back was against the wall.

"This is most extraordinary," he gasped, and caught one of the men flush on the point of the jaw with a powerful uppercut, sending him over backward, striking his head with a thud on the hard pavement.

THE OTHER two attacked half-heartedly; cursing and blaspheming, gasping in pain whenever one of the monocled man's blows got home, and that was frequently, for despite his soft, helpless appearance, he delivered his blows with the strength and precision of a well trained boxer.

Presently his attackers wavered, calling upon the fallen man to get up and help them. When he failed to reply and their intended victim left his position, carrying the fight to them, they lost their courage entirely and, taking to their heels, vanished into the gloom which had spewed them forth.

The Major, scarcely breathed, turned to the woman, intending to offer to escort her to her home.

She was bending over the fallen man whose limbs were now stirring feebly with returning consciousness.

"If you'll allow me, madam," the Major began with a courtly bow.

She jumped to her feet at that and rushed at him, threatening to tear his eyes out, accusing him of attacking her innocent, harmless man, making the night echo with her strident cries.

He retreated before her savage onslaught, protesting feebly, shielding his face with his arms, sighing with relief when she finally left him and returned to minister to the man he had knocked out.

"My good woman," he protested timidly, "I assure you I meant no harm. Had I known that you and your—er— worthy partner were simply indulging in one of the little luxuries of—er—connubial bliss, I wouldn't have interfered for the world. Positively. I thought—I give you my word!— that he was going to knock *you* out. Of course, I couldn't see very well—hence my mistake. I—er—"

His voice trailed off into silence at her wordless snarl of contempt.

He bowed again and said, "Then, in that case, I'll bid you a very good night."

He turned on his heel, but, as if that was the cue for which she was waiting, she rushed after him, wildly brandishing the stick with which only a little while ago her man had appeared to threaten her.

"You ain't goin' to get away as easy as all that, mister!" she cried. "Not if I know it. You killed my man and you're goin' to pay for it."

As she spoke she struck at him again and again, blows meant to kill, blows which missed their objective by reason of the Major's uncanny intuition and agility.

He found breath, beside, to expostulate with the woman and, finally, when fearing that his cries would call out other denizens of Cape Town's cosmopolitan underworld he sought to take refuge in flight, he found his way blocked by a tall man whose bearded face was spasmodically lighted by the red, glowing end of a cigar.

BETTER STAY and have it out with her," the newcomer said sardonically. "Why don't you knock the cat out?"

"Oh, really!" the Major protested, glancing over his shoulder, relieved to find that the woman had gone back to her mate and was sitting on the pavement beside him, holding his head in her lap.

"Oh—I see," the other said. "I thought for a moment you were one of the gang. What was it all about?"

The Major briefly recounted what had happened.

The other laughed.

"God! You must be soft. Don't you realize yet that it was all a put up job?"

"You mean?"

"Why, the man pretended to thrash his woman, pretty sure you'd butt in. Then, they planned to do you in with help of the other two, take all your valuables, strip you—and you'd be another brutal murder."

" 'Pon my soul! And they nearly succeeded. The officer was right. I ought to be tied to my—er—mother's apron strings still."

The other struck a match, shielded it with his cupped hands so that its yellow, flickering light shone in the Major's face.

"A monocled dude, eh!" he exclaimed.

"It's a wonder they didn't kill you."

He let the match fall to the ground, where it flickered for a moment then went out.

The woman came running to them again, sobbing, cursing.

"The blighter! He's killed Piet! He's killed Piet!"

The newcomer interposed himself between the woman and the Major, placed a restraining hand on her arm. Curiously, she submitted willingly to his authority.

"Let me deal with her," he said over his shoulder. Then to the woman, roughly, "Shut your fool squawking, there's nothing the matter with your Piet. He's only shamming so that this gentleman here won't hit him again. Here—let's go and have a look at him."

The two moved away and bent over the man called Piet. A match flared, then another and another. The Major watched them uneasily, half inclined to join them, half inclined to hurry away, wondering at their low, murmuring conversation, impatient at the lengthy time that the inspection of Piet's injuries took.

"I say—" he began nervously, and moved an impatient step toward them.

THE TALL man rose swiftly and came to intercept him. The woman remained on her knees, sobbing softly.

"He's in a bad way," he whispered. "I am no doctor, but I should say he's split his skull. You'd better get away from here before those others come back with more of their kidney to help them. Where are you staying?"

"At the Mason. But—"

"Good," the other interrupted. "You go on there, and I'll stay here and help the woman get her chap to a doctor. I'll bring you the doc's verdict to the hotel. Who shall I ask for?"

"Major—Aubrey St. John Major. But I say, this is awfully good of you. I—"

"Not a word, old man. You'd do the same for me, I know. Off you go now. I'll bring you word as soon as I can."

The Major hesitated; he wanted to see for himself the extent of the fallen man's injuries. Then Piet groaned dismally; the woman cursed the author of her man's ills. The Major took to his heels and ran. The others waited in silence until his footsteps had died away in the distance. Then, as the injured man and woman rose to their feet, the bearded man laughed softly.

"You ought to give up highway robbery and go in for acting, Piet," he said sarcastically. "You fool, you ought to be more careful who you select as easy marks."

Piet groaned, a hand to his aching head.

"Hell!" he swore. "He looked as simple as a cooing dove; looked like a bloomin' know nothin' dude, he did."

"He's a dude, all right, and brainless. But he's got muscle, Piet. He's got muscle." He laughed, as if the idea amused him.

"I'd 'a' muscled him," Piet growled, "if them other two 'ad 'ad any guts! The swine! I'll get even with them for that—leavin' me in the lurch they did. And look here—what did you let him go for, Soapy?"

"You call me Richards, *Mister* Richards, and I'll like you better, Piet," the other replied suavely. But there was a heavy threat underlying his softness. "I let him go for reasons of my own, because I think I can use a fool dude who can use his fists the way he can. Glad I happened along this way when I did."

"As if you wouldn't have been 'angin' around, anyway," Piet countered, "to make sure you'd get your share of the pickings."

"Yes of course," the other agreed easily. "You see, Piet, I'm not sure that I can trust you to divvy up fairly."

Piet growled inarticulately.

"Beside," put in the woman, "we don't want the dude, Piet. I've got all he had worth having. Look! It ain't much. I imagine his remittance is overdue."

PIET STRUCK a match and by its feeble light examined the watch and chain and the small handful of gold and silver coins which the woman held out on the palms of her hand.

Richards laughed.

"You'd be rich, Piet," he said, "if you'd let Bess boss things. She's artistic, you're too fond of the rough work. Now I'm going to the dude's hotel, and I'll take his watch and chain with me. Maybe, as I've said, I can use him. If I find I can't, why I'll make him pay through the nose for killing you, Piet. So long." And he strolled slowly down the alley on his way to the Mason Hotel.

CHAPTER II

The Major Looks at Himself

ARRIVING AT his hotel, Aubrey St. John Major went directly to his room on the ground floor at the rear of the building, lighted the gas, partially undressed and donned an elaborate, gold brocaded dressing gown. That done, he sat down pensively in a Madeira wicker-chair, lighted a cigarette and gazed thoughtfully about the room.

It was in a state of utter confusion. The floor was covered with trunks of all shapes and sizes; some were packed, locked and strapped; others, their lids open, empty, waiting to receive whatever their owner decided to put into them. Hanging from hooks in the wall was a small armory of weapons—two Lee-Metford service rifles; hunting guns of divers calibers, revolvers and hunting knives, and boxes of ammunition. Arranged in a neat row along one side of the room was an array of boots; brown riding boots with spurs attached; stout walking-boots; rope-soled deckshoes, a pair of mosquito-boots and several pairs of patent-leather pumps. The huge, four-poster bed was piled high with clothing—white drill riding breeches, white silk shirts, underwear and sleeping suits; white sun-helmets. On the floor a pile of thick, woolly blankets and, nearby, another pile of linen sheets, pillow cases, table napkins and towels.

The Major sighed, and looked thoughtfully at the thumb of his right hand and rubbed it tenderly; it was slightly swollen and very painful.

"Piet's jaw must have been frightfully tough," he muttered. Then he frowned, remembering his late adventure, wondering how it was going to turn out. "Hope the bounder won't peg out. If he's as soft as all that he had no bally business in the footpad trade. It'll be frightfully awkward if I have killed him. No one would be prepared to believe my evidence if it came to a murder trial. No!" He smiled bitterly. "No one would be willing to believe the word of an—er—ex-convict, while the woman would undoubtedly find a lot of witnesses to swear that I attacked Piet with no provocation whatever. My word, yes!"

HE ROSE to his feet and, with the sureness of a much traveled man, busied himself in packing his equipment, clearing the things off his bed.

As he worked his thoughts ran on.

"Yes, it 'ud be deucedly awkward if I were arrested for murder. That would just about finish the governor back home. The dear old boy, for some reason or other, is always too willing to believe the worst of his youngest son. Of course I've been a bit of a lad—but nothing vicious. Harmless scrapes at the worst! Oh, well! Maybe it's because the governor's so darned upright himself that he can't understand my little—er—failings. Just the same—" and once again the bitter smile hardened the lines of his face—"he was not playin' the game about that last affair. I wrote and told him all about it; I gave him my word of honor that I was innocent, that I'd been 'framed'! But does he believe me? He does not. He sends his—er—final blessing-and five hundred pounds with the instructions that I'm never to darken his doors again. That means I'm an exile from home. Oh, rather! I must learn to forget all that England ever meant.

"And there you are. At least the worst is over except for the sentimental side of it. I've served my two years on the breakwater, less time off for good behavior—punished for buying a diamond illicitly—only I didn't buy it; it was given to me. And I didn't know it was a diamond. That's that! But let's see, now: How do I stand? By Jove! I think I'll draw up one of these—er—balance sheets or whatever the clerk laddies call them. Yes, I'll do that."

Chuckling softly at the humor of the idea he sat down in his chair and on a large sheet of writing paper wrote, awkwardly by reason of his injured thumb, the following items on the "assets" side, making running verbal comment as he set them down:

Four Hundred pounds (cash). "And I'm glad I know how to play poker. Judging by the way I've succeeded these last few days I might make a good livin' as a professional. But the company I would have to keep is not very—er—entertaining. So that's out."

Plenty of clothes, guns and ammunition; horse; buckboard with eight mules. "And poker won me all that. I didn't like taking the buckboard and mules from that bally Boer. But then, the blighter shouldn't have tried to play with an extra ace or two up his sleeve."

Good health—quite strong. "Thanks to the governor who always insisted that games were worth more than brain."

Good rider and shot. "Thanks again to the governor."

Some knowledge of native languages. "Thanks to hours of most fatiguing study while a pupil at—er—Breakwater Prison College."

Speak the taal fluently. "Thanks to a Boer warden bribed—" he sighed heavily—"with the ring returned to me by the girl I thought I was going to marry.

"And that would seem to be the sum total of my assets. Except—'pon my soul I almost forgot him—except Jim, the Hottentot. Now how about my liabilities. First of all:

Wear a monocle. "Of course I might cease wearing one. And yet, I rather fancy it has its uses. And I'd be blind as a bat without it. At least I'd feel deucedly bare. No: I'll continue to wear it and accept it as a liability, if it is one."

Look and talk like a silly ass. "Well, I can't help that. Maybe I am one. I think it quite likely when I consider how easily I was trapped two years ago, and how simply I walked into that bally business tonight. 'Pon my soul! I don't believe I'm safe alone."

No knowledge of the country. "That, of course, only time can rectify. But I'll start about it at once. Yes. Tomorrow I'll go on trek up country. I'll pick up Jim, if he's still waiting for me, at Umbalose's kraal and get off the beaten track for a while."

An exacting conscience. "Which is a bally nuisance. But maybe I can kill it in time if I try hard enough.

"An' now how does this balance up?"

He read what he had written and smiled ruefully.

"I don't seem to be anything for a fond parent to be fond of. Perhaps the governor was right."

HE TOSSED the paper down on the table, rose to his feet, lighted another cigarette and continued his packing.

There was a covert knock on the door.

"Come in," he shouted, not bothering to look up from his task.

The door opened to admit Richards.

He looked around the room, stroking his yellow pointed beard with one hand, nervously fingering his high collar with the other. His prominent Adam's apple moved up and down like an agitated thermometer.

"Here, Major," he said in a hoarse whisper, "it's a good job you're nearly packed. You'd better get out of town first thing in the mornin'. I'm afraid it's all up with Piet."

The Major straightened himself slowly and turned to face his visitor, let his monocle drop into the palm of his hand, polished it absently and stared, slack-jawed, at Richards.

"Are you trying to tell me," he said, "that our mutual friend Piet has—er—been gathered to his fathers? Why it's incredible, I broke my thumb on his bally jaw, thus proving his jaw was harder than my blow."

Richards smiled mournfully.

"Yes—and when he fell he cracked open his head which proves anything—or nothing."

"Is the blighter dead?"

"Not yet, but I don't think he'll last long. The girl thinks he'll be around in a day or two and I bribed her to keep her mouth shut. But she's in love with him, and if he dies she'll be out for revenge. So you'd better make tracks up country without delay."

"I'll start in the morning. I was going to anyway." The Major's wave of the hands indicated the packing he had been doing. "But sit down, have a cigarette, and a drink? There's the whisky, help yourself. I'll join you as soon as I've got this trunk strapped up."

He turned to his packing while Richards sat down, helped himself to a large drink, lighted a cigar and gazed sharply about the room.

He grinned contemptuously at the piles of clothing and the very new guns.

Then he stared at the Major's broad back and at the man's face which was reflected in the mirror opposite.

The monocle was gleaming again in the Major's eye and it seemed to deprive that man's face of any glimmer of intelligence.

RICHARDS LOOKED his man over, with the eye of one accustomed to appraising the worth of others, from the corners of his well groomed, jet-black hair to his small, well shod feet. He looked again at the Major's kit, at his ornate dressing-gown, at the white hands on which, undoubtedly, much care had been lavished; he thought of the Major's folly in allowing himself to be trapped by Piet's crowd and gave full consideration to the way in which the Major had fought off the men who had attacked him.

Richards carefully considered all this, then came to his decision.

The Major was undoubtedly a brainless fop with little thought beyond clothes, possibly a remittance man undoubtedly well supplied with money. A man who looked soft, physically; who looked less than his five foot eleven, but who was, nevertheless, stronger than the average, and knew how to use that strength.

Coincident with Richards' arrival at that decision, the Major sat down facing him, on the trunk he had been packing. "That's all I do tonight. An' look here, Richards, I'm no end grateful to you."

Richards tugged again at his collar. A large diamond ring sparkled on his middle finger.

"Nothing to thank me for, dear boy, nothing at all."

"Oh, but there is. And look here—just occurred to me— even should this fellow Piet die, why should I—er—depart in haste? You would be witness, surely—"

"You forget, Major," the other put in, "that I only witnessed the girl trying to stop you from leaving the scene of the assault."

The Major lapsed into silence, toying with the frogs of his dressing gown, yet his lazy eyes never left Richards' face.

"And," Richards continued, "as you'd already planned to leave tomorrow, anyway, why take any risk in stopping over?"

"That's true. Never thought of that."

"I suppose you're going on a hunting trip. How I envy you lucky young devils who came out from home, well supplied with money, free from care."

The Major sighed.

"Yes: I envy them myself."

"But aren't you one?" Richards exclaimed.

"Far from it, dear old friend of my bosom. Far from it. You behold in me a limb, as it were, chopped off the family tree. A black sheep, cast out of the fold, and there's no one to hear my bleating, I have spent the last penny which will be given me from the family coffers; with it I bought all this and an equipment to take me way back of the beyond, where, dear man, I intend to find my fortune. The gold mines of Solomon, or buried treasure of the old Portuguese explorers."

"Or diamonds?" Richards suggested softly.

"No! Positively not diamonds—not yet."

RICHARDS RAISED his eyebrows skeptically but made no remark. His cigar had gone out and he reached over for a piece of paper which was lying on the table, intending to make a taper of it to light at the gas jet above his head.

It was the Major's balance sheet.

He looked at it covertly, stared slightly when the Major said laughingly:

"Yes, go ahead and read it."

Richards read, cleverly masking his feelings, finally expressing great astonishment.

"You must have been out here a long time to be able to speak the *taal*."

The Major nodded.

"Over two years—but I spent most of the bally time in prison. You see, when I first came out I went up to the diamond fields and some one made me a present of a diamond. I thought it was deuced kind of him until, a little later I was arrested, tried and found guilty of I.D.B. I learned the *taal* in prison, and a lot of other things." A smirk of satisfaction passed over Richards' face.

"So that's why you're not interested in diamonds, eh? But I should have thought you'd want to get your own back on the chap who framed you."

"And so I do, and so I shall." The Major's voice was now hard.

Then almost immediately the old, vacuous expression returned to his face.

"And so I do," he repeated smoothly. "And I want to get even with the bally syndicate responsible for the law which made my arrest possible. Yes. And I know exactly how I am going to do it—I worked it all out while I was working out my—er—sentence. I shall write to all my friends and tell them not to buy any more diamonds; and I'm going to form a society for 'The Abolition of Diamonds in Engagement Rings.' That will bring the prices down and ruin the syndicate. Quite a clever plan, eh, what? And so simple."

"Yes, but very slow," said Richards, masking his look of contempt. "But I can set you on to an easier way than that. A friend of mine has a lot of dealings with the I.D.B. gentry in Kimberley and he'd have a lot more if he could only find some one he could trust to run the diamonds down here for him. It'd be easy for you to do it, hardly any risk. No one's going to suspect you of carrying for I.D.B.'s. You'd pose as a silly ass dude, on an hunting trip. You look the part—"

"You are not suggesting, are you?" the Major interposed with a show of dignity, "that I'm a silly ass? Because if you are, let me tell you that I'm not."

"I only said you looked the part," Richards assured him hastily. "And you have to admit that's true."

"Yes, I'm afraid so. This bally monocle—"

"Well, what do you say? Will you do it?"

The Major considered it and then slowly, regretfully shook his head.

"I'm afraid not. It's—er—hardly honest, is it?"

Richards held out his hand.

"Shake!" he said heartily. "And, let me tell you, Major, that it's a pleasure to shake the hand of an honest man. I'm glad to see that your past unpleasant experience has not made you bitter. I was trying you out just now. Had you agreed to run diamonds for my mythical friend, our acquaintance would have ended here and now. As it is— shake!"

THE MAJOR, evidently greatly embarrassed, took Richards' hand in his left. "My right hurts like the deuce," he said by way of apology, and having shaken the other's hand he fidgetted with his eyeglass.

Richards nodded complacently and, leaning forward, tapped the Major on the knee.

"Look here," said he, "you say you've made plans to leave here tomorrow and that you're practically broke, save for all this equipment. Are you heading anywhere in particular?"

The Major shook his head.

"No, save that I have to go first to Umbalose's kraal and pick up a Hottentot servant of mine. Then I—er—head for the wilds, as it were."

"If you'll go on an errand for me, I'll give you five hundred pounds and a fifth share in the profits, if any."

"Sounds interesting," Major drawled. "What do you want me to do?"

Richards rose and tiptoed to the door, his finger on his lips warning the Major to keep silent. He opened the door suddenly and looked up and down the corridor. Satisfied no eavesdropper lurked outside, he closed the door and locked it, then he drew the curtains across the French windows which opened out onto the grass plot at the rear of the hotel.

"Can't be too careful," he said in answer to the Major's puzzled look, and returned at length to his chair.

CHAPTER III

Treasure of the Veld

"**NOW, LISTEN,**" he began in a low voice. "Ever hear of a place called Devil's Kloof? No, I see you haven't. Well, that's where I want you to go for me. I'll tell you why. You must have heard the story the niggers tell about the blasted place? No? That's surprising. Thought everybody had heard of it in one form or another. The niggers say it's the place where all the wicked spirits live. They say they have been appointed by the Big Spirit to keep guard over a hole in the Kloof which is full of diamonds. They say as any man who goes near the place'll die a nasty death before the day's out."

"Oh, I say," the Major protested, moving uneasily, "and you want me to go there? Really!"

As if seeking to cover up his nervousness he took down his monocle and polished it vigorously.

Richards looked at him contemptuously, ran his finger around the inside of his collar, and continued, his Adam's apple moving uncannily as he spoke.

"Wait a minute. I haven't told you all yet. Now seeing how this niggers' tale is pretty generally known, and seeing how there's always a smattering of truth back of stories of this sort, you won't be surprised when I tell you that a lot of expeditions have been fitted out in the past years and've gone searching for Devil's Kloof. And the queer part about it is this: Although most every nigger knows the legend you can't hardly find one who'll admit to knowing where Devil's Kloof is; and them who says they do know where it is won't tell, no matter how you treat 'em." He laughed harshly. "And I ought to know, I've treated them all sorts of ways myself—from nearly killing them with kindness, giving them all the rotgut their bellies would hold, to stripping the skin off their backs with a *sjambok*. But not a peep could I get out of them. And here's another thing, not so funny. Some of them expeditions was never heard of again, and I knows of two or three men who had gone looking for the pit whose bones were afterwards found out on the veld."

"My!" the Major exclaimed in awed tones. "That would seem to indicate that there's something in this bally story, eh, what?"

IT MIGHT mean most anything," Richards said sourly. "But the only thing I'm interested in is that nobody has found the Devil's Kloof. Nobody, that is—" he dropped his voice to an impressive whisper—"except me."

"You!" the Major exclaimed incredulously. "But you're not dead."

Richards laughed.

"Not so as you'd notice it. And that means, I take it, that there's nothing in this story of the niggers."

The Major looked crestfallen.

"What a shame," he murmured. "I hoped you had found the pit full of diamonds."

"The pit's there, all right—it's a deep black hole in the ground and don't seem to have any bottom to it. It's hidden in the middle of a thick clump of thorn-bush and ain't hardly wide enough for a full-sized man to get into. If there are any diamonds in there, then they're at the bottom, an' the bottom's too far down to be reached anyway I've ever heard of."

"Then," the Major said slowly, "I don't see what you want me to do."

"Wait a minute," Richards replied. "I ain't finished yet. I got to tell you first how I happened to find the place. I was gold-prospecting up country with an old California miner as partner, Tom Wallace was his name. And one day when Tom had gone to some nearby kopjes to see if he could get a buck for supper, I goes in the opposite direction, following up a dried up river bed, thinking I might happen on a pocket or something.

"Well, this dried up river course led me after an hour or so between two steep banks and finally through a 'gate' between kopjes—regular mountains they was with steep sides as shiny as glass; sheer up and down they was, and black like polished ebony. Then I found myself in a sort of blind alley—there was hills all round me and the only way I could get out of the place was back the way I came. I ain't what you'd call an imaginative man but, somehow, that place frightened me. For one thing, except for a few thorn bushes, there wasn't a living thing to be seen, nothing but this black, shining rock; not an animal, or a bird— not even a vulture. Nothing but a lot of snakes tied up in knots and me.

"Well, I determines to look around a bit before I start back and it was then, quite by accident, like, I stumbled across the pit. And then it comes to me where I am: I realize that I'm in Devil's Kloof and that this pit is the place where the diamonds are supposed to be. Excited? What do you think? Well, I throws myself down on my belly and tries to look down the hole—but it's as black as hell and I can't see nothing. I throw a stone down—but don't hear it touch bottom. I made a sort of fire-ball and chucked that down and watched it drop out of sight. And then I rolled up a big black boulder and rolled it over the edge, an' listened. Man, I believe that boulder's dropping yet!

"And then I got really frightened and left the place at a run, sure in my own mind that, supposing there was diamonds in the pit—an' I don't believe there are or ever were—there was no way of getting them out.

I DIDN'T look back until I was well away an' then, believe me or not, I couldn't see any opening in the hills where I'd gone in and out. It looked as if the bloomin' hills had moved and closed up the entrance."

"Now you're spoofin' me," the Major said reproachfully. "The hills couldn't move."

"Of course they couldn't—don't be a damned fool. I only said it looked as if they had. I only told you that to show how hard it 'u'd be for anybody to find the place unless they followed up the river bed. An' who 'u'd think of doin' that?"

"You did," the Major pointed out.

"Yes, I know, stupid, but I wasn't looking for the Devil's Kloof. If I had been, I'd have looked at them hills through my field glasses at a distance and I'd have found no opening an' gone on. As a matter of fact you couldn't see that opening a hundred yards away. Look here, give me a pencil and I'll draw you a picture map of the place."

And on the back of the Major's "balance sheet" he made a little sketch.

"You see," he explained, "the rock being black like it was, and them two ends of the range of hills lapping over like they do, made it seem as if the hills was all in one unbroken line.

"Well—all that's interesting, but ain't much to the point.

"But, as I was saying. I got back to the camp and told old Tom Wallace of my find. He got all excited; would have it that I was keeping something back an' that I'd found enough diamonds to fill a sack. The old fool wouldn't be pacified. An' that night he went down bad with fever."

"Then there is something in that part of the story," the Major murmured in awed tones. "The curse works."

"Don't be a damned fool. He didn't go near the place, did he? Besides, he'd been ailing for a long time. Anyway, I had the devil's own job getting him to a place where he could be looked after. He never really recovered. Sort of lingered for a few months. He wouldn't have lived so long if it hadn't been for his daughter's careful nursing. And he was sort of crazy all the time. Got it into his head that *he'd* found the Devil's Kloof—not me—and that there was diamonds there an' that I'd tried to kill him. What d'you think of that?"

The Major muttered a few inarticulate words of sympathy. Adding, "But I'm still mystified as to what you want me to do?"

"I'm coming to it. But first I want your word of honor that you'll not go blabbing what I tell you."

"I give you my word—on my solemn affy—er—davey. Is that enough?"

"Good enough for me," Richards said in bluff, hearty tones. "Now listen: Old Wallace's daughter believes all that her father told her and she's gone up country to try and locate the Kloof. An' because she's my old partner's daughter I want to protect her, see? I can forget an' forgive all old Tom said about me—he was not responsible at the time, anyway—an' for his sake I'm ready to protect the girl."

"But why bother, old thing?" the Major questioned. "You say yourself there's nothing in the legend. Why not let her go and find out the truth for herself?"

YES, I might do that, only—look here, I wouldn't want a daughter of mine to go up country with no one to protect her save a damned fool of a Boer who drives her ox-team. Just think, man, of all the things what can happen to a white girl, a damned pretty girl, at that, alone up country on a trip like that: Lions, an' fever, an' niggers on the warpath as like as not—not to mention certain white men who might get on to what she's after and get on her trail for their own dirty ends."

The Major nodded comprehendingly.

"Yes. By Jove! Come to think of it, it's not safe for a young female to wander alone unprotected in this bally country. It's not safe for a man, for the matter of that. Just look at what happened to me!"

Richards smiled covertly.

"And besides," he continued, "there's another reason why I want to send some one I can trust up to Devil's Kloof. There might be diamonds in that pit after all. I didn't have a chance to really examine it at the time; had no rope with me, and then I had old Tom sick on my hands. And I haven't had a chance to go back since. But, as I say, if there are diamonds in the pit, they're mine by right of discovery. Mine to share with my old partner's daughter and the man who's willing to help me, and that's you."

"Deucedly kind of you, I'm sure. But I still don't see just what you expect me to do."

"It's easy. You travel as fast as you can for Devil's Kloof. The girl's got two weeks' start on you, but she's trekking in an ox-wagon an' you'll get there before her, easy. Maybe you'll pass her on the way. If you do, don't let her find out what you're after, an' don't try to get her to turn back. She wouldn't believe anything you was to say to her anyway; she's suspicious of everybody, specially anybody she thinks is connected with me. What you've got to do is go on for the Kloof, camp inside it, there's plenty of water, an' wait. When the girl comes along to the Kloof, you hold her prisoner an' keep her there until I join you."

"It all sounds fright fully complicated," Major protested wearily. "There's a thousand an' one questions I want to ask you."

"Don't ask any of them," Richards interrupted impatiently. "What do you want to ask questions for? All you've got to do," he continued meaningly, "is remember that I'm keeping my own mouth shut about things I know an' offering you a way of escaping from being arrested an' sentenced for murder. Why don't you remember that, be satisfied and obey orders?"

"I do," the Major replied quickly. "I am, and will."

"Now you're talking," Richards approved and rubbed his hands briskly together.

"And, I take it," the Major continued, "orders are to go to Devil's Kloof and keep everybody out of it except the lady and you?"

"Right first time," agreed Richards.

"And right it is," echoed the Major. "But where the deuce is Devil's Kloof? How am I to find it?"

RICHARDS HESITATED a moment, then taking the paper on which he had already sketched a crude plan of the Devil's Kloof, itself, now made another sketch.

"It's easy to find when you know where to look," he explained. "You make for Steinberg—that'll be easy—and from there head due north four or five days' trek until you see a kopje what looks like a camel's hump. Then you make for the kopje, trekking east and you'll strike that dried-up river I told you about. Trek along the bed of that, and there you are. Easy, eh?"

"Very."

"An' you'll do it? You'll start tomorrow?"

The Major nodded.

"But first, I'd like to ask you one of the thousand an' one questions: Why not go after the lady yourself? Why take a third person into the—er—business?"

"That's easy: First because I'd find it difficult to deal with Miss Wallace, I told you she didn't trust me. An' then I daren't go openly to the Kloof, I'm being watched by some of the most desperate criminals in the country. They think I've got valuable information about a new diamond field and if I went to the Kloof and did everything openly, like I'd rather, why I'd have this gang following me. Damn 'em! So I've got them on a false scent. I've spread the news around that I am now on my way to a place north of Kimberley. What's more, it is my intention to go there and then, when I've thrown them off my trail I'll double on my tracks and come down to meet you at Devil's Kloof. An' what 'ud happen to Miss Wallace while I'm gadding about up country with no one to look after her welfare? You can see for yourself that she wouldn't be safe at all."

Richards yawned and rose to his feet.

"Now I'll say goodby and leave you to your packing. The earlier you start tomorrow the safer you'll be. I think I silenced Bessie, but Piet may die during the night and then Bessie 'ud split to the Force an' you'd be in a hell of a mess. And don't forget to keep your mouth shut about this job you are doing for me. There's sure to be some of the gang that will try to get information from you. But you play the dude part an' you'll be left alone." He took a gold repeater from his pocket and made a pretense of listening to its tinkling chimes; actually his eyes were riveted upon the Major's face and he smiled covertly when that man's face remained a vacuous mask. Evidently the monocled dude could not recognize his own watch when he saw it; as likely as not he did not know yet that he had lost it.

"Well," Richards continued, returning the watch to his pocket, "I must go now. S'long!"

"S'long," echoed the Major with an airy wave of his hand.

He escorted Richards to the door, bowed him out, shut and locked the door and then threw himself down full length on the bed, holding his sides, his face red with suppressed laughter.

CHAPTER IV

Turned Tables

PRESENTLY HE sobered and rising from the bed went over to the chair and, sitting there, closely examined the maps which Richards had sketched on the back of his "balance sheet." Then, having committed the maps and the instructions to memory, he tossed the paper onto the table, closed his eyes and endeavored to sift the false from Richards' long story.

"I have a feeling," he muttered, "that the bally fellow did not tell me the whole truth—far, far from it. It was, on the face of it, such a fishy sounding story; absolutely full of flaws. On the other hand, there is undoubtedly a lot of truth in it. I think Mr. Richards—he reminded me, rather, of a—er—Sunday School teacher gone to the devil— prides himself on being able to estimate a man's qualities at one glance. And he's probably quite clever that way. He no doubt thinks that I am an awful bally ass who happens to be able to use his fists an' can ride an' shoot. He took my word for that. And he thinks I've swallowed that yarn he told me and that I'll therefore obey orders. He thinks, too, that he has a hold over me from my little encounter with the man Piet. He should know better than that. Oh, well! And why did he exhibit my watch? I think that was a little bravado on his part; a little, shall we say—conceit. Wonder what he would have done had I claimed it? Not that that is important. But, let me see: it would seem that I'm committed to this undertaking. It may be most amusin', an' perhaps I can find a way of being useful to a lady in distress. Yes: I think that quite possible. And now for some more packing."

KNOCKING HIS thumb on the edge of a trunk, he winced, and paused from his task long enough to saturate a small towel in water and wrap it around his thumb, tying the ends around his wrist.

"That's better," he murmured, "much better. It's funny, bally funny, how a little thing like a sprained thumb can be such a bally nuisance. But I have a feeling that Piet's ugly jaw hurts him a great deal more than my thumb! That's a little consolation. I wonder if Piet is really at—er—death's door. I fancy not. In fact I am quite positive he is not. And I'm inclined to think that Mr. Richards, my guide, philosopher and friend, is hand in glove with Piet and Co. Yes. Well, we shall see."

He tensed and was very still as he caught the sound as of stealthy footsteps crossing the grass plot at the rear of the hotel. He smiled and taking from its holster one of his revolvers, dropped it in the large pocket of his dressing gown. Then he resumed his packing, busy now with the things on the bed, his back to the French windows, that opened onto the grass plot at the rear.

Apparently he did not hear the creak caused by the stealthy turning of the handle of the French windows, did not hear them open and close, or the turn of the key in the lock, or the rapid breathing of the two men who had entered.

Not until one of them cleared his throat with a harsh cough did the Major turn to face them.

"Greetings, old dears!" he then exclaimed cheerfully, after a first, well feigned startled cry of surprise. And coming up to the table he picked up the paper lying upon it, folded it lengthwise with exaggerated care and then, using it as a spill, held it in the gas flame and lighted his cigarette with it. He offered the two men cigarettes and when they cursingly refused dropped the paper to the floor and put his foot on the flame.

"I hope you are not deaf and dumb," he said lightly, his face beaming with innocent good nature, while he inwardly reproached his carelessness in having left the paper on the table, thus making it necessary for him to resort to strata- gem to get it out of sight. "I said, you know, 'How do you do?' In reply you simply snarl at me. Most extraordinary, really. And, come to think of it, just what do you mean by coming into my room quite uninvited, as it were?"

"You stow yer gab an' listen to hus." It was the smaller of the two men who spoke—an undersized, rat faced little man who was redolent of the vice and petty meanness of the London slums. "We wants ter 'ave a tork with you. Wot's yer nime?"

"Aubrey St. John Major, dear lad. And what is your? Fagin or Bill Sykes, or the—er—Artful Dodger or some other of the Dickensonian appellations?"

"Never mind wot my nime is," the other replied sourly. "I wants ter ask you a few questions. An the first is this: Wot was Soapy Sam adoin' of 'ere?"

"Soapy Sam!" the Major exclaimed. "What a most extraordinary name. But I know no one of that name. Really!"

"Oh! Come off yer perch, Percy," the little man growled. "I means Richards—Soapy Sam them as knows calls him. He was 'ere to see yer, ain't been long left, I should say. Didn't the chap who was 'ere try to wash 'is hands with nothin'? Course he did. Well, that was Soapy Sam. Smooth all over, Sam is; so smooth in his way of torkin' that yer'd think butter wouldn't melt in his mouth. But he's the biggest crook in all Africa, for hall of that.

"Well, we wants to know, me an' Demper 'ere"—he jerked a thumb toward his companion, a tall, skinny Boer—"we wants ter know wot Soapy Sam was torkin' to you about."

"Well, really," the Major began hesitatingly, "I do not like the tone of your voice and I do not like your attitude. Upon my soul, I don't. Whatever business I transacted was quite confidential and not meant to be—er—shouted from the housetops. He—"

"Cut it short," the little man interrupted. Then, to his companion, "Show 'im a gun, Demper."

STOLIDLY, HIS face totally devoid of expression, the Boer drew a revolver which he leveled at the Major's head.

"Hands up!" he growled in a harsh, guttural voice. "I say, 'Hands up,' you *verdoemte roinek!*"

The Major backed a few paces and as his hands shot with rapidity above his head a vacuous smile spread over his face.

"Most astonishin'," he drawled. "You must be wicked bandits. And so bold. All I have to do, though, is to tug this"—his hands closed on a bell-rope which hung down beside the bed—"an' all sort of chappies-would rush to my assistance."

"You take yer 'ands off that," the little man snarled vindictively, "less yer want a bullet in yer brains. Dutch 'u'd be only too glad of a hexcuse. So I'm warnin' yer."

With a gesture of alarm the Major moved away from the bell-rope.

"That's better; an' now, per'aps, seeing as yer life ain't worth much, you'll tell us wot you an' Soapy Sam was torkin' about?"

The Major moved uneasily.

"I don't think I ought to tell you," he stammered. "It was—er—most secret. A secret business deal, as a matter of fact."

The little man took this up quickly.

"I'll lay it was somethin' to do with Devil's Kloof an' diamonds, wasn't it now? Sure as my name's 'Arry 'Ewins it was. Ain't that right?"

"I'm glad to know your name is Harry—you meant that, didn't you?" the Major replied. "But you're quite wrong. And as I can't see that it really matters, I'll tell you what we were talking about. Although, mind you, I don't at all see what it has to do with you; neither do I approve of the way in which you have come about trying to get this information from me. However, let me tell you that Mr. Richards has sold me a most marvelous idea. You know, of course, that when an elephant feels that he wants to—er—shuffle off this mortal coil, he leaves all his bosom companions and toddles off to some place of solitude to die. An' they all go to the same place—a sort of bush cemetery, as it were. An' that place, you know, has never been found, although hundreds of hunters have searched for it. But Mr. Richards' plan will enable me to discover the place with ease. He was most generous. He told me his plan first, saying I could give him what I thought it was worth to me. And I gave him one hundred pounds and half share in the profits, if any. What I have to do is this: I trek for elephant country—I start first thing in the morning—and, once there, I wound an old tusker and follow the old fellow wherever he goes. Of course, realizing that death is close upon him, he'll make at once for his private burying ground. And there you are, dear lads. I shall be simply rolling in wealth. Just think of all the ivory tusks which will be mine for the taking!"

Hewins chortled and nudged Demper in the ribs.

"Ain't Soapy Sam a oner," he said. "There ain't nobody like 'im, blast 'ins! Ain't that just the sort of game 'e would put over a damn fool dude like this chap?"

Demper stolidly scratched his head with his left hand, but his right did not waver.

"I don't know, *ma-an*," he said slowly. "It may be that this dude is not the fool he looks. Maybe, yet, he is playing a game of us. *Ach sis!* No man could be such a fool as to believe a story like that."

"That's because you ain't never met a dude like 'e is, afore. But I 'ave. I knows 'is sort. Plenty of 'em in Lunnon. Soapy Sam—'e could make a bloke like this fink the moon was made of green cheese."

"Am I to—to understand that you think Richards was spoofin' me?" stammered the Major.

"I don't fink," Hewins answered with a laugh. "I know."

"You mean that there's no elephant's graveyard? My word! If that's true, I'll have the bally blighter arrested for obtaining money under false pretenses. 'Pon my soul I will. An', I say. Can't I take my hands down now—I'm sure I must look like a bally fool holdin' them up like this."

"You keep them where they are, I tell you, *ma-an*," the Boer said and exchanged a few whispered words with Hewins.

"LOOK HERE, Aubrey," Hewins then said easily. "My mate finks you ain't as soft as you look. So, to put 'im in good humor, I'm goin' ter 'ave a look through this stuff an' see if I can find anything worth 'aving."

As he spoke, Hewins turned to one of the trunks, turning its contents onto the floor.

The Major yawned and took a few steps nearer Demper.

"You're both beastly rude," he said, "and were it not for my love of peace I should be tempted to raise my voice in a wild cry for help."

"If you did," Demper replied slowly, "it would be, *ma-an,* the last time you would ever use your voice. So be wise, and silent."

"Wot a 'ell of a mess!" Hewins sneered as he turned his attention to another trunk. "Wot's the idea of taking so many pretty clothes on a 'untin' trip, Aubrey? Lumme! Men who go 'unting in this bloody country fink 'emselves well off if they've got one shirt an' a pair o' patched trousers to 'ide their nakedness. But you! Blimey! You've got a regular wedding trussoo! An' ere's a bloomin' dress suit! Wot the 'ell do yer think you're goin ter do with that?"

"A man must observe the—er—conventions, dear Hewins, even in Africa," Major drawled. "An' I say, I do wish you'd be more careful. Look at your bally dirty finger marks on my dress shirts. Really! It is too much!"

In his eagerness to prevent his linen from being soiled any further, the Major took a step or two forward. He was very close to Demper now. His hands were clasped on the top of his head and his attitude was reminiscent of a schoolboy who was being punished for some breach of discipline.

Hewins had now turned to a third trunk.

"Look at this!" he cried presently. "Gawd love a duck! I be damned if 'e ain't got a whole box-full of winders for 'is bleedin' eye." And from the velvet lined case he had discovered he took a monocle, fixed it awkwardly in his eye, and postured theatrically, burlesquing the mannerisms and drawling voice of the Major.

"My word, Demper," he simpered. "I'm a bleedin' toff. Take yer 'at off an' call me 'Dook.'"

For an incautious moment Demper turned his head to look at his partner; for just that one fraction of time his hand wavered.

And in that fraction of time the Major had taken the wet towel from his injured thumb and flicked it forward.

It snaked around Demper's revolver, jerking it from that astonished man's hand.

Then before either Hewins or Demper could make a move the Major was lounging in the wicker chair, covering them both with his revolver.

"And that's that," he said pleasantly, toying with his monocle and smiling at the men who were dumbfounded at this sudden turning of the tables.

Then he was silent for a little while, amused by the angry recriminations which passed between the two men.

"I think you were both to blame," the Major put in placatingly. "But we won't endeavor to apportion the blame now. There are so many other things to do. I am torn, for the moment, by quite different desires: one, to be relieved of your—er—contaminating presence without delay; the other, to make you clear up this bally mess you have made."

"Look 'ere," Hewins whined. "I know as we did wrong coming in 'ere and 'olding you up the way we did. But we thought as 'ow you and Soapy were doin' us out of our rights. He stole the plan of 'ow to get to Devil's Kloof from us afore we 'ad 'ad time ter look at it ourselves, an' we thought we'd try to get it back. That's all!. An' now we knows you ain't the fool dude we took you for at first, we knows you must be in with Richards on the Kloof job. Well, we knows things about it Richards don't, an' we're ready to come in with you. You an' us 'll go an' get the diamants an' old Soapy can go to the devil. Wot do yer say?"

"MY DEAR chap," the Major drawled, "let me assure you that you're barking up the wrong tree. Oh, quite! How could I be partners with you—I ask you?" Then he turned sharply on Demper and, for a moment, the inane grin left his face. "And I advise you," he continued, "to stand quite still and not try to pick up the revolver you dropped—kick it over here, thanks—or try to draw any other you may have secreted about your bally person."

"Did I not say he was no fool, Hewins?" Demper growled.

"But I am, very," the Major said laughingly. "Quite a bally ass in fact. And I'm so soft hearted. Of course I ought to call the police and give you in charge. Instead—and I must insist on obedience—I am simply going to ask you to refrain from speech and pack up my kit. I think that that is only fair. So, get to work. Quick, now! And be very careful that you fold everything neatly."

The two men hesitated a moment and then, because they did not care to face the alternative, silently set about the task appointed them.

Their task at last ended; every trunk packed, the lids closed, strapped and locked, Hewins made one last appeal to the Major to accept them as partners.

But he laughingly refused to listen.

"No," he said. "The best I can offer you is a nice downy bed for the night. You, Hewins, take a length of that rope and truss up your partner very securely.

"That's good," he said presently with a nod of approval. "Now gag him. I don't like his curses."

Again the way in which Hewins obeyed earned the Major's approval.

"I suppose," that man drawled, "you wouldn't care to come with me and let Demper, as well as Richards, go to the devil?"

"Wouldn't I?" Hewins said fervently. "Just you try me. Demper's nothin' to me. An' every man for 'imself, I says." He laughed triumphantly at the scowling Dutchman. "Wot do yer say, Major? Are me an' you goin' to be pals?"

The Major sighed.

"I don't see how we can. You seem to find it so easy to be off with the old and on with the new. I'm afraid I wouldn't be able to trust you."

"Ah, but yer can," Hewins said eagerly. "I wouldn't go back on a real pal like you'd be. But a bloomin' Dutch-man—Dutchies don't count."

"Well, you and Demper must settle that between you. I rather fancy your late friend will have quite a lot to say to you. Now turn round and I will see if I can truss and gag you as well as you have Demper. I rather fancy that I can. Perhaps better."

In a very little while he had fulfilled his promise. Then, with effortless ease, he picked up Demper and carrying him into an adjoining room, placed him on the bed. There, too, he carried Hewins. He examined their bonds once again, made them even more secure, then pulled the covers up over them, tucked the mosquito netting carefully around them, wished them "pleasant dreams," and tiptoed out of the room, locking the door behind him.

Ten minutes later he was in his own bed, chuckling softly.

Presently he got up again, lighted the gas, and picked up from the floor the paper on which he had made out his "Balance sheet," and on the back of which Richards had drawn the maps.

"I have been very careless about this," he murmured. "I think I had better destroy it before it gets into bad company. I think that I have everything clearly impressed upon the little brain I have. So I'll burn the incriminating papers. But first, I want to change this."

He read through the statement he had drawn up then, chuckling as he did it, crossed out under "Liabilities," the items, "Wear a monocle," "Look and talk like a silly ass," and wrote them down under the heading "Assets."

Then he lighted a match and set fire to the paper which he held until the flame reached his fingers, then dropped it and ground its black ash into the carpet.

A few minutes later he was fast asleep.

CHAPTER V
The Kraal of Umbalose

IT WAS nearly noon. Overhead a fiery sun floated in a sky of brass, not a breath of wind was stirring and the fine red dust of the veld when disturbed by some wayfarer or grazing beast, hovered like a pall a few feet above the ground before finally settling.

At the kraal of Umbalose all was peaceful. All around the tiny collection of huts perched precariously on the slopes of the kopje, cattle and goats browsed contentedly or huddled together in the shade of the trees, placidly chewing the cud and gazing incuriously at the antics of their naked little native herd-boys.

The kraal itself was a hive of activities—the men making ready for the morrow's hunt, the women preserving skins, grinding corn or preparing a meal, singing in very shrill, but not unmusical voices as they worked. Occasionally a man's heavy deep bass bellowing would join in the song until he was loudly scolded by the women to silence.

Flies swarmed everywhere and their loud drone formed a monotonous accompaniment to the other noises of the kraal.

A heavy, pungent scent pervaded the place. It was, in its intensity, as cloying as the thick red dust which needed but a little rain to turn it into thick, clinging mud; it was, in a way, redolent of Africa and Africa's people.

Outside the largest of the bee-hive shaped huts, the hut of the headman, Umbalose, sat two men.

THEY SMOKED filthy, battered old pipes, long since discarded by some white men, and drank occasionally from a large calabash of thick, native beer which stood on the ground near by.

One of the men was Umbalose, a man who boasted, with no little ground for his boast, that he was a full-blooded Zulu. He was very fat; so fat that his chin seemed to descend to his waist in a succession of billows.

His eyes were almost lost in rolls of fat, but they were bright and intelligent; and, if they hinted at cruelty, they promised hearty goodfellowship toward all who did not actively oppose their owner. Umbalose had been a mighty warrior in his youth, but the onward rush of civilization had entangled him in the soft vices of peace.

His companion was an altogether different type of man.

His skin was of a dull, dirty yellow color, his face flat and in some ways suggestive of the Orient. His wiry hair stuck out in queer corkscrew twists all over his head. His nose was very broad, his ears outstanding. His teeth flashed white and his homely face indicated loyalty, keenness and a highly developed sense of humor. He was not very tall, but, evidently, abnormally strong; every time he moved, no matter how slightly, splendid muscles rolled under his skin. There was not an ounce of superfluous flesh on him and as he now sat, or rather squatted on his haunches, his hands gripping his ankles, he aptly represented the spirit of Africa; looked like a study in ivory, yellowed by age, carved by a master hand.

"Why remain thirsty, Hottentot?" said the headman, "if there is still beer in the pot?"

The Hottentot laughed.

"I have drunk my fill, Umbalose," he replied. "To take more would be folly."

The headman spat contemptuously and, picking up the gourd, held it to his lips, tilted back his head and emptied the gourd with a long, appreciative gurgle.

"It is always folly," he remarked, wiping his thick lips on the back of his hand, "not to drink what it is possible to drink. The time will come, Hottentot, when you will greatly desire this beer which you now refuse."

The Hottentot laughed again.

"Maybe, Umbalose," he said. "And when that time comes I will think of this I now refuse and my thirst will be satisfied."

Then he sighed and looked with longing eyes at the empty gourd.

The headman chuckled and clapped his hands, ordering the woman who appeared at the opening of his hut to bring more beer.

She scowled, asking, "Why should good beer be poured down the throat of a pig of a Hottentot?"

Then, cowering slightly at the headman's angry frown, she brought out another pot and set it humbly at their feet.

"Now drink, Hottentot," the headman invited.

But the other shook his head.

"No. That I cannot do. Maybe today my Baas will come. He must find me with my eyes open and my legs ready to take the trail."

Again the headman spat contemptuously.

"All Hottentots are liars and fools; there is nothing of worth in them. And of all Hottentot you are the biggest fool and liar of them all. For two years now I have suffered you to dwell at my kraal and have had scorn heaped upon my head because I called a Hottentot my friend. But that scorn I can put on one side; it is no more to me than the bite of a mosquito. Though you are a Hottentot and thus less than the dogs, I know you to be a man and therefore on an equality with great chiefs. There is not one among my young men as strong as you or who can read the spoor as well. Not even old Gante, the witch doctor, has greater wisdom. And your courage—that has been tested and proved many times during the time you have been with us. So I say that you are a man and I can forget that you are a Hottentot. But I also say that you are a liar, and, maybe," he laughed, "it is because of that I have allowed you to stay with us. Never was a man born who could tell lies with so serious a face as you, Hottentot." He smote his thick thighs, chuckling as he thought of one of the experiences narrated by the Hottentot.

"It is," he continued, "that I am now thinking of the story you told of the killing of a lion with only a broken assegai for your weapon. *Wo-we!* To think of that!"

"And yet, Umbalose, that was true," the Hottentot replied gruffly. "See! Here are the marks of his claws." And he pointed to a long scar which ran from his right shoulder down across his chest, ending at the waist.

The headman laughed.

"You may say it was a lion, Hottentot, that marked you so, but I think it was done by the finger nails of an angry woman. *Wo-we!* I tell you that a woman is more dangerous than any lion."

THERE WAS silence for a little while, broken only by the headman's wheezy breathing and his gurgles of satisfaction as he sipped contentedly of the new gourd of beer.

"But wherein am I playing the part of a fool, Umbalose?" the Hottentot asked presently.

"Do you ask?" countered the headman. "Is it not plain? You came to me, seeking my hospitality, saying you wished to wait here until a white man, your Baas, joined you. For two years you have been here, hunting with my young men, helping to train my cattle, doing at times the work of women in order to pay for the hospitality I was willing to give you. And for nearly two years you were a good companion. You drank until there was no beer left and my women could not make beer strong enough to weaken your limbs, blind your eyes or weaken your stomach. But this past month you have been more like an old woman awaiting death. You have kept close to the kraal like a child who is frightened of evil spirits. And you have set your mind against the kindness of beer. No longer are you a companion fit for a fighting man. As well might one drink with a new born babe.

"And all this you do, say you, for the sake of your Baas, for the sake of a white man you have seen but on two days—and that so long ago. *Au-a!* The folly of it. Maybe this man you call your Baas is dead; or, if not dead, maybe he has forgotten you. Or, if he is not dead and has not forgotten you, then undoubtedly he is without wealth—for what man just released from *trunk* is possessed of wealth—and so in no way able to reward you for the services you intend to give him.

"So I say, Hottentot, drink and forget all white men."

The other shook his head.

"No," he replied. "That I cannot do. You do not know my white man. He is a man amongst men. He is in all things different from others. It is true that only on two days have I seen him. But on the first of those days he saved me from an evil white man who was thrashing me with a *sjambok*. And because of what he did on that first day, the second day he was caught in the snares of that evil man and sent to *trunk*. For my sake, he was punished. For two years he was sentenced to heavy punishment. Would you, then, have me false to the debt I owe him?"

The headman sighed heavily.

"Maybe you are right, Hottentot," he said. "But I shall be sorry to see you go from me, and I am eager to see this white man of yours."

"You shall, Umbalose. Maybe today he will come. And I will be sorry to leave this place. But my white man will need me. Although he is a *man*, he is as helpless as a babe unborn. He knows not this country or us black ones. He cannot speak our tongue. Should he stray but a few yards from an outspan, he would be lost. But he will learn; he will learn quickly. And I shall teach him."

The noises of the kraal gradually died away. The women, with calabashes balanced on their heads, passed out in stately file on their ways to the river for water. The men also departed upon their separate errands and presently the kraal was deserted save for Umbalose and the Hottentot.

The day's heat increased, the glare was blinding. But the two men did not seek the shade of the huts, neither did their naked bodies seem conscious of the sun's scorching rays.

A white man, mounted on a raw-boned mule, rode up to the kraal and came to a halt before the headman's hut.

AT THE first sound of hoofs the Hottentot jumped to his feet, his eyes agleam with expectancy. Then, seeing the rider, he dropped back again on his haunches, grunted a sullen reply to the white man's greeting, and stared owlishly before him.

The white man dismounted awkwardly and took from his saddle wallets two square shaped bottles which he set on the ground close to the headman's feet.

"You are thirsty, headman," he said ingratiatingly. "I have brought you white man's *puza*." He spoke the vernacular very haltingly.

He was a heavily built man. His face, shaded by the large sunhelmet he wore, was that of a man who revelled in moral slime. He was dirty and unshaven; his clothing torn. In his hand he held a large *sjambok* which he tapped nervously against his thigh.

"I have brought you these, headman," he continued, indicating the two bottles. "They contain a drink worthy of men like you."

Umbalose nodded and closed his eyes as if to shut out the vision of happiness the bottles had conjured up.

"I know white men," he said slowly, "and I know that you do not bring me this *puza* expecting nothing in return. What do you want of me?"

The white man laughed harshly.

"Very little I want, headman. Almost less than nothing."

"Still, I would know what that little is?"

"Only a guide to take me to that place of the spirits, that place, so the story goes, to which all the spirits go in order to watch over the treasure left there by Chaka."

"*Wo-we!*" the headman exclaimed angrily. "And again you come to me full of that folly? When you first came to me I said I knew not of the place; that if I knew where it was I could not take you to it because it is a thing forbidden. And as I said to you then, I have said to other white men who have come to me seeking information of the place which is forbidden. And I say the same to you again. I have spoken."

"But there is such a place," the white man insisted craftily. "You have heard of it?"

"*Au-a!*" the headman replied. "I have heard of it and undoubtedly there is such a place. But I have also heard of a land where the souls of white men go after the great sleep has fallen upon them, and, undoubtedly there is such a place. But I cannot take you to the one, or the other."

The white man's face fell and it was with difficulty that he restrained his temper.

He whistled, tunelessly, a few bars of a song then popular in the London music halls and endeavored to formulate a plan which would secure from the headman the information he so greatly desired and which, he was sure, the headman could give.

He started with surprise when Umbalose, apparently reading his thoughts, said: "It is useless, white man! I do not know where the place is, and if I did I could not tell you. It has been forbidden. Know you not that all the spirits of Chaka's dead warriors guard at that place?"

The white man nodded absently. Having arrived at a plan of sorts he did not now press the headman further. Instead, he drew the cork from one of the bottles and then held the bottle under the headman's nose.

ALL THIS time the Hottentot had been looking straight before him, apparently uninterested in the conversation of the headman and the white man. But now the cork had been withdrawn from one of the bottles, his nostrils dilated and he turned toward Umbalose, an expression of great longing in his eyes.

He stretched out his hand as if desiring to take the bottle from the white man.

The headman grunted and speaking swiftly, so that the white man could not catch the portent of what he was saying, exclaimed. "So a white man's *puza* makes you forget your folly, eh, Hottentot?"

"Maybe," the other replied, "it makes me remember. But let us not waste time talking, let us drink."

He snatched the bottle from the white man's hands and drank greedily, not even gagging as the raw stuff, doctored with acid, passed down his throat.

The headman laughed uproariously.

"Almost, Hottentot," he said, "I would be willing to tell this white man the secret, did I know it, in exchange for this *puza* which has made you a man again."

The white man who had been on the point of snatching the bottle back from the Hottentot, hearing this, opened the other bottle and gave it to Umbalose.

"You drink, too," he said, "and we will all be men together."

The headman accepted the bottle and for a time there was no sound save the greedy smacking of lips and the *tot-tot* of the liquor pouring out of the narrow-necked bottles.

Presently, the bottles emptied, the Hottentot and the headman began to sing one of the wild chants of Zulu warriors, accentuating the rhythm by softly clapping their hands, swaying drunkenly from side to side.

The white man, thinking his opportunity had arrived, questioned the headman again regarding the whereabouts of the Devil's Kloof. But he had over-reached himself. The foul drink he had given the two natives—one small drink of it would have been sufficient to knock out a white man—had made them both impervious to time or place. The headman apparently was unconscious of the white man's presence, deaf to his voice and, as the latter repeated his questions in a louder, bullying tone, only sang more shrilly and clapped his hands with greater vigor.

A long hour passed; the singing of the men died away and they now sat as if in a stupor, staring blankly before them, their eyes inflamed.

Thinking the propitious time had arrived, the white man again questioned the headman.

He was answered by a peal of derisive laughter, and the two natives exchanged a number of ribald and very pointed jokes anent the folly of white men and of this white man in particular.

Thereat the white man suddenly remembered his dignity and the respect due to a white man from a black, the respect which he had forfeited long since.

Jumping to his feet, he stood over the Hottentot, his *sjambok* raised threateningly.

"You damned rascal!" he swore savagely. "Do you dare to snigger at me?"

"I always laugh at fools, white man," the Hottentot answered with drunken solemnity. "And is it my fault that you are a fool?"

For answer the white man brought down his whip on the native's naked back, drawing blood and laughing callously at the half-suppressed moan of pain which came from the Hottentot's lips.

He struck again and again, laughing continuously, vowing to kill the native who had dared to laugh at him.

SEVERAL TIMES the Hottentot attempted to rise to his feet and run from the biting torture of the lash. But each time his legs failed him and he dropped to the ground in a huddled heap, his strength stolen from him by the rotgut he had drunk. Umbalose, too, was helpless; the liquor had made him drunker, even, than the Hottentot. He could only look on with wondering eyes, muttering words of sympathy, hoping that some of the young men of the kraal would return.

Breathing heavily, the white man paused for a moment from using the *sjambok* and lashed the Hottentot with a vicious tongue.

And so intent was he on his outpourings of wrath, that he was not aware of the approach of a light, tent-topped wagon drawn by sixteen mules.

The wagon came to a halt in a cloud of choking dust a few hundred feet away and the Major, dressed in spotless duck semi-uniform, highly polished riding boots, a white helmet and his monocle gleaming in his eye, jumped down from the wagon calling, gaily:

"*O-he*, Jim! Jim!"

The other white man turned at the voice and, seeing who the newcomer was, noticing particularly the monocle and the dude-like attire, turned away from the natives and made as if he desired nothing so much as to get away from the place with great speed.

And now the Major, noting with eyes of steel gray the recumbent natives, the blood-stained whip in the other's hands, the empty bottles and Jim's bleeding back, came hastily forward.

"My word!" he exclaimed. "This is beastly—positively beastly. It is absolutely criminal. First you make these two drunk on some rotten concoction and then you thrash them. Why?"

The other sneered. Having mounted his steed he now felt quite safe and looked down contemptuously at the Major.

"That's my business," he said.

"Really! Then it's a damned rotten business!"

"Well—supposin' it is; what are you goin' to do about it, Percy?"

The Major raised his eyebrows, allowing his monocle to fall into the palm of his hand. He put it carefully into his breast pocket.

"I'll tell you," he said. "I am goin' to make your business mine. So—dismount." The other laughed.

"If I dismount," he blustered, "it'll be to finish what I started doing to you last night. If it hadn't a' been for my woman I'd have knocked your bleedin' head off."

The dude stared at him incredulously.

"It can't be Jake, surely," he cried. "It is, though!" He fished his monocle from his pocket and fixed it in his eye. "Yes, by Jove, it's Jake. Or is Piet the name? Really, I've met so many laddies within the last twenty-four hours that I find it almost impossible to keep you straight. But, now I come to think of it, I see that you're Piet, the chappy I knocked out; that is, I mean the chappy who hit my bally thumb with his jaw. Well! I am glad to see you. Our mutual friend, Mr.—er—Soapy Richards, told me that you were waiting for cherubs to carry you up to the Pearly Gates. I am afraid it will be a long time before they are opened to you. We must celebrate this little reunion and I think the best way will be to continue our little argument, so unfortunately stopped by your heavy fall, of last night. So—dismount."

"Don't talk like a fool," Piet replied. "Don't you know nothing? Don't you know it ain't the thing for white men to fight where niggers can see them? It gives the niggers wrong ideas. But you come on back to town and—"

"There may be something in what you say," the Major murmured. "But I can't think that witnessing two white men fight would be half as bad for—er—niggers as drinking the stuff you've been ladling out to them. Besides, I don't think these two laddies can see much. So, for the third time, dismount!"

To add emphasis to his order a revolver suddenly appeared in his right hand.

"Blast you," Piet whined as he slowly obeyed, "What right have you got to interfere between a white man and a little argument he is having with a couple of niggers?"

"SIMPLY," REPLIED the Major, "that I do not like the way you conduct your argument."

Piet whined some incoherent reply and the Major continued:

"And now shall we continue last night's pleasant little argument?"

He smiled and tensed himself slightly, expecting a mad, bull-like rush.

Instead, Piet only answered sullenly, "I tell you I ain't goin' to fight. It's bad for the niggers."

Major sighed.

"So much consideration does you credit but—I have none. Give me your *sjambok*."

Cursing, Piet handed it to him. He ran it through his hand, testing its suppleness, glancing in disgust at the blood which stained it.

"Won't you put up your fists?" Major asked hopefully.

"No, I tell you. An' look here, don't let on to Soapy Richards that you saw me out here. He'll have me murdered, mister, if you tell him that."

"My word!" Major exclaimed wearily. "He'd deserve a vote of thanks if he did. And now—get out. Quick!" He struck Piet across the legs with the *sjambok*, making that man howl and curse. "I haven't begun to treat you as you deserve," the Major continued. "If I did, I'm afraid I'd be arrested for murder and, really, I have no desire to hang for vermin like you. And now—" with one final cut of the lash—"if you will take my advice you will go hence and never return."

He threw the whip at Piet and watched that man clamber up into the saddle and gallop away, whimpering loudly.

Then he turned to the two natives and stooping over the Hottentot, gravely scrutinized his bleeding back.

"Jim!" he said.

But the Hottentot made no reply. Despite the cruel beating he had received, the fumes of the liquor had mounted to his brain and he slept, snoring hoggishly.

The Major turned to Umbalose.

"You are his Baas?" that man asked, grinning fatuously.

The Major nodded.

"*Wo-we!* You are all that he said you were. But your heart is too soft. You should have killed that evil white man."

"Why did he beat the Hottentot?"

"He asked me where was the place the spirits of Zulu warriors go. And when I said that I could not tell him he was very angry and cursed us. Then the Hottentot laughed at him; then his anger increased and he beat the Hottentot. That is all. But had you not come—" He shook his head doubtfully.

"And the Hottentot?" the Major asked, looking at the sleeping man anxiously. "You think he has not come to any great harm?"

Umbalose chuckled.

"His head will pain him when he wakes, and his back will be stiff. That is all. He only sleeps now. *Au-a!* And that is a strange thing: I have seen men fall asleep whilst they were being beaten, as if the beating had sapped all their strength, and they had not partaken of the white man's *puza* as the Hottentot had." The headman scratched his head and looked dubiously at the white man. "But if you are the Hottentot's Baas," he continued, "how comes it that you speak our tongue? He told me that you did not know it."

"Two years have passed since he last saw me. In two years a lot can be done."

Umbalose nodded sagely.

"True: Two years have taught me to like a Hottentot. He is a man, this one. But a fool. Truly a great fool. For these two months past he has had but little beer to drink because, said he, 'tomorrow my Baas may come and he must find me ready for him; he will need my help; my legs must be strong and my eyes clear!' *Wo-we!* And today that evil white man and the smell of the *puza* he brought was too much for the Hottentot and he drank. *So-a!* Then you come and he is not ready for you. He will be very shamed when he wakes. Be kind to him, white man. He has waited a long time for you."

"**I WILL** always remember that," the Major said gravely. "And now I must trek on. Come you to the wagon with me that I may in some part repay you for the hospitality you have given to the Hottentot."

"Hospitality is given, white man," the headman replied with dignity. "It is not a thing to be bartered."

The Major threw up his hand with the gesture of a man who has been hit.

"The fault is mine," he acknowledged. "But it is permitted, surely, to offer a present?"

Umbalose grinned.

"Truly! And if the present is desirable, it will be accepted."

"Then come down to the wagon," the Major said again as, picking up the Hottentot, he led the way.

With difficulty the headman struggled to his feet and staggered after him and was rewarded, as soon as Major had made the Hottentot comfortable on a pile of blankets, by a rich assortment of gifts: pocket knives, axes, mouth-organs and rolls of gaily colored cloths.

"It is a chief's wealth you have given me, white man," he stammered in delight.

"I have only given you my thanks," the Major replied. "And now we trek on." He climbed up into the wagon.

"But where do you go?"

"To that place of the spirits."

The headman scowled.

"And you know where it is?"

"Truly."

"Be warned by me, white man," Umbalose said earnestly. "Do not go. It is a place forbidden and there are warriors whose duty it is to see that none enter."

The white man hesitated, then, with a farewell wave of his hand, drove off at a gallop, much to the disgusted surprise of the chestnut horse tethered to the tailboard of the wagon.

CHAPTER VI
The Lady of the Wagon

IT WAS early morning. The sun had not yet risen far enough above the horizon to make its presence felt The grasses were still laden with the night's dew; the bushes bespangled with globules which sparkled like gems. North, south, east and west stretched the vast, undulating veld. In all its vast expanse there seemed to be no moving thing except the white tent-topped wagon, no living creatures except the mules which drew it, the squat Hottentot who drove them and the Major, mounted on his horse, who rode beside the wagon.

And yet the bush was teeming with life, invisible to the untrained eye, but as obvious to the Hottentot as the printed page of a book to a student. And even the Major's eyes were beginning to see things which, but a little while ago, would have been hidden from him.

These past days of trekking with Jim, the Hottentot, had been for him a marvelous education in the ways of the bush and the creatures inhabiting it. And he had been an apt pupil. So that now when Jim pointed ahead, exclaiming softly, "See! There are springbuck, Baas!" the Major did not strain his eyes looking for the form of this most graceful of buck. Instead, with no effort of concentration, he would gaze casually in the direction indicated by the Hottentot, looking for something which *moved*. And then "something"—perhaps it would be only the switch of a tail, or the pricking up of an ear, or the stamp of a foot— would move in the vast stillness and focus his attention. And immediately the thing he sought would leap into his vision with the suddenness and clearness of a picture thrown upon a screen.

IT WAS proof somewhat of his newly acquired veldcraft that he presently pointed to a clump of trees ahead and turning to Jim, said, "There we will camp. There we will find water."

The Hottentot chuckled softly.

"The Baas learns," he said. "In a little while there will be nothing that I can tell him. But" he chuckled again— "not for a little while."

The Major looked at him wonderingly.

"But there is water there, Jim," he insisted. "I can smell it."

"Yah, *Baas,*" Jim agreed. "Undoubtedly there is water at that place, but not yet is it sure that we will camp there."

"Why, Jim? What cause for doubt?"

"I have known caves," Jim said sententiously, "which offered a dry place in which to sleep in times of rain. But there were leopards in those caves, and when the rains came I slept in the open."

"You mean," the Major questioned swiftly, "that there may be leopards at the water-hole? And that because of them we will not be able to camp there? What folly. Of what use is this—" he picked up the rifle which he carried before him on his saddle—"if we are to be afraid of leopards?"

Jim looked admiringly at his Baas.

"I think," he said, "that you fear nothing. And yet, sometimes, it is wise to be afraid. I think it would have been best had you been afraid of the man on whose errand you now go. I do not like this place you call Devil's Kloof. It is an evil name and all things connected with it are evil. The man

Richards is evil—I have heard of him. He will not play a true game with you. You, my Baas, risk much in order that he, who risks nothing, may grow rich. Therefore, I say that it would have been wiser to be afraid of that man and his doings. But most of all, Baas, you should be afraid of this trail we are following."

"And are you afraid of all these things, Jim?"

"Undoubtedly, Baas, but chiefly of the last."

The Major scoffed.

"It is only a woman's trail, Jim," he said lightly.

"And therein, Baas, is all the danger, all the evil, the world contains. A woman's trail is always dangerous, it always leads to folly."

"*Wo-we!*" the Major exclaimed. "And this from a man who boasts of four wives."

"It is because of that, Baas," Jim said mournfully, "that I know the truth of what I speak."

"But this trail, Jim," the Major protested. "We are not following it. It happens to go the way we are going, that is all. And it is an open trail. And I think that by tomorrow, or the next day, we will have caught up and passed the woman's wagon and be making a trail of our own."

"The Baas' eyes are not yet fully open," the Hottentot said. "If he will look closely at the droppings of the cattle which pull that other wagon, he will see that by sundown, at the clump of trees where he says there is water, we will have caught up with them."

"I see," the Major said gaily, speaking now in English. "That is what Jim, the old fraud, meant when he said that perhaps we would not camp at the water-hole. But I do not believe he knows they are so close ahead just by looking at the spoor. I believe the old blighter can see the wagon and oxen ahead of us. But, come to think of it, that's just as marvelous!" He shaded his eyes with his hand and stared directly ahead of him, endeavoring to pick out against the dark, olive-green of the veld a slowly moving wagon. Then he shook his head. "I can't see the wood for the bally trees," he confessed. Then, to Jim, in the vernacular, "I am going to ride on ahead, Jim."

"The Baas will take care?" the Hottentot said anxiously.

The Major laughed and spurring his horse, galloped swiftly away, sitting gracefully in the saddle, looking as if he and the horse were one perfect whole.

"What a man!" the Hottentot exclaimed. "There is nothing he cannot do, and do well. And he is my Baas!"

Even in the little while they had been together, a wonderful understanding had sprung up between these two, white master and black servant, both *men,* both embued with the spirit of eternal boyhood. Between them there was no question of race or color. But there was no mawkish, falsely sentimental "love for a black brother" about the Major's treatment of Jim; neither did the Hottentot ever presume or in any way seek to proclaim himself to the world as the equal in all things of a white man. It was rather that each recognized the other's essential manliness and was content to let it go at that.

AN HOUR later the Major drew rein, shaded his eyes with his hand and gazed over the veld. The clump of trees which marked his destination seemed no nearer than they had done when he first left Jim. Through the heat waves the trees were distorted and danced grotesquely. Far beyond them a low range of hills, blued by the distance, loomed high on the horizon.

"By Jove!" the Major exclaimed, licking his dry lips. "This is a bally frightful country. I expected to be at the water-hole by now."

He turned in his saddle and looked back, half-inclined to wait for Jim. To his surprise he could see nothing of his white-tented wagon and for a moment felt alone and a little awed. The veld was so vast and he, by contrast, no more than a puny insect. Then presently, the wagon crawled into sight, topping a rise. He could hear Jim's strident voice and the rifle-like reports of the long driving whip. He grinned happily, feeling that no matter what happened there would always be Jim to back up any play he made—good natured, grumbling Jim, who feigned to be greatly afraid at the times when he showed his greatest bravery.

"He has taught me a lot already," the Major muttered. "But there is yet more, lots more to learn from him still. As old Pim would say: I am innocent as a new born babe. And so, until greater knowledge comes to me, I must be very cautious. Oh very!"

With that he turned his face once more in the direction of the water-hole, and rode on at an easy tripple, a rocking-chair gait which well trained and good conditioned animals can keep on tirelessly through a long African day.

Many times during the next hour the clump of trees ahead of the Major vanished altogether from his sight as he crossed one of the wide wave-like depressions of the veld. At other times it appeared so near that it seemed as if by stretching out his hand, he could touch the nearest tree. At times the heat waves obliterated all form and shape, and the earth about him seemed to dissolve into the electric blue haze of the sky; between sky and veld there seemed to be no dividing line.

At long last he came within shouting distance of the clump of trees, and with difficulty restrained his horse from breaking into a gallop.

He drew rein for a moment and scrutinized the place, making sure that all was safe, before he went on; he saw a number of oxen grazing contentedly nearby, and a large ox wagon, with a much patched canvas top, drawn up in the shade of the trees.

Riding on again he heard a woman's voice, a full rich contralto, raised, he thought, in angry expostulation.

Coming still nearer he heard a man's voice, sullen, interlarded with expressions peculiar to the South-African Dutch.

A few minutes later he arrived at the water-hole outspan and, reining in his horse, sat looking down at the girl who was seated on the disselboom of the wagon, and the gaunt, shaggily-bearded Boer, who stood stolidly before her. Both of them were so intent on their argument that they ignored the Major's presence seemed, indeed, to be unconscious of it.

The Major looked keenly at the girl, noting with approval her workmanlike dress and appearance. Her hair close cropped—not an affectation of fashion, but a necessity if one was to consider cleanliness and comfort on the veld—clinging in tight brown curls about her well shaped head. She wore heavy, cord riding breeches, a gray flannel shirt, open at the neck, its sleeves rolled up above her elbows, brown leggings and boots. A rifle rested across her knees, and one sun-browned, capable hand rested lightly on the stock whilst the other pointed accusingly at the Boer.

"She is pretty," mused the Major. "No! That is wrong. She is beautiful!"

THIS LAST thought was induced by the girl's suddenly jumping to her feet and threatening the Dutchman with her hand, stamping her feet, crying, "You are a fool, you big senseless lump of clay. You will mend the wagon, and tomorrow, maybe tonight, we shall inspan and trek on. You hear me?"

"*Ja!*" The Boer replied stolidly. "I hear you, little spitfire! Tomorrow we will trek; but not on. We go back! Unless—" He leered at her provocatively and stretched out his arms as if intending to clasp her, but backed away with a startled oath of dismay, as she suddenly leveled the rifle at him.

It was then that the Major decided to make his presence known.

"Can I," he drawled, taking off his helmet, and bowing low in his saddle, "can I be of any assistance, dear Miss?"

The Boer turned with a startled exclamation, and the girl looked up with signs of relief showing in her clear brown eyes. But almost instantly the look of relief gave way to one of suspicion.

"And who the devil are you?" she snapped.

The Major seemed taken aback and covered his embarrassment with an exhibition of inanity.

"Just a wanderer on the face of the globe, dear Miss," he said lightly. "I come and go as the wind blows."

"I should say you are mostly wind," the girl interposed.

"What is your name?"

"Aubrey St. John Major. I—"

Again her cutting voice interrupted him. "And your business?"

"Dear Miss," he protested in mock injured tones. "I am no bally tradesman. Actually I am on a hunting trip, for my health's sake, in company with a bally Hottentot, and

I cannot begin to tell you how delightful it is to me in this outpost, as it were, of civilization to see a member of the—er—so-called weaker sex."

"Yes, I imagine you would be more at home at one of Lady What-Not's 'At homes.'"

He stared at her in blank amazement.

"But I do not know the lady I assure you."

She laughed again, then, suspicion again clouded her eyes.

"It is funny," she said slowly, "that you come up into this country on a hunting expedition, where there is so little game."

"I was assured," he began hastily, "that it was absolutely teeming with game; lions, elephants, rhinos and what not, all dwelling together like the lion and the lamb of the fable, you know. You do not mean to tell me, surely, that I have been spoofed?"

"No," she replied, "I do not think that you have been spoofed and I do not think that you are as big a fool as you look."

"Really!" he exclaimed. "That is a bit too thick! I may look a fool—for that you must blame my parents—but I have plenty of brains I assure you."

The girl shrugged her shoulders.

"I suppose," she said, caustically, "That you do not happen to know a man named Richards? Soapy Richards?"

"OH RATHER, yes!" the Major replied gaily. "He is a most astonishing blighter and been no end good to me. At least," he amended, "I thought he was good to me at first. You see I was being beaten up by a gang of beastly thugs one night, in Cape Town, and I believe I should have been killed had not Soapy Richards interfered. I was no end grateful to him, I assure you, and I had no hesitation in buying from him stock in a mine he was trying to sell and which he assured me would in time make me rich beyond the well known dreams of avarice. And I was so pleased with my acumen in getting hold of so valuable a property that I did not think of questioning him, when, on bidding me good-by, he pulled out a watch to consult the time, and that watch, dear Miss, was my watch. It had been stolen from me by the afore-mentioned gang of desperadoes. I say I did not suspect Mr. Richards of anything at the time—I was, understand, so bally grateful to him—but later—" he sighed—"when I discovered that the mine existed only in Richards' imagination, then I began to think things, and, do you know? I have come to the conclusion that the mine and Richards' good Samaritan act were all so much froth and bubble. The sort of thing one would expect to be produced from soft soap."

The girl laughed again; a clear musical laugh, and her eyes danced with merriment.

"You are an even greater fool than you look," she gasped. "But somehow, I am inclined to like you, Mr. Aubrey St. John Major."

The Major beamed with pleasure.

"Then I may dismount?" he asked, "and outspan, as the bally Boers put it?"

She nodded assent.

"There is room for us all," she said, and frowned when the Boer, who had been a silent listener to the conversation between herself and the Major, uttered a loud protest.

"There is not enough water for us all, *roinek,*" he said. "It is best that you trek on to another water-hole that is only five miles away; and that is nothing. You have a horse and a wagon that is drawn by mules, is it not? You go on and I will tell your Hottentot when he comes where you have gone."

There was a threat underlying the Dutchman's voice and the girl looked at the Major keenly as if wondering how he would take it.

"I think," that man said slowly, "I will stay here at least until my Hottentot arrives. Then, if he says that there is not enough water, we will go on." He turned to the girl continuing, "He should be here by noon, and I hope that you will do me the honor of lunching with me."

"I will be charmed," she said. "And now, if you will pardon me, I must dress in honor of the occasion."

With a wave of the hand she climbed up into the wagon and disappeared under its tented-top.

CHAPTER VII

Vanderspey Shakes Hands

THE MAJOR turned to the Boer, glancing speculatively at his gigantic frame, the thick red lips, tangled tobacco-stained beard and the small, piggish, red-rimmed eyes.

"Your name?" he asked sharply, speaking the *taal*.

"Ach sis!" the Dutchman replied. "Must I tell my name to any damn fool Englisher who asks it?"

"Of course, old dear, if it is a name you are ashamed of I will not press the matter."

"Almighty!" the Dutchman roared. "I have no shame in my name. It is a good name, man! There is no better name than Vanderspey in all this land."

"That is all right then, Van, old dear. Now suppose you take me to the waterhole; there is enough I take it, for my horse?"

"Turn your horse loose, he will find the water."

The Major nodded, and, turning loose his horse, followed it to a jumble of rocks, where was a large pool of crystal-clear spring water. He drank himself then returned to where Vanderspey stood scratching his head in puzzled indecision.

"There is difficulty?" asked the Major.

"Ja!" the Dutchman replied wrathfully. "She wants to go on, this fool girl, and I say we should go back. This journey she takes is a folly. She goes seeking much treasure where there is no treasure, where only danger is, and puts to scorn the other treasure which is close to her hand."

"And what is this treasure which she scorns?" the Major asked.

Vanderspey laughed.

"Is it not clear to you, Englisher?" he asked. "I am a man! I have a big farm—three thousand *morgen*—with many niggers and sheep. Man! I tell you! By men who know, I, Vanderspey, am counted rich, and I offer all to this fool girl who goes searching for treasure that is not."

The Major laughed softly.

"But perhaps there is a string attached to the gift."

Vanderspey stared at him with dull, uncomprehending eyes.

"A string you say?" he muttered.

"Yes," the Major agreed. "Not that you, old chap, can be exactly called a string. But I suppose that with all this you offer the young lady, you also offer your hand?"

The Dutchman nodded.

"*Ja!* That is it, and, look you, it is a good hand." He stretched his big right hand out toward Major. "Shake it," he said, "and judge for yourself."

As he spoke he grinned maliciously.

"Yes," the Major drawled, fixing his monocle more securely, and gazing at Vanderspey's hand as if it were some freakish curiosity. "It would seem to be quite a good hand; very large and muscular. Judging by the heart line I should imagine you are going to be disappointed in love."

HE TOOK Vanderspey's wrist fastidiously between his thumb and forefinger and turned Vanderspey's hand over. "Very hairy," he continued, "and the condition of the finger nails leaves much to be desired. However, as a hand it is a good hand."

And then he held out his own right hand, slightly tanned, long-fingered, the nails neatly trimmed and polished; a plump, almost effeminate looking hand.

He grasped Vanderspey's, and instantly the Boer stiffened; his hand tightened about the Major's. The Major tensed slightly, standing with his feet apart. His biceps swelled under his white silk shirt as he summoned up his strength to meet the vise-like pressure Vanderspey was exerting.

The Dutchman stared incredulously. He had expected the Major to drop to his knees, to cry out in pain and beg to be released from the torturing grip; instead the dude only smiled. Worse yet, his fingers contracted about Vanderspey's hand in a grip of steel; each finger feeling like a wire, slowly but surely tightening.

Vanderspey's eyes dilated, beads of sweat formed on his brow, rolled down his nose and dropped into his tangled beard. He endeavored to put more force into his grip and, failing, bit his lips in order to suppress a groan of pain. His fingers grew numb, he felt that drops of blood must be dripping from his finger tips; suddenly he relaxed his efforts and at that moment Major twisted his hand upward, and to the right, pulling him off his balance, sending him with a crash to the ground.

"Yes," the Major drawled, wiping his hand on a handkerchief. "Yours is a very good hand but I fancy it has been rejected in a manner of speaking. Eh! What!"

"Almighty!" the Dutchman roared, rubbing his benumbed fingers, rose to his feet and glared angrily at the Major. "It was a trick, Englisher."

"Of course. And now perhaps you will tell me what you have decided to do. Do you go forward in the morning or back?"

"Almighty! That is easy. We go back. I will see to that."

"And if the young lady insists on going forward, what then?"

"I know how to deal with women. She will go back. In the beginning I agreed to do all she said, knowing that if I did not come with her she would get someone else to bring her on this fool trip. But I came. And, now she has spent all her money, she will be glad after a time of all the things I offer her."

"You mean to marry her, of course?" the Major said.

Vanderspey leered.

"Maybe. But at least I have promised to send away my nigger women so that she will have no rivals. That is most dangerous of me, is it not?"

The Major sighed.

"I am afraid, Vanderspey, that you are born to trouble as the sparks fly upward, and I think that tomorrow you will go forward. Yes, I will make it my business to see that you do that. But here comes Jim, he shall help you mend the wagon. But first he will prepare a meal."

AS HE spoke, Jim, the Hottentot, drew his mules to a halt with a flourish, and jumped to the ground shouting a greeting to his Baas and the scowling Dutchman.

"Outspan, Jim," the Major ordered. "There is plenty of water for the mules. Then prepare skoff."

With great efficiency Jim turned the mules loose, then busied himself for a while in the interior of the wagon. Half an hour later he had set up a canvas table in the shade of some trees, had covered it with a white damask cloth, on which silver gleamed, and highly polished crystal ware; on either side of the table were set two canvas chairs.

And then the girl appeared at the opening of her wagon and the Major leaped forward, offering her his hand.

She took it gracefully and stepped down daintily.

"My name," she said demurely, "is Marjorie Wallace."

"Charmed!" the Major murmured conventionally and led her gravely to the table.

As the meal progressed a feeling of restraint between them ceased and they talked merrily of this and that, finding they had many tastes in common, not once did either of them by word or act indicate that there was anything unusual about so well served a meal in the wilds of a rawly new country.

To all intents and purposes they might have been any good looking, well dressed couple lunching at a fashionable resort in London or New York. When Jim brought them their coffee the Major took from his pocket a silver cigarette case, opened it, offered it to the girl and held the match to her cigarette.

For a little while they were both silent, happily content with each other's company.

Jim and the Dutchman were now engaged in cutting a new disselboom and the ring of their axes against the hard wood was the only sound which broke the silence.

"I think," the Major said presently, "that by late afternoon you will be able to trek."

"I am quite sure I shall."

"But are you sure which way you are going to trek?"

"Naturally," she replied. "We are heading north."

"But Vanderspey has different ideas," the Major objected.

"Oh, Vanderspey!" She made a little grimace of contempt. "He will go the way I order. It is rather embarrassing at times, but he is devoted to me."

"I should think," the Major suggested, "that would be dangerous rather than embarrassing."

"Dangerous? How?"

The Major fidgetted uneasily. "My dear Miss Marjorie," he said, "consider your situation! You are here alone on the veld, your only protector a coarse Boer."

"You mean I am in danger of being abducted by Vander-spey! Poor old Van! He is as harmless as a sheep dog."

"Sheep dogs have been known to get rabies and then they are not altogether harmless."

"Oh well then," she said, with a seriousness befitting the subject, "if Vanderspey goes mad, I shall make sure of shooting before he—" she dropped her voice to a whisper—"bites."

THE MAJOR sighed. He believed this girl needed his protection, yet he could not see any way in which he could force that protection upon her. She seemed so competent.

The girl, as if in answer to his thoughts, suddenly produced a revolver. "This," she said, "is always with me, and I find that it is a very competent protector."

"But can you use it?" he asked.

"Better than most men," she replied. "I lived through rough times with Daddy in the Californian gold fields, and often this was my only companion. Daddy saw to it that it was not just meant for show.

"Look," she said, and pointed to a small battered tin plate. "I will turn my back to you, put my revolver on the chair here, and you shall throw that plate up in the air. Then you call 'right'—and we shall see."

The girl turned her back to him, and he threw a plate high up into the air.

"Right!" he called.

Quick as a flash the girl whirled, picked up the revolver and fired twice.

The plate leaped in the air at the impact of the bullets, and then dropped to the ground. The Major picked it up, examined the two jagged holes and returned it to the girl.

"Are you satisfied now?" she asked triumphantly.

He shook his head.

"It is not always as easy as that, and I wish you would let me join your expedition."

Instantly the atmosphere of friendly good comradeship disappeared.

"I go my own way," she said curtly, "And I go alone. I warn you that should I have reasons to suspect that you are following me, I shall shoot at sight."

The Major sighed.

"Then will you accept my Hottentot, Jim, for your driver, and let Vanderspey come with me? I think I can handle him."

"No!" she said.

"At least," the Major said despairingly, "you will accept my horse, won't you? Then, if anything goes wrong you might be able to ride away."

She hesitated a moment, then:

"I think I will accept that," she said softly. "And thank you!"

And with that the Major had to be content. The only thing he could do now, was to make clear to Vanderspey that the girl was not alone in the world but had a protector, namely, himself. With this end in view, he rose carelessly from his chair, explaining in response to the girl's questioning look that he must be toddling along.

THEN HE gave a few orders to Jim, instructing that man to pack up the luncheon things and inspan. And Jim having set about his task with a will—the Hottentot was strangely eager to get his Baas away from feminine influence—the Major excused himself to the girl and went over to where Vanderspey was slowly working on the new disselboom, and watched him.

The Dutchman evidently resented this scrutiny, for presently he threw down his ax with a curse, and asked: "Why do you stare so at me?"

"I was attempting," the Major said lightly, "a little mental telepathy. I wanted to convey to your brain that you must obey Miss Wallace in all things. I want you to bear very closely in your mind that from now on I shall be only a half-day's trek ahead of you, sometimes less; and at night, when you may think you are safe from prying eyes, I shall take it upon myself to pay secret visits to your outspan. You will not see me; Miss Wallace will not see me; but I shall be there. And so, dear man"—he rose to his feet and stretched himself—"You will be very grateful, will you not?"

Vanderspey scowled.

"If a hyena comes prowling around my outspan at night," he growled, "I shoot the skellum."

"And that's very wise. Only, at the risk of appearing boastful, I must point out to you that I am not a hyena, and that you won't see me."

Vanderspey muttered inarticulate oaths. His face was white with fury and in his piggish eyes was a killing light. Yet the Major knew that the Boer would hesitate a long time before attempting any overt action.

"Well that's that!" he said, "S'long!" And rising to his feet he turned his back on Vanderspey and returned to his wagon.

Jim had inspanned the mules, and all was ready for the trek.

"Good-by, Miss Marjorie," the Major said. "I hope we shall meet again very soon."

"It is not likely," she replied coldly, then her eyes softened. "But I, too, wish it were possible. You have been very kind. I will take good care of your horse and, when this trek is over, will leave him for you at the livery stables at Steinberg. Good-by!"

She held out her well shaped, sun-bronzed hand, and took Major's in a firm cool grip.

"Good-by, Miss Marjorie," the Major said again and climbed into his wagon.

"Trek!" he called sharply to Jim; and the Hottentot shouting wildly, flourishing the long stocked driving whip, urged the mules into a gallop, and the wagon rolled swiftly away.

WITH HER hand shading her eyes, the girl stared after them, until no sign of them was left save a swiftly moving cloud of dust. Then she turned slowly, a thoughtful expression on her face, and climbed up into her wagon.

CHAPTER VIII

The Galloping Trek

AFTER LEAVING the water-hole inspan, the Major was very quiet and had no answer for the Hottentot's ceaseless banter and the rough homespun philosophy with which he sought to point out the folly of the Supreme Being in creating women. And at length, as they drove on, his Baas' silence infected him and he sat sullenly silent, applying the whip with unnecessary vigor.

The speed of the wagon increased, and it swayed perilously from side to side.

"This is folly, Jim," the Major said presently, reining in the mules. "Put away your whip. You are a wicked heathen, Jim. You rail against women, yet had there been no women there would have been no Jim!"

The Hottentot grunted disdainfully.

"As long, Baas," he said, "as women remember the one purpose for which they were made, I have no words of complaint to make against them. But when I see them taking to themselves the dress of man, and the work of man, then I say there is no evil so great. That Missy back there," he continued, warming to his theme, "should be at home in her hut, making beer, drying skins or preparing her man's food."

"She is a white woman, Jim, and has no hut and no man."

"*Wo-we!*" Jim exclaimed. "Then she must be a witch, for she is without doubt past the age when maidens are given in marriage. I say—"

"You have said enough," the Major interrupted abruptly. "There are some things which even you, wise one, do not understand; and it is folly to talk of what is not understood."

"I understand," Jim muttered sullenly, "that she is a woman, and has fascinated my Baas with her eyes."

Again there was silence, unbroken, until Jim viewed a horseman ahead of them. He looked slyly at his Baas, asking: "And can you see nothing Baas, or have your eyes been blinded as are the eyes of a love sick youth?"

The Major roused himself.

"My eyes are open, Jim," he said. "They are not blinded, and I see—" he hesitated—"a buck ahead of us."

Jim chuckled.

"You are blind, Baas," he said. "That is no buck. It is a man on horseback. The horse is gray. It is lame in the off-fore. The man who rides it is small but, I think fat. He is a policeman." He paused looking triumphantly at the Major, noting the look of incredulity on that man's face. Then, "Shall I tell you more?" he added. "To prove how blind my Baas is?"

"Tell me more if you will, Jim," the Major replied. "But it will not prove me blind, but rather how wide open are your eyes—or how big a liar you are."

Jim laughed.

"I am no liar Baas. At least, I do not lie to you. I will tell you no more. You shall see for yourself when we have got up to the man."

AND HALF an hour later, when they had drawn rein beside a man on horseback, the Major found himself exchanging greetings with a short, rotund little man, dressed in the uniform of the mounted police. His horse limped slightly on its off-fore.

"What is your name, pardner?" the little man asked, and though his phrases were of the American West his accent was that of a London-bred man.

"Major. Aubrey St. John Major. And yours?"

" 'Emmings. Trooper 'Emmings. And I am pleased to meetcha. Have you a drink you can offer a thirsty man?"

The Major nodded.

"Suppose you climb up into the wagon with us," he suggested, "and tie your horse to the tailboard of the wagon. A little rest will do you both good."

"Blimey! Yes!" exclaimed the other, mopping his beet-red face with a white spotted, blue, cotton handkerchief. "It's blamed 'ot ain't it?"

A few minutes later he was seated on the driver's seat between Jim and the Major.

He continued:

"This is an 'ell of a trip I am on. Got to go to a kraal way back of beyond of somewheres because there is a rumor that the niggers are giving trouble. My corporal, he is there already, and he sent a special messenger to me to hurry along and join him, I ought to have been there yesterday, but my blinking horse put its feet down an ant bear hole and sprained his fetlock, I couldn't ride him yesterday, had to walk, and by rights, I ought not to have been riding him today. Poor devil! And say, pard! Look here! There is a farm about ten miles on. I could get a horse there, if you will take me."

The Major nodded. "Charmed," he said. "I am always ready to do all I can to help the long arm of the Law. I hope," he added anxiously, "that you do not expect any great trouble with the natives of this district. You see I am on a hunting trip."

"Oh no!" The trooper reassured him. "It won't be much, just a little trouble about some bloomin' superstition. Something to do with Devil's Kloof. Me and my corporal will soon be able to put them right. Nothing to worry about, nothing whatever."

The Major nodded.

"I'm very glad of that," he said. Then: "You will pardon me, I know, but sometimes you talk like a man who has lived most of his life within sound of the dear old Bow Bells, and yet, your figures of speech, if you get what I mean, are those of an American. How is it?"

THE TROOPER grinned somewhat sheepishly. "That is all my corporal's fault," he said. "He is a real, honest-to-God Westerner. I am ready to gamble that he can sit a horse, and ride and shoot, and knows the niggers of this country better than I does the palm of my hand. You ought to meet him Aubrey, if you will pardon me being familiar. It sure would be an education for you. And Blimey! You look as if you need one."

The Major laughed.

"I'd like to meet him, trooper," he said. "Maybe I will someday. I suppose being with the corporal so much, you have unconsciously, as it were, adopted his mannerisms?"

"There's no unconscious about it," replied the trooper flatly. "Corporal Greenway is wot I fink a man ought to be, so I tries to be as like 'im as possible, only— Blimey! it's blinking hard. He stands nearly six foot and he's as thin as a beanpole. And me! You can see for yourself wot I am!"

The Major sighed in sympathy for him. Then he remembered the girl he had just left at the water-hole.

"Look here," he said excitedly, "couldn't you give up this trek you are on and go back and look after a lady?"

The trooper shook his head.

"It ain't possible," he said. "I've got my orders and I've got to obey them; but 'oo is she and wot's the trouble?"

The Major told him, briefly, his fears for the girl.

"I don't see there's nothing I can do," Hemmings said, "though I sure'd like to take a hand and bash that blighter Vanderspey in the jaw. But I can't. But, say, wot's her name?"

"Miss Wallace, Marjorie Wallace."

"Wot?" Hemmings exclaimed excitedly. "Has she brown 'air, cropped short, with sort of curls about 'er 'ead, dresses like a boy, and eyes with a sort of 'I can take very good care of myself' about them?"

"You have described the girl exactly," the Major said, and continued, with a growing curiosity, "You know her?"

"Lumme!" Hemmings replied. "I should just say I do, and this 'ere is an 'ell of an 'ole I'm in! Look here, my corporal, I'm finking, is in love with this girl. He met her down at the last post where we were stationed at. You understand we have only been in this district a little while, and don't know it like we ought. Well, the corporal he meets this Miss Wallace and gets mighty interested in her, and she in him, for the matter of that. The corporal he lets on to me that the only reason he is interested in her is because she is a Yankee, the same as 'im, but I know better. And as for Miss Yankee! It may have begun that way, but it ain't like that wiv 'er now, and Lumme! 'Ere's a 'ell of a mess for me. Here's the corporal's girl in a funny situation, and I feels as if I ought to go back. But I don't see how I can.

"It's 'ell! No matter wot I do, it'll be wrong. But this is wot I am going to do: I am going to push on as fast as I can to this farm and get another horse, and then ride like 'ell to the corporal and tell him all about it."

The Major nodded agreement with the idea, and tightening his grip on the reins said to Jim:

"We trek fast now!" The Hottentot grinned, flourished his whip and urged the mules into a frenzied gallop.

CHAPTER IX

Jim

IT WAS nearing sundown of the following day, when the contour of the ground over which the Major's wagon was traveling suddenly changed. Before it had been gentle and undulating, dotted with thick clumps of mopani bush and tall coarse grass. But now the ground ahead was as smooth as a billiard table, and totally devoid of vegetation. Directly ahead a low range of hills loomed up forbiddingly, looking, Jim said, "As if they marked the outer edge of the earth."

A little to their right the veld seemed to be scarred by a deep cut, which ran directly toward the hills.

"There," said the Hottentot, "is a river. Let us make for it and camp on its banks before the sun sets and darkness falls."

The Major laughed.

"True, oh wise one! There is a river, but there is no water in it!"

The Hottentot looked at his Baas with an expression of astonishment.

"The Baas has been here before?" he questioned.

The Major shook his head.

"But I know there is no water there," he said.

Jim looked at the sun, and then around the dreary plateau.

"Then where shall we camp, Baas?" he asked. "Remember that we have but little water with us."

"We camp on the other side of those hills," the Major stated.

The Hottentot looked at his Baas as if thinking he had gone a little mad.

"The sun has been very hot," he muttered, "and we have trekked far; undoubtedly the Baas is tired. How could we reach the other side of the hills by night? We cannot fly over them, having no wings; and to go around them means a day's, or maybe two days' trek."

The Major laughed.

"Therein it is shown, Hottentot," he said grandly, "that some things are hidden even from you."

As he spoke he turned the mules toward the river, and, reaching it, drove along its banks a little way until he had discovered a place where the banks were less steep and it was possible for him to drive the wagon down on to its firm, sandy bottom.

This dried-up river—it was now only a wide crack in the surface of the veld—was about forty feet wide, and the bed free from obstructions of any sort. It led straight toward the hills, with none of the twists so typical of African rivers.

The Major put his mules to a gallop.

AS THEY neared the black hills the banks became steeper, towering high above the top of the wagon, formed of black rock which glistened like marble.

Jim was frightened, and made no attempt to disguise his fear.

"Where do we go, Baas?" he asked, his teeth chattered. "I like not this place. It looks like the approach of the place of the dead."

"It is there we go, Jim," the Major replied, laughing.

"You mean, Baas?"

"I mean that we go to the Devil's Kloof; the place guarded by the spirits of dead Zulu warriors; the place where, so goes the tale, great treasure is hidden."

Jim looked at his Baas with an expression of profound amazement.

"What a man!" he exclaimed softly. "There seems to be nothing hid from him, and yet I thought, in my folly, that he would have need of me; I thought I could teach him many things."

"As you have, and as you can, Jim," the Major replied earnestly. "The little I know about this place I have been told; there is no credit due to me."

"But, Baas," Jim said earnestly, "learn from me now. I say that it is folly to come to this place. Evil will come of it."

The Major shook his head.

"It comes to me," he said patiently, "that no harm can come to us, even supposing that spirits live in that place. I think that they will be kindly disposed toward us, for look you, we are not Zulus, neither have we any evil designs in our hearts. And so, we go!"

Jim was silenced, his eyes were glued on a sandy stretch ahead of him. Presently it narrowed so much that there was very little margin on either side of the wagon and the Major drove more slowly.

"It is best that we turn back," Jim grumbled, "while there is yet time, for look, Baas, there the river ends and we can go no further."

He pointed ahead and it seemed as if the sheer sides of the hill completely blocked further passage. But on nearing, they saw that the river bed had turned sharply to the right, and then after a few hundred yards again to the left. And left again, passing through mountainous banks. Presently it opened out into a crater-like valley in the heart of the hills, where vegetation was luxurious.

"And there, Jim," the Major said, pointing to a rock-circled pool of water which gleamed blood red, reflecting the sunset glow of the sky, "there we will camp!"

Quickly they outspanned. In a very little while they had erected a bell-tent, and a fire was blazing, before which Jim was grilling a joint cut from the buck the Major had shot earlier in the day.

THE MEAL ended, the Major prepared for bed, and turned in. But owing to the excitement of the past two days and his relief at finding the Devil's Kloof, he could not sleep and, after an hour of restless tossing to and fro, he rose, donned a warm gown, lighted a cigarette and joined Jim, who, wrapped in a vivid red blanket, was walking up and down before an enormous fire, speaking soothingly, reasoningly, to the mules, which were tethered close by the fire.

"There is no need, Jim," said the Major, "to keep watch in this place. No one can get at us. Neither is there any need to tether the mules; they will not try to get out of here."

Jim chuckled grimly.

"Say you so, Baas?" And as he spoke he took a burning brand from the fire and threw it with angry curse out into the darkness beyond the circle of the fire-light. There was a loud rustling noise in the bushes, and a cat-like, spitting snarl. As the flaming log came to earth, the Major fancied he saw, silhouetted against its light the skulking form of a leopard.

"By Jove, Jim!" he breathed softly, and went into his tent for a rifle. Emerging instantly, his eyes ablaze with the joy of the hunt, he asked hoarsely, "Where is it?"

Jim shrugged his shoulders.

"It?" he replied. "There—and there—and there—and there!" He pointed all about the camp. "There are hundreds of them, Baas."

The Major chuckled softly.

"Somewhat of an exaggeration," he drawled in English, adding in the vernacular incredulously, "Hundreds of them?"

"Truly, Baas," Jim replied gravely. "I think that they are inhabited by the souls of the dead Zulus and have come to drive us away from this place of theirs." He put more wood on the fire, and threw another flaming log into the bush.

Again it was greeted by a spitting snarl of defiance and for a fraction of a second the Major saw another leopard, and on that instant he fired. A tawny black smeared shape leapt into the fire-light and dropped with a lifeless thud to the ground.

"The hundreds, Jim," the Major said gleefully, "are at least lessened by one."

"Yah," agreed Jim in alarmed tones. "But listen to the voices of the spirits demanding vengeance!"

The echo of the Major's shot was still reverberating back and forth between the high hills encompassing the valley, sounding like the rattle of distant machine-guns.

THE LEOPARDS' voices were answered by several others, and their spitting snarls, too, were multiplied by the echoes; and then, when all these sounds had died away, somewhere up in the hills a dog-ape barked, and his voice was the signal for a chorus of imprecations shouted by the apes which lived in the hills. Leopards screamed an answer to the challenge, and for a while the valley was a bedlam of howling noises, to which the mules added their raucus clamor.

"Well," said Jim grimly, "said I not, Baas, that this was an evil place?"

"This is no place for a bally Sunday School picnic! My word, no! But on the morrow we will go hunting. Sit down, Jim, and rest or sleep. I will keep watch!"

"The Baas said," Jim observed sarcastically, "there was no need to keep guard in this place. And I will not sleep. Together we will keep watch."

"Then, Jim," said the Major, "we must find a task for our hands or sleep will take us unawares."

He caught hold of the leopard he had shot and dragged it by the tail closer to the fire-light.

"This will be a good time," he said, "to teach me how to take the skin from a beast."

The Hottentot nodded approval and whetted his short-bladed bushman's knife on the sole of his foot.

"First, Baas"—stooping over the carcass of the leopard—"we make a cut here—"

For a time the two men forgot their surroundings; the Major closely following Jim's directions, questioning him, learning the anatomy of the beast, cutting and pulling until finally the skin had been removed with but few slits to show that it had been the work of a novice.

Jim nodded approval.

"The Baas will do better than that very soon. And now to remove this offal." When he came back from disposing of it he squatted down on his haunches close to the Major, who was proudly fingering the skin of the leopard.

"In the morning, Baas," he said, "we must peg it out, and I will show you how to preserve it."

Night wore on. Overhead the stars shone startlingly bright. In the clear air they seemed very near; looked, indeed, as if they were set in a black velvet ceiling, stretched across the top of the hills. Weird moaning shrieks presently filled the valley with an atmosphere of supernatural fear.

"More devils," Jim said, moving uneasily.

The Major listened intently, then laughed. "A wind is blowing, Jim," he explained. "It is blowing through the cracks in the hills."

Jim nodded. "Maybe, Baas," he said uneasily, "but I think they are evil spirits."

THE MAJOR was silent for a moment, then said earnestly, "Now, listen, Jim. You have taught me many things, you will teach me many more things. Now I will teach you a little of the wisdom of the white man. I think the noise we now hear is the noise of an upspringing wind. But you in your folly say that it is the voice of devils. And if you say that, believing that, then it is the noise of devils, and you are afraid. Is that clear? Do you understand the road along which I desire to take you?"

Jim pondered on this for a moment, then chuckling, softly exclaimed, "Yah! I think I see, Baas. It is as if a witch doctor said to me that should I drink of such and such water, I should die, because it was taboo. And if later I drank it, I know that I should die; but not because of the water, but because of the fear the witch doctor had planted in my mind concerning it. Is that what the Baas would teach me?"

The Major nodded assent.

Jim sighed.

"It is a big lesson, Baas. Some day, maybe, I will learn it, but now it is too hard for me, and"—he shivered—"I think the noises we hear are the voices of spirits."

He turned his back on the Major and muttered a charm, guaranteed by the witch doctor from whom he had purchased it, to preserve him from sorcery. "And now," he continued, turning again to his Baas, "I have no fear, for that is a powerful charm." The Major laughed.

"The charm was no other than the one I gave you. Think it over, Hottentot."

The wind died down, great clouds blotted out the stars; suddenly the air was heavily impregnated with moisture; thunder rolled continuously and lightning flashed, running along the tops of the hills, silhouetting them in an outline of fire. And then, after a devastating thunder clap, the clouds burst and spilled their contents. The fire went out with a sharp hiss, and though but a few yards away from the tent, the Major was saturated before he could gain its shelter.

CHAPTER X

GHOST OF THE PIT

THE MORNING broke swiftly, the rain had ceased, and a few clouds which were in existence dissolved rapidly before the rising sun.

Having broken their fast, the Major and Jim set their camp in better order, building a *scherm* in which to put their mules at night. That done, Jim carrying a spare gun and a belt of cartridges, they explored the valley.

It was, the Major decided, evidently of volcanic origin, and the fact that the hills had strong indications of iron-stone explained the intensity of the night's electric disturbances. The valley was almost circular in shape, and of a scant two miles in circumference.

Jim's keen eyes detected a faint trail leading up the steep slopes on one side, and, climbing this, their way challenged by apes, they reached the summit, and from there gained a wonderful view back across the country they had recently traveled.

Again it was Jim's keen eyes which detected, crawling sluggishly over the plain, the wagon drawn by sixteen oxen, of Miss Wallace.

"I think, Jim," the Major said gaily in English, "we will be proper explorers, and give names to anything that appeals to our fancy. And this we will call 'Look-out Point.'"

Jim nodded and grinned as if understanding what his Baas had said.

"Yah, Baas," he replied, parrot-like. "Golly! Dam, yes, no, if I don't see you so long, hallow!"

The Major looked at him in amazement.

"By Jove!" he chuckled, "the old lad has been hiding his light under a bushel. The beggar speaks English most fluently!" Still chuckling, he led the way slowly down into the valley. As he was pushing his way through a patch of long grass the ground suddenly seemed to drop away from under his feet.

He threw out his arms just in time to save himself from falling down a deep pot hole. Clambering out with Jim's alarmed aid, he gazed down into the yawning chasm. He could not see the bottom. It was lost in total blackness. The sides of the hole were polished smooth, looked almost as if it had been bored by some gigantic drill.

"By Jove!" he exclaimed softly. "I had almost forgotten the business of my friend Soapy Richards. This must be the so celebrated pit. Funny that I should stumble on it in this way!"

He gave a few curt orders to Jim and then waited by the pit mouth until that man had been to the wagon and returned with a long, stout rope and a bundle of papers.

OF THE papers he made a sort of torch, lighted it and lowered it into the pit at the end of the rope. It flamed brightly until, about fifty feet down, it flickered as if caught by a strong crosscurrent of air. Then as it was lowered still further, it burned steadily again. At length just before the end of the rope was reached, the lighted paper came to rest on the bottom of the pit.

"I'm going down, Jim," the Major said.

"*Wo-we!*" Jim exclaimed. "That is folly. Undoubtedly this place is evil and at the bottom of this hole waits death."

The Major laughed, and, hauling up the rope—the torch had by now burned itself out—carefully knotted the end around his waist. The other end Jim, protesting worriedly, tied about the trunk of a nearby tree.

"Pay out the rope slowly, Jim," the Major ordered and disappeared into the darkness of the pit.

The diameter of the pit was so small that, by pressing out his knees and arms against the walls, he was able to lighten the strain on the rope and was enabled at times to light matches and by the feeble illumination they cast in the abysmal darkness of the place, examine the smooth, shining walls.

When he was about fifty feet down he shouted excitedly to Jim, his voice echoing hollowly:

"Hold fast, Jim!"

The Hottentot, his face dripping with the sweat of anxiety, took several hitches of the rope around the tree and gazing down into the darkness, broken by the little jets of flame as the Major lighted match after match, called hoarsely:

"What is it, Baas? Are you all right?"

"All right, Jim," the Major's voice boomed up reassuringly. "I have found a shaft leading off this one. I am going up it a little way. Let me have plenty of slack."

"But, Baas—" Jim started to protest.

"Obey!" the Major's curt order cut short Jim's expostulations and, with fear filled eyes, he loosened the rope.

Minutes, long minutes passed. It seemed to Jim that the earth had swallowed up his Baas. No sound came to him, no glimmer of light. His superstitious mind pictured nameless horrors which had taken his Baas.

He wanted to flee from the place, but loyalty held him fast.

"Baas!" he called despairingly and tugged gently on the rope. There was no resistance! He tugged it again, hauled up several feet. Still no answering tug. He pulled up more of the rope, his fears increasing, until it was obvious that his Baas was no longer fastened to the other end. And then misery completely possessed the Hottentot and throwing himself face downward on the ground he wailed his loss. He shouted curses, cursing the spirits who had taken his Baas from him; he swore vengeance upon them. Then, presently, regaining control of himself, his eyes shining with determination, he prepared to lower himself into the pit.

And then a voice called from the bushes just to the left of him.

"Jim!"

"It is his ghost," Jim muttered, looking fearfully in the direction of the voice.

And then the Major appeared, his clothing torn and soiled, carrying a large, iron box.

"I AM no ghost, Jim," he exclaimed breathlessly, and continued swiftly, noting Jim's look of unbelief. "I went along that shaft, Jim, and I saw light ahead of me. So I undid the rope so that I could go forward unimpeded. And I found that the shaft opened into another pit, a very shallow pit, Jim. And out of that I climbed very easily. That is all."

"It is a lot, Baas," Jim said grumblingly. "I thought the spirits had taken you."

"And you were intending to come and take me from the spirits, Jim? You would dare the unknown for your unworthy Baas?"

"There is nothing I would not dare, Baas—"Jim began, but broke off abruptly to ask, "And what is that which you carry?"

The Major put the box down on the ground.

"I do not know, yet, Jim. I found it in that shaft just where it opened out into the other pit. We shall see."

He opened it with difficulty and exposed to the brilliant sunlight a shimmering array of jewels—rubies, sapphires and emeralds, gold crosses and rings of antique pattern, jeweled cameos of exquisite carving.

"By Jove!" he exclaimed softly, while Jim looked at him as if wondering that so many pieces of colored glass should so affect his Baas.

"I wonder," the Major continued in English, "how they came here? I imagine one of the early explorers—Spanish or Portuguese—must have got to this place somehow. Maybe he was chased by—er—natives and hid the treasure here, meaning to come back for it some day. Perhaps he was a priest—certainly they seem to be church jewels. But it's useless tryin' to form a theory as to how they got here. The fact is, here they are. And they're worth thousands—thousands! By Jove, yes! We're rich. Jim! Rich beyond the—er—dreams of avarice. Rich, Jim! You hear?"

"Golly, damme, yes, no," Jim replied stolidly. "If I don't see you, s'long, hullo!" Then in the native vernacular, "It is time we had *skoff*, Baas."

The Major laughed.

"You are a true philosopher, Jim," he said. "Of what use riches when the belly is empty? Lead on, then, and we will eat."

He closed the lid of the box, picked it up and led the way to the wagon, followed closely by Jim, who kept looking furtively behind him as if fearing that evil spirits would yet emerge from the pit and claim vengeance.

CHAPTER XI

Diamonds and Death

THE MIDDAY meal over, the Major examined his find again, emptying the treasure into
a large chamois leather bag, and sat dreamily in a chair
endeavoring to reason out the circumstances which led to
the jewels being secreted in such a place. He tried, too, to
estimate Richards' claim to the treasure—and the girl's.

And so the long afternoon hours passed until Jim, who
had been out collecting firewood and exploring the valley,
came back with the information that he had found many
more pits.

"Does the Baas want to go down them, too?" he asked.

The Major shook his head.

"No, Jim," he replied thoughtfully. "At least, not yet."

Jim grinned his relief, then held up his hand in a warning for silence.

"Some one comes, Baas," he said. "Someone rides a horse
fast this way."

They quickly took up positions behind rocks which
masked their presence from any one riding into the valley.
Hardly had they done so when the girl, Marjorie Wallace,
appeared riding furiously along the river bed, rounding
the bend.

She rode almost up to the wagon before seeming aware
of its presence, then reined in her horse with a startled
exclamation, wheeled and rode as if intending to go back
as fast as she had come.

The Major then stepped out from behind the rock, full in the course she would take and held up his hand, signalling her to halt.

She reined in her horse and looked at him contemptuously.

"So you are in Soapy Richards' pay after all," she said slowly.

"If it pleases you to think that," the Major drawled, "then, perhaps, I am. At any rate, I can't allow you to leave here."

"I'd like to see you stop me," she stormed, and drew her revolver, leveling it at him. "Out of my way!"

He smiled up at her, but did not budge.

"Out of my way," she demanded again, "or I will ride you down."

She spurred her horse forward and it seemed, for a moment, as if she would carry out her threat. But at the last moment she reined in suddenly, pulling her mount back on its haunches and, when it reared frantically, wheeled it with a masterly exhibition of horsemanship.

"That was quite cleverly done, Miss Marjorie," the Major drawled when, having calmed her horse, patting its arched neck, she sat there looking scornfully at the Major and Jim, who now joined his Baas.

Once again she pointed her revolver. "I will give you one more warning," she said. "Out of my way or I shall fire!"

"I THINK not," the Major said gently. "It would be so much like murder, wouldn't it? And besides, why do you want to go from this place, considering the trouble you took to get here?"

She answered that with a look of contempt.

"And," continued the Major easily, "I think you will be much safer here, than back out there on the veld with Vanderspey."

She was silent for a moment, then, "How did you know of this place?"

"Who doesn't know of it?" he countered with a laugh. "Every one must have heard the story of Devil's Kloof."

"Yes, perhaps. But not every one knows where it is. Though many have looked for it, no one has succeeded in finding it—except my father."

"I am here," the Major pointed out. "Therefore I must have found it, and it is most extraordinary, I assure you, the way I did find it. We rode along the dried up river, looking for water, and found ourselves here. And here we are!"

"If I could believe that," she commended, then checked herself. "But I cannot. You are lying, of course. You must be in Soapy Sam's pay. And because of that it is not safe for me to be where you are. I ought to shoot you." She sighed. "But I cannot. That, I suppose, is because I am a woman and too soft!"

"Will you accept my assurance," the Major then asked gently, "that I have not received one penny of Soapy Sam's money?"

She looked at him sharply. "And will not?" she demanded.

The Major hesitated.

"I think," he said slowly, "that under certain conditions, I can promise you that I will not."

"Conditions!" she stormed. "And what are they?"

"Simply," he said, "that if you can convince me that you have prior claim to this Devil's Kloof, I will place my services unreservedly at your disposal."

As he stood there, his monocle reflecting the rays of the lowering sun, his clothing immaculate, his pose that of an effete dandy, it seemed almost an impertinence that he should offer his assistance.

She suppressed a desire to laugh. Her womanly intuition told her that the foppishness, the attitude of inane boredom was merely a pose.

"Suppose," she said, relaxing slightly, sitting easily in the saddle, "suppose you tell me what you know."

HE NODDED, and in a few short pithy sentences outlined for her Richards' account of looking for Devil's Kloof, and his treatment by her father and the girl herself.

She laughed softly, a little sadly, when he had concluded.

"And you believed that?" she asked.

"No!" he admitted. "I am afraid that I consider Mr. Richards' story was not entirely free from—shall we say—inaccuracies. Suppose you tell me the truth."

A few minutes later they were both smoking, whilst Jim, having unsaddled and turned loose the girl's horse, cooked an extra batch of bread for the evening meal.

"The truth," the girl said suddenly, "is this. Many years ago, my father, Tom Wallace, found in an old, deserted Spanish mission in Old Mexico, a diary of one Brother Sebastian. The parchment was yellow with age and in places the spidery handwriting was faded so that a translation was impossible. What we could translate was mighty interesting.

"It told of the writer's adventures—he was a Jesuit— with Francisco Barreto, up the Zambesi Valley. That was in 1596. But the part that so greatly interested father was this—remember that I am condensing it:

"Fifteen men deserted from Barreto's force, taking with them an iron bound box containing church jewels. Brother Sebastian described the jewels very fully in his journal.

"Well, Barreto could not spare any soldiers to send after the deserters and Brother Sebastian—the responsibility of the jewels was his—appointed himself to track down the deserters and recover the property of the Holy Church.

"The account of his ensuing adventures is thrilling."

The Major nodded.

"Well, after many months of wandering through bush and jungle, in constant peril from savages, wild beasts and fever, Brother Sebastian caught up with the thieves. And it was here, at the Devil's Kloof.

"He found the thieves reduced to two, and they nearly dead.

"He took the jewels from them—and then killed them. He must have been a very terrible man.

"Before he could get away from the Kloof a party of natives appeared and he hid from them down one of the pits. During the night he succeeded in frightening them, playing on their superstitious fears, and they stampeded.

"On the morrow he started on his long journey back to join Barreto, hiding the box of jewels in a sort of tunnel which led off one of the pits. He explains that he thought that safest, doubting his strength to carry the box any great distance.

"And then there's a big break in the diary. Apparently Brother Sebastian's account was not believed by his superiors. But the rest is not of interest to us now.

"But what I have told you so took hold of father's imagination, that he sold out his holdings in California and we came to Africa to search for the treasure Brother Sebastian had hidden so long ago.

AT FIRST we wasted much time and nearly all our money, searching in Portuguese territory and the Zambesi Valley. You see Brother Sebastian was no geographer and had only the vaguest ideas of his directions. Then, by chance, we heard of the legend of Devil's Kloof and that immediately localized the search. We came south to Cape Town, arriving practically penniless.

"It was then that father met Sam Richards and got him to finance an expedition, promising him a third share.

"I wanted to go with them, but father would not let me. So he and Richards set off alone.

"All went well, father afterwards told me, until they came within sight of the kopjes which guard the Kloof here and which corresponded to Brother Sebastian's description.

"Then Richards pretended that he was discouraged, that father was but an optimistic dreamer, and insisted on going no further. He would return, he said, on the morrow.

"But circumstances ruled otherwise. That night their camp was surrounded by a band of natives, evidently out for mischief. And Richards, riding the only horse with the outfit, made his escape, leaving father to his fate. With the break of day, the natives rushed the camp. They burned the wagon and most of the provisions. Then, for some unknown reason, possibly because they suspected Richards had ridden off for help, vanished, leaving father stabbed through the thigh.

"I shall never know how father managed to come on to the Kloof here, lame as he was, taking what little provisions he could carry. But he did. And he satisfied himself as well as he could—you must remember he had no rope and could not investigate the pits—that the story told in Brother Sebastian's diary was true.

"For a few days he rested here at the Kloof, then set out for Steinberg. He was found, half-crazed with hunger and thirst and the pain of his wounded thigh, about twenty miles from here, by a corporal of the police. The corporal took care of him at his camp, and as soon as possible brought him south to me.

"But, before that, Richards had returned with the news that my father had been killed by some unknown savages; and that he himself, after nearly losing his own life in defence of father's, had barely managed to escape. He assured me, with tears in his eyes, that he had held father in his arms when he died, and that he, too, would have been content to die with him, only father had begged him to make his escape and take care of me.

"Part of his scheme of protecting me"— she smiled rather bitterly—"was a constant endeavor to get from me the secret of the kloof; offering me, in exchange for the information, his honorable hand in marriage.

WHEN FATHER returned, Richards was dumbfounded until he discovered that father could not live very long, and that he had a very vague recollection of things which happened up country.

"But father had a few lucid moments when he told me of all that he had discovered. And just before he died he summoned up enough strength to draw a map of Devil's Kloof, showing the location of it, and of one of the pot holes. That map Richards stole from me at the one moment in my life when I was completely off guard. It is rather difficult, you know, to be on guard against men like Richards at a time when you are first made conscious of the fact that the best pal you ever had has died."

The Major nodded with a sympathetic smile.

"Though the map was gone," the girl continued, "I knew that I could find that place and decided to come on as soon as possible, knowing that Richards would not be able to make a move himself at once; knowing, too, the fact that he was being closely watched by men of like kidney to himself. Richards was greedy. He has no intention of sharing the treasure with anyone, if he can possibly help it. So I went to Vanderspey, and tried to make a bargain with him. He agreed to bring me here. And," she shrugged her shoulders, "the rest you know."

Again the Major nodded. "But why go to a man like Vanderspey?" he questioned softly.

"He was the only man I knew rich enough to finance the expedition," she said. "And," she flushed in a somewhat shamefaced manner, "I am afraid I took advantage of him. You see I knew that he thought himself in love with me, and I used that knowledge. Otherwise he would not have come this trip, which he calls stupendous folly. I regret that now. I thought at first that he was a stupid, good natured giant of a man who would eventually consider himself well rewarded for his trouble and outlay of money with a share of the proceeds. Instead"—her voice wavered—"Instead I discovered him to be a beast, absolutely devoid of morals."

"And that is why you rode on ahead?" the Major asked.

She nodded.

"But surely," he expostulated, "it would have been wiser to have ridden for the nearest police post. There is one I believe not very far from here. Coming to the kloof you were running into a cul-de-sac, you would have been absolutely at Vanderspey's mercy."

She nodded agreement.

"I did not think," she admitted, but added in a lower voice, "I think at the back of my mind was the belief that

I should find you here; and that you would not withhold your protection. Besides," she continued hurriedly, a look of determination on her face, "I had no intention of giving up all hope of finding the treasure just because a big, fat, hulking Boer dared to make love to me."

"Aren't you anxious to see the treasure?" She looked at him sharply.

"You mean you have found it?"

HE NODDED, and going into the tent brought out the jewels he had discovered. He poured them from the chamois bag out into her lap, watching her with an indulgent air as she toyed with them, and uttered exclamations of delight, loading her slender fingers with the heavily jeweled rings.

He smiled at her and waited.

She hesitated a moment, and then giving him back the jewels, tearing the rings reluctantly from her fingers, said in hushed tones:

"Will you take care of these for me?"

He nodded, put them back in the bag and gazed with speculative eyes about the camp.

"They will be safest here, I think," he decided, and, taking the top off a small water barrel, dropped them into it. Then: "You must not forget that Jim has already sounded, in a manner of speaking, the warning to dress for dinner. Perhaps you would like to wash? The tent and everything in it is at your disposal."

He bowed, and walked away, making for the rear of the wagon, where, with Jim's expert aid, he quickly erected a shelter for himself.

The girl stood a few minutes gazing after him with dream-filled eyes. Then, rising, she went into the tent, exclaiming with delight at its luxurious fittings.

What chiefly appealed to her after the long dusty days of traveling, was the canvas tub, filled with water, which stood invitingly in the center of the tent.

"To judge from all this," she murmured, "one would say that he was soft. But who knows! Is it soft to desire cleanliness and comfort? Then I'm soft, myself."

They ate dinner that night—and dinner was the correct name. This was no crude bush travelers' repast.

The Major looked more like a leisured clubman than ever, wearing a dress suit, with starched shirt. Yet, somehow, he did not seem incongruous in that environment. And the girl, although at first astonished that he should so dress in the bush, realized intuitively that it was no senseless pose— that it was his way of keeping in touch with civilization.

As they ate, illuminated by the soft glow of candles, they talked animatedly, with the good-natured freedom of friends of long standing.

AND THEN, the meal over, they still sat for a while and talked, watching the flickering flames and the yellow gleam of eyes beyond the firelight, listening to the snarling of hungry beasts.

The soft soughing of the wind through the cracks in the hills made lullabys in place of yesternight's hideous shrieks. The air was filled with the good scent of mother earth and an atmosphere of rest pervaded the place.

Jim, his duties finished, was now squatting on his haunches before the fire, a blanket draped about him, singing one of the songs of his people.

The Major raised himself suddenly.

"Good night, Miss Marjorie," he said softly.

"It has been very pleasing, sitting here. I shall always remember."

He climbed up into his wagon and disappeared beneath its tented hood.

And the girl rose, too, and went into the tent.

CHAPTER XII

Besieged

BEFORE THE rising of the morrow's sun the Major rose and having indulged in the luxury of a primitive shower bath—it consisted of Jim's throwing several buckets of icy cold water over him—toweled himself vigorously, dressed, and told Jim that after *skoff* they would trek. So that when the girl emerged from her tent, freshened from her night's sleep, most of the preparations were completed. The crisp morning air was filled with the appetizing smell of frying bacon, tinctured with the aroma of coffee.

"You slept well?" Major asked gently.

"Never better in my life," she replied. "You travel in great comfort."

"We will eat now," he chuckled, and escorting her to where the table was spread invitingly, seated her in a chair, and then sat down opposite her. "And after we have eaten," he continued, "we will trek."

She made a little gesture of expostulation.

"But why?" she queried. "Why be in such a hurry to get away from this very delightful, peaceful spot?"

"I would be quite willing to stay, but we have to consider so many things. The conventions, for one thing."

"I think we are both above considering them; and besides, what is the difference, my trekking with Vanderspey, or staying with you?"

He did not answer that, but continued. "And the second point is, that very soon Vanderspey will be along, and his presence is not desirable in this place. It might be awkward to handle him."

"I can handle Vanderspey all right," she assured him confidently.

"Are you so sure?" he asked. "Remember that you rode away from him yesterday."

She flushed, and bit her lip.

"And the third point," the Major continued, "is that I am not at all sure how soon our friend Richards will arrive on the spot. And I would much rather be away from here when he does come. It will save a lot of explanations."

"But," she objected, looking round the place, "we have no cause to fear anyone. We can easily keep Vanderspey out of the place if we wish. Why! We can hold it against an army!"

"Hardly," the Major objected. "But it is true that they can hold us in here, stop us from getting away, I mean, much more easily. So you see that it is best that we leave before anyone arrives to challenge our departure. Out there"—he waved his hand to the open veld—"we need fear no one. As a matter of fact, I am sorry that we did not trek out of here last night."

SHE OPENED her mouth as if intending to raise more objections to leaving the Kloof, then closed it firmly.

"I am ready to trek," she said suddenly, "as soon as you give the word."

"We'll go as soon as I have struck camp."

The meal finished, they arose, and helped Jim take down the tent and pack its contents onto the wagon. When this task was almost completed, the Major sent Jim up to "Look-out Point," in order, as he explained, to see that the coast was clear.

Jim departed on his errand, happy at the thought that they would soon be leaving the Devil's Kloof; grumbling because they were to be burdened by the presence of a woman; feeling that his Baas had been entrapped by a woman's smile, which would bring an end to the life of adventure they had planned to follow.

The Major and the girl, finding merriment in almost everything they did, completed the packing. And so engrossed were they in their task, so light hearted in each other's companionship, that they became oblivious to their surroundings and the passing of time.

They did not see a man appear around the angle of the terrain guarding the entrance to the Kloof; did not see him come forward eagerly, craftily, revolver in hand, dodging from tree to tree, taking advantage of every scrap of cover; moving softly, despite his big bulk and clumsy hobnailed boots. Indeed, the first indication they had of an interloper was when Vanderspey, emerging from behind a tree, not eight yards from where they were standing, snarled:

"Hands up!"

They wheeled quickly at that. The color fled from the girl's face, leaving it an ashen white, and a little gasp of dismay came from her lips.

The Major, an expression of helpless incredulity on his face, raised his eyebrows and let his monocle fall to the ground, where it smashed to pieces.

"But I say," he exclaimed, in tones of great consternation, "my bally eye-glass is broken, I shall be as blind as a bat! I must go and get another."

He turned as if meaning to climb up into his wagon, but halted at Vanderspey's order, raising his hands abjectly above his head.

"And so," the Dutchman continued easily, his face black with wrath, "it is to this you come, eh, missy? You leave my wagon. You laugh at the love of an honest burgher like me. You pretend to be insulted because I whispered of certain things to you. And you ride away pretending that my presence will soil you. Almighty! As if I did not know your *slim* cunning ways! You leave me and come to this *verdoemte roinek*. But I have got you like love birds caught. And now, knowing what I know, I shall know how to treat you. First I will kill this *verdoemte* dude! Almighty! Yes! And then no longer shall I talk of marriage to you!"

His voice was full of base insinuation, and the girl flushed. She looked at the Major, as if expecting that he would answer the Dutchman's implied accusations. At the same time she feared that he would, and would thus bring upon himself the Dutchman's insensate wrath.

Major's face was bland and as lacking in determination as a child's. If he expressed any emotion at all, it was one of regret for his broken eye-glass. Sighing a little, feeling somehow that she had placed her trust in a broken reed, she turned again to Vanderspey.

"You are mistaken, Van," she said winningly. "You jump to conclusions. And that is bad. As you see, my horse is saddled, and I was going to ride back and join you."

HE CLUMSILY turned this over in his mind, nodding his head as if in acceptance of her statement.

"*Ja!*" he said stolidly. "That may be so. But why did you play a trick on me yesterday? Why did you leave me?"

She shrugged her shoulders and held out her hands appealingly.

"I was afraid of you," she replied. "You are so big and strong. Your love making was"—she smiled in his face—

"was so rough. And I have told you many times there must be no talk of love between us till this trip is over. Then, if it seems good to us, we can go to a predikant and be married as is proper. And you broke your promise. And so I rode away. And I came to this place not knowing that this gentleman"—she inclined her head toward the Major—"was here. I was planning to get the treasure, and then come back to join you."

She looked at him anxiously to see if he would accept this statement, sighing softly with relief when he once again nodded and the fierce scowl left his face.

But almost immediately it clouded over again and suspicion filled his black beady eyes.

"And you have found the treasure? Yes?" he queried.

She shook her head.

"Then maybe," he continued, "this dude has already found it? If he has, we will take it from him. Then I shall kill him."

"No!" she cried sharply. "He did not find it. My father was mistaken, Van. There is no treasure."

The Dutchman nodded, a grin of satisfaction spreading over his face.

"Then if there is no treasure," he said slowly, "how are you going to pay me for the use of my wagon and oxen? How will you pay me for the provisions that I bought so that you could come on this so foolish trip?"

"A way will be found," the girl replied.

"Almighty! Yes!" he bellowed. "I shall be paid and paid in the way I most greatly desire."

He grinned possessingly at her. Then once again his eyes lighted with suspicion as for the first time his slow-thinking brain took in the evidence of the Major's preparations for departure—noted the tethered mules and the loaded wagon.

"Almighty!" he roared. "You have been lying to me! From the beginning you have lied to me. You were getting ready to leave this place—you were going away with the *verdoemte roinek*, and I should have lost everything!"

HE PEERED about the place, craftily, yet keeping his revolver leveled at them, and asked with a sudden show of cunning: "But where is the Hottentot? Is he hiding somewhere or"—he leered—"did you send him away so that you could be alone?"

"You are quite wrong, dear lad," the Major drawled easily. "Jim is not hiding; I sent him a little while ago to spy out the land as it were! To see there were no hyenas and whatnot to bite us as we left this place. I cannot for the life of us understand how he overlooked you and failed to give us warning. But doubtless that is explained because he expected to see you coming with your wagon. He could not have thought that you would come in on foot."

The Dutchman grinned.

"And so," he said, "in that way I showed how *slim* I am. The pace of the wagon is very slow and so I came on foot. *Ja!* Through the night I traveled and before the rising of the sun I was close to the kloof, where no one would see me."

"You are wonderful," the Major drawled, "upon my soul, you are. You think of everything. Except there is one thing you have overlooked. If you will pardon me, your great weakness is a childlike credulity. You are so willing to believe the obvious.

"For instance, you put quite a wrong construction on Miss Wallace's coming here, though I admit it was an obvious one for a man of your type. But on the other hand

you are too ready to believe Miss Wallace's statement that
the treasure has not been found. That is where you make
your big mistake."

The Dutchman looked at him, but vaguely understanding the Major's persiflage.

"Yes," the Major continued, "you are too, too credulous.
Let me assure you that the treasure has been found. And
a most wonderful treasure it is!"

The Dutchman looked swiftly at the girl and grinned
knowingly at her facial expression.

"So," he said, answering the Major. "The treasure has
been found? Eh? And you are willing to give me that treasure in return for your life."

"Naturally," the Major drawled. "I value my life far above
rubies."

He glanced swiftly at the girl and sighed softly at her
look of contempt.

"And where is this treasure?" Vanderspey demanded.

The Major chuckled.

"If you will allow me," he said, "I will show you."

"I do not allow you to go out of my sight," the Dutchman bellowed.

"No, of course not," the Major drawled. "And there is
no need to do so. You see we racked our brains for the best
place in which to hide them. And if you will kindly open
the spigot of this water barrel"—he pointed to the water
cask which had not yet been loaded onto the wagon—"and,
when the water is drawn away, you will find at the bottom
of it rubies and whatnot without number."

IF THE Dutchman had doubted before, the girl's
indignant cry of despair put all doubts on one side. Yet he
had no intention to be caught off his guard.

The Major, noting his hesitation, continued, "If you wish, dear old thing, I myself will open the spigot and let the water drain off, or, if you wish, I will tilt the barrel over; maybe that will be quicker."

He lowered his hands as if intending to carry out his idea.

"No you don't!" Vanderspey replied quickly. "You keep your hands up."

The Major shrugged his shoulders and obeyed. He looked again at the girl, as if wishing to take her into his confidence. But her immobile face and the cold glance of her eyes told him that she was not in the mood to receive whispered explanations.

The Dutchman walked slowly over to the barrel, ordering the two to step backward, keeping them always in line with his revolver. When he reached the barrel, he kicked it over and watched the water rush out. With the force of the flow came the chamois leather bag in which the Major had put the jewels the previous night. And as it lay on the muddy ground he looked at it wonderingly, doubt and belief struggling for mastery on his face.

The girl made a little rush forward, but stopped at the menace of his revolver, and the Major drawled easily, "Your self-control is amazing, my dear Vanderspey. You have the treasure of kings lying at your feet and yet you do not stoop to pick it up."

And then Vanderspey hesitated no longer. With a hoggish grin he stooped over, with difficulty because of the stupendous girth of his waist. One ham-like hand closed on the bag, and then a heavy weight hit him between the shoulders and sent him sprawling face downward on the muddy ground. Before he could recover, the Major had

snatched the revolver from his hand, and Jim, the Hottentot, emerged grinning from a clump of bushes.

The girl, shaken out of her calm by this sudden reversal
of fortune, turned with a gesture of apology to the Major.

"I thought," she said falteringly, "that you were—"

He stopped her, a finger to his lips, and, as Vanderspey
scrambled awkwardly to his feet, scowling malevolently,
picked up the bag and righted the water-keg and tossed
the bag carelessly into it.

"As I said once before, Van dear," he drawled, "you are
too bally credulous. You are too ready to believe any little
fairy story told you. I will admit that you showed great
cleverness in creeping upon us unawares, as it were, but
you were not clever enough to think that Jim might have
seen you and would exercise great caution in coming here.
But I was on the lookout for him, of course, and in order to
distract your attention and so make it sure that he could get
within striking distance, I told you the little story about the
treasure. It was not difficult for Jim to pick up a large stone,
quite a rock, in fact, and propel it in your direction. And
now will you be a good boy or must we bind and gag you?"

VANDERSPEY'S VEHEMENT curses
were answer enough and he was forced to submit to being
bound and gagged by the Major's expert hands, aided by
Jim's knowledge of intricate knots. And then they picked
him up and carried him away and put him in the wagon.

Rejoining the girl the Major laughed pleasantly.

"And that's that," he said. "And now we can trek on at
our leisure."

The girl nodded happily.

Jim was scurrying about, catching mules, harnessing them, working like one possessed; on his face an expression of great determination.

"*O-he*, Jim," the Major called banteringly. "The world does not end today. There is plenty of time; there is no need of haste."

"There is great need, Baas," Jim shouted back grimly, not slackening his efforts. "We have already wasted too much time. Had it not been for the Dutchman, I would have told you before."

Realizing from Jim's tone that some new danger was menacing them, the Major went over to him and under cover of helping him harness the mules questioned him in a low voice as to the need of haste.

"Baas," Jim said in reply, "as you know I climbed up the hill from which all the country around can be seen. At first I saw only the Dutchman's wagon and his oxen a day's trek distant. And I thought all was well. And then I saw a man riding on horseback, swiftly, along the bed of the river. Behind him, riding as if they sought to overtake him, were two other white men. All heading this way. And then toward the east I caught the sparkle of sunlight on the spear tips of warriors. And for a while that was all I could see, because my eyes were blinded by the sun. Then I saw, Baas, an *impi* hastening this way. And though, Baas, you may, without difficulty be able to deal with several white men, I do not think that you, as yet, have quite sufficient wisdom to defeat an army of Zulu warriors. Therefore, I say, you must make haste."

"But, Jim," the Major expostulated, "How do you know the warriors mean any evil toward us?"

"I do not know," Jim replied gravely. "But this I know: when Zulu warriors go on the warpath they have no friends and they kill without reason, grinding under their feet whoever may be in their path. Just as a bull elephant, gone mad, permits nothing to stand before him. And I think these warriors are angry because we have dared to come to this forbidden place.

The Major nodded gravely and returned to the girl.

"It must be stupid for you to hang about here," he said lightly, "while we are getting ready for the return journey. So I venture to suggest, Miss Marjorie, that you mount your horse and ride on ahead."

She shook her head, her eyes dancing with merriment.

"No," she said. "You will not get rid of me as easily as that."

"BUT I must insist," he continued. "It is much better that you go now, and go quickly. You see we are likely to have other visitors very soon. And I would like you to get away before it is too late."

"And who are these important visitors?" she asked banteringly.

"I rather fancy," he drawled, "that Soapy Richards is one. Who the other two are I have no idea."

She laughed scornfully.

"We have nothing to fear from them—three white men. Why, you could handle them easily."

He bowed.

"Thanks for the compliment! But that is not all. Jim tells me that there is a Zulu *impi* heading this way. And while they may not know of our presence here, or harbor any evil intention toward us, yet I think it best to play safe. And I should feel much happier to know that you are safely out of the way. So please go!"

She shook her head determinedly.

"I will not go!" And her tone was final. "I go when you go and not a moment before. If it comes to a fight you will need my help. I can shoot as well as a man. You know that."

He nodded.

"I thought perhaps that you could ride for help."

She laughed.

"You know that you had no such thought in your mind at all. Besides what need for help, or what need for haste. For the matter of that, if the Zulus are on the warpath we are much better here than riding along between the high banks of the river, or out on the open plain beyond. We can defend this place easily. But out there they would surround us and in a little while all would be over."

The Major nodded agreement.

"By Jove!" he exclaimed. "You are right! Jim," he called to the Hottentot, "we have decided not to trek. Here we will be safe. We can hold this against the Zulus without difficulty. We have plenty of provisions, plenty of water. And today or tomorrow or the next week—what matter—help will come."

Jim considered this, and replied, "Maybe your plan is best, Baas. Had we trekked as soon as I first sighted the *impi* we could have got well away. But the affair with the Dutchman delayed us too long, and now perhaps it is too late. No, we will stay. And if you and the Missy will keep watch from that rock there"—he pointed to a large boulder overlooking the entrance to the valley—"no one could enter without first getting your permission. Yah! And we will roll down the rocks to close up the entrance so that the warriors can only come in by ones and twos. But how about the white men, shall we keep them out also?"

"No, Jim!" the Major replied decidedly. "They must enter."

"And that is folly!" Jim grumbled. "A man does not willingly pen up hyenas with his herd of goats."

"Nevertheless, Jim," the Major answered, "they must enter. Now we will free the Dutchman that he may help us in the work we must do."

A FEW minutes later, having freed Vanderspey and explained to him the threatened danger—and he, despite his wrath, was wise enough to see that for the time, at least, he must forget his own troubles—they made all possible preparations to meet the threatened attack.

Actually, there was little they could do to better their position; already it was practically impregnable unless attacked in great force. But, on Vanderspey's suggestion, they decided to make of the wagon a sort of fort. They filled up the water keg and loaded it on to the wagon, then got out all of the Major's firearms and opened the cases of ammunition.

"Unless," said Vanderspey, nodding sagely, "the niggers have guns themselves and do not charge—we are safe."

CHAPTER XIII
Divided Counsels

WHILST THEY were thus occupied, a horseman spurred frantically around the bend. And, so overcome with fear was he, that he rode almost up to the wagon before he was aware of its presence.

Then he fell off his sweat-drenched horse with an exclamation of triumph.

"Good, Major," he panted as that man went forward to greet him, noting the preparation which had been made for defending the place. "We are ready for them and can give them hell!"

Lying down behind a rock he leveled his rifle and aimed down the bed of the river.

The Major's rifle was hanging from the ridge pole of the wagon. He took it now in his hands, loaded the magazine, pulled out the "cut-off."

"Yes, Mr.—er—Richards," he agreed. "I think we are ready for anyone who comes. But who do you expect?"

"Hewins and Lemper, the swine!" Richards snarled. "They have been on my trail ever since I left Cape Town. But I can handle them now."

He toyed lovingly with the trigger of his rifle and, as two horsemen appeared in sight, fired. But his shot went astray, for the Major, stooping over quickly, had knocked the muzzle to one side. And then, before the newcomers could answer to the shot or Richards could fire again, he had run forward to meet them, waving a white handkerchief.

"You fool!" Richards screamed. "What in hell are you doing that for?"

"You'll know very soon, *ma-an*," Vanderspey replied. "Listen!"

He held up his hand for silence as he spoke.

And then they heard the wild chant of native warriors and the dull, hollow booming noise made by the beating of spear heads on bullock hide shields.

Richards blanched.

"My God!" he exclaimed. "What is that?"

The girl looked at him disdainfully.

"A Zulu *impi* is out on the warpath. They are coming to attack this place. That is why the Major is waving the white flag to those other two. We need all the defenders we can get. That is why we allowed you to come in. Otherwise we should have kept you out. As it is, I think it would have been just had we left you to the mercy of the warriors as you once left my father."

Richards growled some inarticulate retort then turned to watch the two men who had halted at his shot and had dismounted, seeking cover behind the boulders which were strewn in the water course at that point.

Then, suddenly, as the singing and the beating of shields ended in loud, exultant shouts, they mounted and spurred forward with frantic haste just in time to escape a shower of assegais rained on them from the heights above.

Coming to the wagon they dismounted and listened sullenly whilst the Major outlined the situation and appointed posts for each member of the tiny garrison.

"An' who the blinkin' 'ell do yer fink you are?" Hewins demanded. "Wot do yer mean by givin' hus orders. Me an' Lemper knows 'ow to 'andle niggers, don't we, Lemper?"

"*Ja!*" the Dutchman replied stolidly. "But I think the *roinek's* plan a good one, so we will do now what he says. Afterward, when this business with the niggers is finished we will deal with him. And, Almighty! How we will deal with him!"

"Me, also," Vanderspey, scowling malevolently, chimed in. "I, too, have something to say to the monocled dude— yes; and also to his *verdoemte* Hottentot. *Ja!* And to the girl!"

"You'll keep your hands off the girl," Richards snarled. "I'll take care of her, and don't you forget it, you big hunk of hog."

"DON'T FERGET," Hewins put in, "that me an' Demper'll 'ave somefink to say to you, Soapy; tryin' to give hus the slip like you did. Yus! An' I wants ter tork to the Major bloke, too."

The Major chuckled.

"And I may have something to say to all of you," he said. "So it would seem that we are going to have a very pleasant little chat together. But, for the present, suppose you forget your little differences and—er—keep your eyes peeled. I think it would be best if we went up to the bend—you see there they cannot get at us from above, not if we keep a little this side of it. Then, if they prove too strong for us, we can retreat to the wagon."

Sullenly they agreed and moved slowly forward to take up position behind boulders commanding a view of the river bed beyond the first bend as far as the second.

Richards, walking by the Major's side, asked anxiously, "Have you found the diamonds yet?"

"Diamonds!" the Major exclaimed. "Positively no! I haven't even looked for diamonds. Things have been happening too fast here for me to think of anything like that. You see," he continued easily, "I did not get here until the day before yesterday at sundown. And the next day, of course, I was busy making camp. And then, in the evening, Miss Wallace appeared on the scene and I had my work cut out persuading her to stay. And this morning Vanderspey arrived and was quite violent in his language and actions. Oh, quite. He required very careful and diplomatic handling—very!

"Then you came, *and* your friends, *and* the howling savages. So you will understand that, far from searching for diamonds, my time has been occupied—very fully occupied—receiving guests, the bidden and the unbidden."

Richards looked at him keenly then nodded in complete satisfaction.

Confident that he had successfully gauged the Major's mental processes, he accepted that man's statement absolutely. He glanced quickly toward the rocks which sheltered Demper and Hewins.

"We will have trouble with them two," he said, turning again to the Major, "when this business is over. To hear them talk, you would think that they had been my partners; and that I had double-crossed them. When the truth of the matter is that they are well known criminals and have dogged my footsteps ever since they heard the rumor that I knew where the Devil's Kloof was."

"Beastly annoying for you," the Major drawled in reply. "And I can understand how you feel about it. I have met the gentlemen before. They came to see me in my hotel at Cape Town, shortly after your visit. They wanted me to go into partnership with them; but they seemed so very tired that I thought it best to put them to bed." He laughed pleasantly. "No doubt they will tell you about it sometime. But why are you here so soon? I did not expect you for another month at least. You told me, if you remember, that you intended to go north, Kimberley way, hoping to throw off your trail anyone who might be following you. Of course, under the circumstances, I am glad that you did not. Still I am interested to know why you changed your plans."

Richards scowled, but made no reply.

"And, oh, yes! the Major continued. "And how's our dear old friend Piet? Still in the land of the living, I hope?"

RICHARDS FROWNED thoughtfully. Then his face lighted, and with an affectation of good humor, he clapped the Major on the shoulder.

"You know he is alive!" he exclaimed. "And I will admit that I made a mistake in telling you that he was so near death. You see," he continued suavely, "I needed your help very badly in this business, and I thought that that was the best way to make sure of you. Once you were on the way, well away from Cape Town, I intended to send a messenger after you, telling you that Piet was all right. But Piet himself saved me the trouble. You saw him at Umbalose's kraal and gave him a thrashing he greatly deserved. He got another from me of a different sort when I heard that he had disobeyed my instructions. So there you are."

"I still do not see why you changed your plans."

"It is plain enough," Richards insisted. "I saw that Piet suspected that you were heading for the Kloof, and so I followed you, meaning to warn you to be on your guard."

"It is a soapy sort of reason," the Major drawled, "but I don't think that it quite washes. However, it is of no great matter. You are here, and I think very soon your marksmanship will be put to the test."

Richards looked worried.

"Do you really think," he stammered, "that the niggers will attack us."

"It is impossible to say," the Major replied lightly. "But if they do, we must be ready for them. So I suggest that you get to your post."

Richards hesitated a moment, and then went forward, but not to the boulder the Major had indicated as his station, but to one to the right, and slightly in the rear of Demper and Hewins.

"None of that," Hewins protested, wriggling uneasily. "I ain't going to have you behind me! You might get excited later on and think I was a nigger and put a bullet in my hide. So you just get up in the line with us. Or in front of us if you like. It would please me better. But you don't get behind me. Come on!"

And when Demper and Vanderspey added their voices to Hewins, Richards shrugged his shoulders and crawled forward to a point which was in line with the others.

"There is no need for you to carry on like this," he whined protestingly. "We are all white men here together; and we have got to stick to each other. I vote we forget our little quarrels, so that we can fight these blinking niggers without worrying about getting a bullet in our backs."

"Sounds all right," Hewins growled. "But what about afterwards?"

"Why afterwards!" Richards said smoothly, "We will still be partners, and share up equally."

"I don't share with no blinking dude and the girl," Hewins snarled. "Or with Vanderspey here. Wot 'as 'e got to do with it? And for the matter of that; I don't see why we should share with you Soapy! Me and Demper 'ere, we're pals. We share and share alike. And I reckon we have got the casting vote in anything that goes on in this place."

AND THAT was the signal for a long, acrimonious debate between the men as to the proper division of the treasure. Partnerships were formed and broken. Promises and threats winged through the air with delightful abandon. And as the debate continued, the voices of the men grew hoarser; more fraught with murderous lust. Blows were exchanged. Revolvers levelled. And then the Major's voice, bitingly sarcastic, drawled out, putting an end to the argument.

"If you dear lads are not very careful, by tomorrow your bones will be bleaching in the sun. Look!" He pointed down the river bed, where they could see the natives climbing down the steep banks. Immediately the bickering ceased. The men returned to their posts and waited, looking to the Major for their orders.

Save for the first objections of Hewins: they had all accepted, without question, his right of leadership.

"We do not fire," he said. "Until we are sure that they mean mischief. And then not until the range is good. They are too far away now; a chance hit or two might only serve to infuriate them to such an extent that an attack would be driven home, despite heavy losses. When they have reached that boulder—" he pointed to one about two hundred yards away— "we will retreat to the next bend—you going first, Miss Wallace, then you, Richards, then you Hewins, then Vanderspey, then Demper. The Hottentot and myself will bring up the rear. You understand?"

They scowled assent, and all watched the assembling of the warriors along the sandy bed of the river, about a quarter of a mile away.

"How many of them?" the Major asked, turning to the Hottentot.

"Five hundred at least, Baas, all fighting men."

The sunlight gleamed on the assegai tips of the warriors as they massed together in close formation. Before them capered their leader. His loud shouts of exultation were carried clearly to the ears of the whites.

When he came to an end of his harangue, the warriors beat loudly on their drum shields, finishing with one deafening crash and a loud piercing yell.

Then they came forward, slowly, moving with the perfect rhythm of a machine. Silent, dour, ominous. Silhouetted against the white silver sand, their red shields making a fantastic splash of color against the walls which hemmed them in on either side.

With a nervous half-hysterical cry, Richards fired. And a warrior in the front rank pitched forward on his face. Swiftly the other men fired, the Major and the girl withholding their shots. Three other warriors fell. But the column of marching men did not check. The gaps in their ranks were filled up, and the rest came on at the same slow pace; as grimly implacable as a river in flood.

"By Jove!" the Major exclaimed softly. "They are magnificent. But it is too like murder."

He sprang to his feet and ran forward a little way toward the warriors.

AND WHEREAS the bullets of the white men had failed to check the warriors, this strange action of the white man brought them to a bewildered halt.

Their leader came on alone to within a couple of hundred yards of the Major.

"Come back, you fool!" the men behind the Major shouted, withholding their fire.

"Come back, Baas!" Jim pleaded.

But he ignored them.

"What do you desire, warrior?" he asked. "Why do you come against us with an *impi?* Know you not that there is peace between the white man and the black?"

The other's reply came back clearly.

"With white men we are at peace, it is true. But there is no peace between us and those who dare to defile the place made sacred by the spirits of those warriors gone on before us."

"Then let us parley," the Major continued. "We have done no evil here. And are ready to leave this place to the spirits whose abode it is. By noon, I tell you, we will be gone from this place, forever."

"If you will promise that," the old warrior replied, "then all will be well, except—" he paused—"except some talk must still be made of those of my warriors you have killed."

As he spoke the *impi* behind him was moving slowly forward.

"Watch, Baas!" Jim shouted anxiously. "It is not wise to try to parley with a Zulu on the warpath. He has only one desire—and that to kill! He can only go one way—and that forward. As well try to reason with a striking snake."

The warriors were moving faster now and had almost drawn level with their leader.

"Stop them!" the Major shouted, "or we fire again and many of them will die."

"They only come nearer," was the reply, "in order that they may better hear the words that pass between us."

Then he yelled an order and several warriors in the front rank aimed their old muzzle loaders and fired.

Jagged pieces of metal buzzed about the Major's head. One, it was so big that he could have watched its flight through the air, tore through his white helmet, grazing his scalp.

And then, shouting their war cries, the natives came on at a fast charge.

The Major turned and ran swiftly for the shelter of the rocks, wondering why only Jim and the girl were visible, wondering why only the girl's rifle should be attempting to check this mad charge.

"To the wagon, Baas," Jim shouted. "Those dogs have already gone there for their own safety."

The three of them, the girl, the Major and the Hottentot, ran swiftly and gained the shelter of the wagon and then looked back, wondering why the natives had halted, had not come around the bend into full sight.

The Major turned contemptuously on the other men.

"We obeyed horders like solgers, Major," Hewins said with a broad grin. "We waited until the niggers reached that 'ere boulder, like you said, and then we ran."

"I'm sure you did," the Major drawled. "But not, I think, in the correct order. You left Miss Wallace to—er—hold the fort, as it were. And, I believe, you call yourselves men!"

"I told 'er to come on wiv us," Hewins growled sullenly. "An' she wouldn't come. Didn't expect me to carry 'er off, did yer?"

"Here they come, Baas!" Jim called.

As he spoke the head of the column of natives appeared round the bend.

A volley of shots checked them and they milled about aimlessly, shouting threats. They did not seem anxious to come forward to the attack. Neither could they regain, it seemed, the discipline which was theirs before their first mad charge.

The white men fired spasmodically, picking off any warrior who became overbold, keeping the rest seeking cover.

FOR A time it seemed as if the white men's marksmanship had taken the fighting spirit out of the warriors, and Hewins was crowing gleefully, boasting that the affair was finished.

And when the attack did materialize, it came in an unexpected guise. There was no wild rush forward, but something much more menacing, much harder to deal with.

The warriors had discovered a gutter like ridge in the bed of the river and, crawling along it on their bellies, had reached the place where the bed of the river was cluttered with boulders. In a very little while each boulder sheltered a warrior. And from those vantage points those who had guns fired at the defenders whilst the rest slept. Slugs tore their way through the canvas top of the wagon. And one smashed Vanderspey between the eyes, killing him instantly.

The Major looked grave and implored Marjorie to hide back in the valley, out of the zone of fire, gripping her hand and calling her a brick when she indignantly refused.

He looked around at the others; noting with disgust Richards' fear distorted face; smiling approval at the set, dour countenance of Demper, and Hewins' tense, tight lipped smile and eyes shining with determination to hold out no matter how great the odds might be.

He looked at Marjorie Wallace again. She evinced no sign of fear or anxiety; neither was her face lighted with a blood lust. She was not a killer; wholly feminine she detested bloodshed. But, being a thoroughbred, realizing that an unpleasant task had to be done, she stuck to her post, taking advantage of every inch of cover and firing coolly, methodically, whenever a target presented itself.

She personified the spirit of the pioneer women of all races, and of all ages, since man's adventurous spirit first led him to essay the conquest of unknown lands.

She met the Major's glance with a light flutter of her hands and an encouraging smile. It was sufficient to assure him that no matter what happened she would play her part thoroughly to the end. She patted the revolver in its holster which hung from a belt slung about her hips.

"If they get too close"—her lips noiselessly formed the words—"use your revolver—and save one for me."

He nodded, his face set stern.

"It won't come to that," he replied, and rising to his full height in order to get a bead on the warrior behind the nearest rock, fired.

"Down!" the girl cried in dismayed tones as the hidden warriors who possessed guns loosed their shots at the target he made.

"Down!" Jim grunted in the vernacular. "Down, Baas!" And diving forward he swept his Baas' feet from under him, so that he was once again behind the comparative security of the wagon.

Presently the fusillade of the shots died away and the defenders of the wagon held their fire, seeing no target to aim at.

The Major whispered to Demper and Hewins. They nodded and presently climbed out of the wagon, lifted out the body of Vanderspey and buried him under a pile of rocks.

RETURNING TO their posts they sat down glumly, looking out through the slits they had cut in the canvas cover of the wagon. Nothing moved. The sun, reflected by the sandy bed of the river, blinded their eyes. The rocks loomed up black, ominous, each one seeming large enough to shelter a thousand warriors.

Here and there a warrior sprawled in full sight, his posture rigidly distorted as are the bodies of men who have died a sudden, violent death.

The heat, penned in, absorbed by the black hills, was intense; under the tented cover of the wagon it was suffocating. The clothes of the men were drenched with sweat; the naked body of the Hottentot looked as if he had just emerged from a swim. The girl's hair dung to her forehead in damp, sticky curls. For a little while all were silent, oppressed by the heat and the seriousness of their position.

The Major presently called a conference, endeavoring to determine on the best course to pursue.

"There's nothing we can do," Richards groaned. "We're caught like rats in a trap."

"Is there no other way out of this place, Major?" the girl asked.

The Major shook his head doubtfully.

"I have not had time to explore it thoroughly. It is possible to climb to the top at one place, but the descent to the other side of the veld is a sheer drop of hundreds of feet. I do not think it would be possible to get down even with a rope. No! The only way to get out is the way we got in. And, by Jove," he cried, his face lighting up with the inspiration of his thought, "that is the way we are going out."

"Tork sense, you bleeding fool!" Hewins growled. " 'Ow are we going out that way wiv 'undreds of blinking savages awaiting for us?"

"Wait a minute," the Major held up his hand. "I want to talk to Jim here a moment first."

He turned to the Hottentot and conversed with him for a time in the vernacular.

Then in English he asked the others, "And what do you think will happen if we stop here?"

It was Demper who replied, basing his knowledge on the many experiences of battle his people had waged against Zulu warriors.

"Almighty!" he growled. "That is easy to answer. The cunning devils are playing a waiting game now. They will not show themselves; not so much as an eyelash will they show. Then in the night's darkness they will creep up closer and closer and with the rising of the morrow's sun they will rush us. And though we killed hundreds, the rest would kill us. And Almighty! They are not gentle in the ways they choose to kill."

The Major nodded.

"Then what is your advice, Demper?"

"That we play their game. We, too, will be *slim*. When the darkness comes we will leave this place quickly, and go back into the valley, climbing up into the hills as high as we can go. Then when they rush the wagon they will find no one there to kill, and I think for a little while they will forget all about us in the joy of looting. And then, in the daylight, all crowded together as they'll be, we can kill enough of them, maybe, to make the rest sicken and go away."

The Major considered this thoughtfully.

"BESIDES," HEWINS urged, "it'll give us more time even if they don't go away as Demper says. An' the longer we can 'old out the bigger chance of a rescue. Gord! You don't fink a lot of niggers like this can go on the warpath an' not 'ave the police after them afore you can say Jack Robinson? Unless," he added dubiously, "there's another rebellion on. If there is we might as well say our blinking prayers—especially you, Soapy."

That man snarled a blasphemous retort; then strongly urged the adoption of Demper's plan.

The Major shook his head slowly.

"I don't think it's feasible. You see in the first place it's almost impossible, save in one place, to climb the hills, and there it is very steep, offers no real foothold. And supposing we did, there's no shelter. We'd be easy targets, while the natives could take shelter in the bushes."

"Why shouldn't we hide in the bush, then?" Richards asked in a quavering voice.

"Say, ducky!" Hewins answered him with a laugh of derision. "If you want to play 'iding-seek wiv five 'undred bloomin' niggers, a-searching for yer, why you're welcome. But don't ask me to play the game."

The Major laughed. "I think that answers Soapy very well, Hewins, old top. But to resume: another objection to taking to the hills, Demper, is that we could take very little provisions or water with us, and, if the natives decided to play a waiting game, they'd soon have us at their mercy."

Demper spat phlegmatically.

"Ja!" he exclaimed. "I am answered."

"Blimy! I should think so," Hewins echoed. "So what's your plan, Major?"

"I have two," that man replied. "Both rather desperate I am afraid. But then our situation is desperate. The longest we can hope to hold out for is until a little after sunrise tomorrow. If one could be certain that a rescue party was on the way and would be here by then we would, of course, hang on. But we have no reason for expecting that. And any move we make we must make before sunrise. After, will be too late.

"So, my first plan is this: there are a number of pits, shafts if you will, back there in the valley. My first suggestion is that we hide down them; we have plenty of time to store them with provisions; and I'm rather inclined to believe that the warriors are somewhat in awe of them and will not dare to explore them. Jim thinks so too. He thinks that they will then be content to take our wagon, mules and horses, willing to believe that the spirits have avenged themselves on us. At any rate, we can hide down the pits until our provisions give out; a week or more. And then—"

"We will have to crawl out of our holes and be killed," the girl finished quickly.

"Exactly," the Major nodded. "Unless the natives have departed; and I do think that a rescue party will appear on the scene by the end of the week."

"They might come and go an' we be none the wiser," Hewins objected.

"That's one of the risks my first plan contains."

"It's too full of risks," the Cockney replied gloomily. "Supposing the niggers ain't afraid of ghosties, supposing they takes it into their 'eads to explore them pits? Suppose—aw hell!"

"Yet it is a good plan, I tell you, man," Demper said thoughtfully. "Niggers do not like holes in the ground. That I know."

"But your other plan," the girl asked gently.

"That we carry the fight to them, as soon as we have made due preparations."

"What!" the three white men shouted in unison.

"**HAVE YOU** gone mad!" Richards gasped. "There are only six of us all told, while the niggers number thousands."

"Hundreds," the Major corrected. "Hundreds, Soapy."

"Hundreds or thousands," Richards exclaimed, "they're too many for us. I like your first plan too well to want to hear any more of the other."

"I wants to 'ear it just the same," Hewins insisted. "We ain't got nothing else to do. Wait a minute, though." He peered through his peep hole. "There's a nigger getting careless. Ought to know better than to show his blooming carcase like that."

As he spoke he fired. His shot was greeted with a yell of pain, and the warrior he had shot at sprang erect, and then, collapsing in a heap to the ground, crawled painfully to better shelter before the little Cockney could fire again.

"Now go on, Major," Hewins grinned. "I—"

But a ragged discharge of the warriors' muzzle loaders kept each eye glued to its lookout hole. Hewins shot had awakened the drowsing natives and they fired blindly in the hope that a stray shot would find a billet.

"They couldn't hit a hay-stack," Hewins grunted contemptuously. "Not wiv good guns, let alone wiv them there pot-bellied things they've got."

Even as he spoke a slug broke through the canvas and hit him in the wind, doubling him up with a loud *Ouch!* of pain. Instantly the girl was over by him, sympathetic consternation on her face, ready to administer any aid he might be needing.

"I'm all right, Miss," he gasped. "Took—the wind away—that's all. Lucky it had to break through the canvas first. That stopped the—force of it. If it hadn't been for that—'ell! My belly ain't as tough as canvas!"

As he straightened up the slug which had hit him dropped to the floor of the wagon. He picked it up and examined it with a look of disgust.

"Well, I'm blowed!" he exclaimed: "If it ain't the leg of one of them 'ere cast iron cookin' pots. Lumme! To think of being knocked out by a blinkin' kettle. Carries me back to me early days, when I was a respectable 'appily married man! My Lizzie, she was decidedly partial to kettles, she was. And many a Saturday night she met me at the door wiv: 'Where's yer blinking wages?' an' if I didn't answer quick enough to please her, I 'ad to dodge the bloomin' kettle. Lumme!"

This little account of past domesticity helped to relieve the tension under which they were all laboring. Then presently they sobered, Hewins' mishap bringing home to them the narrow line between them and death.

"I'll be able to breathe better," Hewins gasped, "w'en I'm safe out of this 'ole. Let's 'ear your other plan Major. 'Ow do you reckon to carry the fight to the niggers?"

"FIRST OF all," he said thoughtfully, "we have got to consider that they're rotten shots, and that though by chance they might once in a while hit a stationary target, the odds against them hitting a moving one is infinitely greater. Admitted? Right! Then we must consider that they have nearly run out of ammunition. Perhaps, or perhaps not. You may have noticed that very few slugs pattered against the canvas at this last discharge of theirs. Neither did they keep up the firing so long."

The Dutchman nodded agreement.

"Yah! That is true," he said slowly. "A nigger who has a gun will always fire it as long as he has any powder left. *Ach sis!* They love to make a noise. I have seen them empty their guns again and again into the body of a buck which was, look you, dead already. *So-a!* I tell you that all those that had guns and ammunition fired a little while ago, and those whose ammunition had given out pretended to fire. Maybe they went *bang* with their mouths. *Ach sis!* In some ways they are very little children. But go on: what next will you say?"

"If all you say's true, Demper, then the next step will be easy. I want to draw their fire and exhaust their ammunition."

"That will be easy." Hewins chortled. "We'll stick Soapy up outside the wagon and—"

"It may be you we'll set up," Richards snapped.

The Major waved his hands soothingly.

"We can't spare either of you, unfortunately. I think that if we stick a helmet on a stick, or rig up a dummy and make a lot of noise, that will be quite sufficient."

"And having drawn their ammunition, what then?"

"Why then they are reduced to assegais only, and—"

"Almighty!" Demper exclaimed. "Only assegais, he says. *Ma-an!* What do you think assegais are? Toys? I tell you they know how to use them. They can throw them—"

"But that's the point," the Major interrupted hastily. "Jim—I am trusting to his knowledge and keen eyesight— says they are armed with short stabbing assegais. They have none of the throwing ones with them, he says, otherwise they would have thrown them long before this, for they are well within range. And so—"

"You are talking like a fool," Richards interrupted snarlingly. "Here we are safe and you would have us go within stabbing distance. A hell of a plan yours is!"

"I am afraid it is," the Major agreed. "It is hell if we go and hell if we stay; and for my part I would rather go."

"Then how do you plan to go?" the girl asked.

"IT IS simplicity itself," the Major said. "First, as I have already suggested, we draw the natives' fire. Then we take most of the provisions out of the wagon in order to lighten it; and then we turn loose twelve of the mules and your horses. Harness the other four mules to the wagon, and then drive the other loose mules before us. We will drive out in the wagon. I think that the very unexpectedness of the maneuver will ensure success. You see," he continued earnestly, "the sudden rush of the loose animals will quite throw a disorder into the ranks of the natives, and then, when they see the wagon coming closely behind, with all of us firing rapidly, I am inclined to think they will be so bewildered that we will be able to pass through before they are aware of what is happening. And get through or not, we will have made an attempt; and if we are fated to fail, we will have at least died fighting."

This plan was received by a murmur of approval from Hewins and the girl; the latter saying enthusiastically. "I think that we should make an attempt late in the afternoon, an hour before sundown, say. That should give us plenty of time to unload the wagon and get everything ready. And here's another thing; we ought to reinforce the wagon. I mean we should make barricades along the sides and rear so that assegais could not pass through easily."

The Major nodded approval.

"And now," continued the girl, "I am going to make a dummy man, which we will stand out in front, hoping that it will draw their fire."

As she spoke she rummaged among the Major's equipment in order to find the wherewithal to carry out her intention.

"It is a crazy plan," Richards said testily. "As long as we are here we have a chance of living through, but your way is just like doing deliberate suicide. Not for me. I am going back into the valley and hide myself down one of them pits."

The Major turned to the Dutchman.

"And you, Demper?" he questioned.

"I am in two minds, *ma-an*," he replied stolidly. "Your plan is the plan of a youngster. Fifteen or maybe twenty years ago, I would have come with you. *Ja!* Maybe ten years ago I myself would have thought of such a plan. But now—" he shook his head—"I think not. It is too risky. It is a chance I will not take."

"Nor me," Richards echoed.

The Major shrugged his shoulders and turned to the girl and Hewins.

"That means, I suppose, we all have to stay here. I am sorry. I think we are passing up a good chance of escape."

"It don't mean nothing of the sort," Hewins said indignantly. "We agreed to follow your orders, an' them as won't come, do as they blame well please. But me, I am coming wiv you, and the young lady will, and the 'Ottentot. That puts us in the majority any'ow. I don't see that there's any call for us to remain be'ind just because these two skunks don't want to come. Tell you wot: put it to them to consider, either they come wiv us or they don't. If they come wiv us, start now getting ready. And if they don't come wiv us, they can start packing their stuff down into one of the pits and crawl into their 'ole like bloomin' worms."

The Major nodded.

"That seems fair enough," he said. "Well, Demper, Richards, what do you say?"

"I have said all I have got to say," Richards replied sullenly. "I stay here down one of the holes, whether I stay alone or not."

THERE WAS a crafty look in his eyes which did not pass unnoticed by the Major. He realized that Richards' thought was that after the wagon had been captured by the natives and its occupants killed, then the natives, believing that they had killed all who were at the Kloof would depart and leave him to search for the diamonds he believed to be hidden here, free of risk.

The Major laughed softly, bitterly. He turned his back on Richards, and turned to Demper.

"And you?" he questioned.

The Dutchman's heavy features bore a lugubrious expression. Evidently he was torn by conflicting desires. Finally, with a shrug of his shoulders, he said, "Almighty! I would like to go with you, but I stay."

The Major nodded curtly. "Then that is settled," he said. "Four of us go, you two stay."

And without further words he turned to the task of unloading the wagon, assisted by the others.

They all worked in dour silence, carrying provisions out of the rear of the wagon, where they were safe from the natives' observations. Then when the wagon was emptied of all its heavier contents, they re-inforced the inside of its tent-topped cover with bundles of twigs, blankets and sacks.

Meanwhile the girl had succeeded in making a very life-like dummy of a suit of the Major's, stuffed with pillows, crowned by a large helmet. And putting this in the front of the wagon, she managed to impart movement to it by cunningly placed strings.

Kneeling down behind it, sheltered by the wagon seat, she levelled a rifle in such a way that the dummy seemed almost to be holding it, and fired spasmodically.

Her ruse had its effect and slugs pattered about the wagon from the guns of the natives.

But they were harmless, causing no damage, for their force was spent before they reached the wagon, indicating that the supply of powder was running short; by the time the men had finished their task, the firing had ceased altogether.

The Major beamed his approval at the girl, then he turned to Jim and Hewins and instructed them to help the two men who had desired to stay, to carry provisions to the pits.

Demper waited long enough to shake his hand and wish him "Good-luck," hesitated so long that it seemed as if he must be considering changing his mind and leaving with the wagon.

And this he probably would have done had not Richards called at the critical moment, "Come on, Demper. There ain't no time to waste!"

Then, nodding his head in farewell, he shouldered a store of provisions and plodded off silently in the wake of the other.

CHAPTER XIV

Raining Assegais

THE AFTERNOON sun sank lower, shadows lengthened, an atmosphere of peace pervaded the place. The Major and the girl, sitting close together, looked confidently out through the opening at the front of the wagon, trying to see what the future held in store for them, indulging in optimistic day dreams. Yet beneath it all they were fully conscious that this was a false security that they were now experiencing, realizing all that had to be done, all the obstacles that had to be overcome, before any of these dreams could be realized.

The girl sighed, and the Major taking her hand pressed it reassuringly.

"It's time," he said, "that Jim and Hewins returned."

"Perhaps," the girl said a little fearfully, "they will not come back. Perhaps they have decided to stop, too."

The Major shook his head confidently.

"No, there is no fear of that; they will both return if they are permitted to return. Demper and Richards may try to keep them by force, but—" He shook his head.

Again they were silent for a little while; the Major moving about uneasily; glancing up at the position of the sun; looking at the rock strewn watercourse where death lurked.

"And if they do not come?" the girl questioned so softly. "Shall we stay too?"

"I think we shall have to," he said with a sigh.

Then his face lighted as he heard the footsteps of the two returning men.

"Demper tried to hold us up," Hewins chortled, explaining their long absence. " 'Im and Richards wanted us to stay wiv them, an' I reckon we would 'ave 'ad to if it 'adn't been for this nigger of yourn.'E's a cunning devil all right. The way 'e pretended to lose 'is footin' and barged into old Soapy, knocking 'im down the blinkin' pit, was a fair caution. And that gave me a chance to get out of Demper's range, an' 'ere we are."

The Major looked questioningly at the Hottentot. Jim grinned reassuringly, and busied himself with the mules' harness.

"It is time we started. Baas," he said presently, and the Major agreeing, they harnessed four of the mules to the wagon.

Because they were not interrupted in this task, and there was no stir from the warriors beyond, they were tempted to hope that the warriors had departed; but Jim's keen eyes soon showed that in this they were mistaken. And following his pointed finger they could see where boulders were moving, seemingly of their own volition, directly in the path the wagon would have to take.

"We must work faster, Baas," Jim said, "or they will have closed the way. It is well that we are only harnessing four mules. It is better still that the warriors think we are going to inspan all of them. If they knew what we plan to do they would work more swiftly. As it is—"

HE BROUGHT the other animals, the twelve mules and the three horses, round to the front of the wagon. And stood there placidly, made lethargic by the heat, quite content to remain still in one place.

"Ready, Baas?" he asked.

The Major looked round at the girl and Hewins.

They nodded. The tension was great. The air seemed charged with suspense. Everything was very still.

The Major hesitated, doubting at this last moment as to the wisdom of the course he had persuaded these others to follow.

He looked at the girl. She was tying herself loosely to one of the struts supporting the tent-top of the wagon, so that she could keep to her post and not be thrown off her balance by the swinging of the wagon. Within reach of her hand was an arsenal of weapons, all loaded in chamber and magazine.

Hewins was similarly occupied on the opposite side of the wagon. And that, the Major thought, was a complete answer to his doubts.

"Yes, all ready," he called to Jim, climbing up into the driver's seat, the long lash and stock driving whip in his hand.

"Until we have started, Baas," Jim said grimly, "you hold the reins; then I will take them, and this day I will show you how to drive mules."

He stood erect, his legs apart, braced for a sudden jolt of the wagon.

He held the whip aloft; the lash hung down limply, not a breath of wind stirred it.

Again there was silence, an ominous silence, a silence which could almost be felt.

Then, with a loud blood curdling yell, Jim's whip became a live thing in his hands. With loud crackling reports it leaped over the heads of the loose animals; it bit into their flesh, stung them, goaded them to a mad panic.

Bunched together, they galloped swiftly down the watercourse and after them, at a speed equally as frenzied, Jim drove the wagon.

At the first sound of the stampede of the animals and the rattle of iron shod wheels, as the wagon lurched and swayed precariously along the boulder strewn ground, the warriors leapt to their feet and drew together as if they would form a living barrier to this living avalanche. But as the onrushing animals drew nearer, their courage faltered and with frightened yells they scrambled to the left and right; falling over each other in their eagerness to avoid being trampled under foot. A few made desperate lunges with their spears as the stampeding loose animals rushed by them; but not even the bravest waited for the wagon, and their retreat was hastened by the Major's shooting.

IN A few breathless moments the first line of the warriors had been passed, and now Jim was swinging the wagon round the first bend. The wagon tilted precariously on two wheels, seemed as if nothing could save it from capsizing. Jim swung the animals to the left to counter-balance the tilt; it righted itself and settled down with a sickening thud on four wheels.

Then on again, their pace increasing, the loose animals thundering before them, driven whenever they showed signs of slackening their speed, by Jim's voice and the vicious bites of his whip. And here the ground was comparatively free from boulders, the distance between the high black walls greater.

And no warriors were in sight!

Hewins and the girl were now firing out of the rear of the wagon, checking the onrush of the band of warriors they had just passed through and who, yelling fiercely, were running with incredible speed after the wagon.

"If we can get round the next corner, Jim," the Major said, "we are safe."

"So *you* say, Baas," Jim said gravely. "But *I* will not say that until many miles are between us and these cursed ones. It wou'd be best that missy and the white man come now to the front of the wagon," he concluded.

The Major nodded, and by the time they had come to the next bend in the river, Hewins and the girl were kneeling at the back of the driver's seat.

Ahead of them they could hear shouts intermingled with cries of pain and panic. Then rounding the corner they saw their advance guard of animals galloping ahead of them, having apparently passed through a horde of natives, cleaving a path.

Evidently their onrush had been so unexpected that many of the natives had not been able to get out of the way, and the sandy bed of the river was dotted with black forms which moved painfully.

Here, where the banks of the river were not so steep, the natives were climbing up out of the river bed; and from vantage points thus gained threw down boulders. Several threw assegais, four of these feathering the off-leader, causing it to drop to the ground. The very impetus of the wagon's movement carried the poor beast forward some yards before Jim could rein in the others. Then he leapt down, knife in hand, intending to cut loose the wounded beast. The stoppage was the signal of a cry of exultation from the warriors.

Descending again to the river's bed, regardless of the rain of bullets from the wagon's defenders, the natives closed in on it, reinforced by the first party who were now coming up in the rear.

Swiftly, with an exhibition of generalship, and well executed tactics, they formed a ring around the wagon, a ring which gradually contracted.

These natives had throwing assegais, and presently the air was filled with them. Another mule dropped and then another. An assegai pricked the Major's arm, drawing blood. The ring was now much smaller, the warriors crawling forward, Assegais rattled continually against the wagon, tearing through the canvas cover.

"Blimey!" Hewins gasped. "I'm beginnin' to think we'd have been better down one of them 'ere pits." Then, quickly, to the Major, "But I ain't blamin' you, cully, not in the least. Don't you think I am. I followed you wiv me eyes open. I thought that your way was the best way, and I ain't agoing back on what I said."

"Thanks, Hewins," the Major said softly. "That is bally white of you."

HE TURNED to the girl. She was white faced, but her lips were set firmly, and her eyes held no look of fear, or reproach, as she looked at him and said: "We will win through yet!"

As she spoke she fired at a fantastically dressed warrior who had crept dangerously close to the wagon.

"It is a pity," she said softly, "that all this killing should be necessary, and simply because we are greedy for treasure. I don't think I will be able to touch it even if we do manage to get safely out of this. It has too much blood on it."

The Major held up a warning finger to his lips; he had intercepted a look of greed and cupidity on Hewin's face, and it seemed as if, for a moment, that man's vices had conquered his virtues.

"I'm afraid I've made rather a mess of things," the Major muttered. "We should have gone down the pits with the others."

The girl patted his hand encouragingly.

"You have nothing whatever to reproach yourself for," she assured him. Then: "Look! They are closing in on your right."

And for a while they had no further opportunity for speech, but fired as rapidly as possible, keeping the warriors from getting any closer.

Several times the Major shouted to them, hoping to bring an end to the bloodshed or, at least, to ensure the safety of the girl. But they would not listen to him, howling in derision at his promises and threats.

And then, it was very nearly sundown, a new danger threatened. Some of the warriors were now throwing spears to which lighted brands were attached. Most of them fell short, but one dropped on to the canvas tent of the wagon, smoldered a little while and then burst into a fierce flame, threatening a swift destruction to the wagon and its contents.

The natives greeted this with wild, exultant shouts.

"We will smoke you out, white men, defilers of the place of the spirits! As jackals are smoked out, so we will smoke you out!"

"Watch closely now, Baas," Jim warned. "Now is the time they are likely to charge."

The Major nodded and he and the girl fired with great rapidity, while Jim and Hewins attempted to beat out the spreading flame.

Hewins, taking down a canvas bucket from a peg driven into the upright support of the hood, filled it with water from the keg and threw it on the flames, working like one possessed until the flames were beaten.

"An' that's olright," he exclaimed, "as long as they don't start any more fireworks. If they do—we're done. They ain't no more water left."

As he spoke he tilted the keg, hoping to find a little water remaining. As he did so something rattled on the bottom of the keg and the chamois bag was exposed. With a furtive glance around to make sure he was not observed, he retrieved it and put it inside his shirt.

"An' wot now?" he asked, hearing a new note in the yells of the savages.

" 'Pon my soul, I'm not quite sure," the Major drawled—his back was to Hewins. "But the mules and the horses are coming back and"—he gave one final, hasty rub to the monocle he had been polishing, fixed it in his eye, and standing up on the wagon seat continued excitedly—"and the natives are retreating! My word! It's like a bally melodrama, what? Saved in the nick of time. Oh, quite!"

HIS ARMS were around the girl's shoulder, holding her close to his side. Hewins and the Hottentot stood close by, watching the return of the stampeding animals and the panic stricken retreat of the natives as they swarmed up the high banks, those below jabbing the ones above with their spears in order to induce better speed.

Some of the animals galloped swiftly past the wagon; the rest came to a halt beside it, their flanks wet with sweat.

And then those in the wagon heard shots and shouts of encouragement, saw horsemen riding along the tops of the banks, saw others, led by a tall, lanky man in uniform, riding fast along the bed of the river.

The girl released herself gently from the Major's hold; her eyes shone with expectant delight and, as the rescue party came to a halt, she jumped down from the wagon and ran forward with a glad shout.

The Major seemed to sag, seemed suddenly to have lost his morale as he watched the meeting of the girl and the corporal.

Jim was grinning happily, murmuring, "The Baas will soon forget."

And Hewins was milling about at the rear of the wagon. Apparently he was not over anxious to be seen by the rescue party.

The corporal of the mounted police dismounted, and, his arm about the girl's waist, came forward to greet the Major.

"Marjorie tells me," he said, drawling slightly, a nasal inflection in his voice, "I have a lot to thank you for. An' I'll thank you later. But now I've got to finish this bit of work, an' I must put Marjorie in your charge a while longer. Got to chase the natives back to where they belong an' read the riot act to them.

"You-all had better go back to the kloof an' wait there. I reckon I'll be able to join you by tomorrow sunrise, sure."

And with that he vaulted into the saddle, waved his hand in a farewell salute and led his hastily enlisted posse back along the bed of the watercourse to a place where they could ride their horses up the steep bank and take up the pursuit of the fleeing warriors.

CHAPTER XV

The Major Writes a Letter

"**T**HE DEAR corporal would seem to be deucedly competent," the Major drawled.

The girl started, surprised out of the dreamy mood into which she had fallen.

"He is," she agreed softly. "Very! We—I had almost forgotten—had planned to marry as soon as he wins a commission. He—I—" her voice faltered.

"Ah!" the Major murmured. Then, briskly, to Jim, "Inspan—we go back to the kloof."

"That is folly, Baas," the Hottentot protested.

"It is an order, Jim," the Major said sternly, and helped the Hottentot inspan the mules which had stopped at the wagon.

The girl, sitting on a nearby rock, watched him intently.

"Major," she began softly.

"Get up into the wagon," he said tersely, "and we will get back to the kloof. I want to make camp before darkness sets in."

She sighed and obeyed.

Then Hewins showed himself, carrying a small parcel of provisions.

"I ain't goin' to no bloomin' kloof," he asserted. "Me. I'm agoin' to ride me 'orse away—barebacked if I 'as to."

"You'll have to," the Major replied coldly. "But why this hurry to depart?"

"I don't want ter see Richards or Demper again—that's why, mister."

As he spoke he caught his horse which had stopped with the mules and put on it the bridle he had taken from the wagon.

"Just a minute, Hewins," the Major drawled, covering the man with his revolver. "Before you go I'd like that bag you took from the water keg. Quick, now!"

Hewins hesitated a moment, scowling fiercely, then, with a broad grin on his face he said, "It's a fair cop. But 'ow did yer know I 'ad it?"

"I was polishing my eye-glass at the time, dear lad, and saw you reflected in it. Quite simple. Now give me the bag."

Hewins fumbled inside his shirt, then tossed the bag to the Major. At the same time he leaped on his horse and galloped away.

"But I 'elped meself to some of the rings," he yelled back derisively.

He flourished his hands; the gems on his fingers glittered as they caught the rays of the setting sun.

The girl struck up the Major's hand just as he fired and the bullet sped harmlessly into the air.

The Major scowled, picked up the bag and climbed into the wagon; and a few minutes later they were driving back to the kloof.

Arrived at the camp she watched the two men prepare *skoff.*

When she suggested that Demper and Richards be apprised of the rescue and released from the pits where they had sought shelter, she was met with an angry refusal.

"Do you think," the Major stormed, "that I'm going to fight for my share of the treasure with those two blighters? Hardly. It'll be all easy sailing for me from now on, and I don't intend to go out of my way to seek squalls."

"Are you trying to make me think," she said merrily, "that you're in the same class as those two? Because, if you are, let me warn you, that you won't succeed. You see"—and her voice softened—"although I've known you only a little while, I know you very well. I—"

He laughed bitterly.

"You do not know me at all well. Not half as well as the police. You see, my dear young lady, I am a man with a prison record. I have only just been released from a long sentence on the Breakwater for a very serious crime. Good-night. Jim will bring you your *skoff.* And if you hear noises in the night, do not be alarmed. It will simply be Jim and myself getting ready for a long trek."

He bowed curtly and left her.

FOR A long time sleep would not come to Marjorie Wallace that night, despite the fact that she was physically exhausted.

She tried to think of the corporal, the man she had promised to marry, and, instead, a vision of the Major always blotted him out of her thoughts.

And when sleep finally did come to her, it was broken at first by restless dreams. But, as the night wore on, these dreams gave place to restful ones of a life of peace lived with a man she thoroughly understood and who understood her.

She was awakened by the rays of an early morning sun pouring in through a vent in the tent.

Rising, wondering at the quiet of the place, she went to the opening and peered out.

The place was deserted; the Major, Jim, the wagon and mules had gone.

She went outside, greatly dispirited, disappointed, and saw, with a start of surprise, two men—Richards and Demper lying on the ground near by. They were both securely bound and gagged.

Bending over them she saw, pinned to Richards' coat, a letter addressed to herself.

Taking it off and opening it, she read:

Dear Miss Marjorie:

Jim has just signaled from Look-out Point that the gallant corporal and his men are on their way here. So I must hurry off. It would never do for me to give him a chance to question me too closely.

I am leaving Messrs. Demper and Richards to your tender mercies. I thought of taking them with me, but they were too impossible. But, if I were you, I would not release them. Let the corporal do that. They might be dangerous!

I had quite a job convincing them that there were no diamonds in this place—their minds seemed set on diamonds! They would have it that I had already discovered them, or that you had. They almost caught me in a nice little ambush, but failed; thanks to Jim.

But, as they were so keen on the matter, I showed them what I had discovered! Poor old Richards, he actually foamed at the mouth! So, to please him, I stuffed all the things in his pockets. I thought it was right that he should possess them for a little while—after all, he has put himself to, so much trouble!

Of course, you or the corporal—I think it had better be the corporal—will be able to get them back from him without any difficulty. And then you won't have to wait for a commission, will you? And I don't approve of long engagements.

And now here comes Jim, grinning like a Barbary ape at the thought of being on trek again.

Good-by, dear Miss Marjorie. Think of me sometimes.

Yours devotedly,

The Major.

The girl folded the letter wistfully, patted it and then put it carefully into a pocket. And for a little while she sat gazing dreamily before her until, roused by the sound of swiftly approaching horsemen, she murmured, "I shall always remember, Major, and I understand."

Then, rising to her feet, she ran swiftly to meet her lover, knowing that nothing could spoil her memories of the man who had, for such a brief time, played such a big part in her life; knowing that those memories would not spoil the life of happiness she was destined to lead with the man she now ran to meet.

WHITE MAN'S STRIDE

JIM, THE Hottentot, looked at the Major, his Baas, in deep disgust.

"*Wo-we!*" he exclaimed softly.

"What folly!" He glanced cautiously around to make sure that a path of retreat was open, noting particularly a heavily thorn-armored tree in the bush a little to his right.

"Mark that tree, Baas," he continued in the same low voice. "You have often wondered if a man could climb such a tree. Presently, I think, you will show me the way—if I do not get to it first. He is getting angry, Baas. He tells you to go way or—"

"Quiet, Jim!" the Major ordered. "I make discoveries in the only way possible to make discoveries. And I—"

"You," Jim interrupted gravely, "will not live to discover what happens when a man pelts a lion with pebbles."

The Major smiled.

"Twice I have hit him on the nose, Jim, and once in the ribs. But he only snarls like a licked cur."

As he spoke he flicked another stone at the magnificent black-maned lion which crouched, belly down, in the center of a small clearing.

The stone hit the ground just before the lion, sending a little spurt of dust into the air. The beast's snarls changed into a comical sounding sneeze but its yellow, basilisk-like eyes did not blink, their hypnotic stare did not shift from the two men—the white master and black servant—who stood facing it not thirty yards distant.

"It is not seemly, Baas," the Hottentot protested. "One does not inflict childish punishments on a great chief. Besides, it is not wise. *Wo-we!* It is folly to play with death."

"It is only that I seek to add a spice to life, Jim. The straight, smooth road often wearies. There is a good sized stone close to your right foot, Jim. See if your aim is better than mine."

"What folly!" Jim groaned. But he stooped cautiously, his eyes on the lion, and when his groping hand closed on the stone he threw it with all the power of his abnormally long, powerful arm. Neither did he permit his personal opinion on the wisdom of this lion-baiting to affect his aim. His Baas ordered, Jim obeyed.

The heavy, jagged stone thudded against the lion's ribs with great force.

The snarls increased in force; the evil, blood curdling, bad tempered snarls of the bush-veld's master-killer; the lion's tufted tail lashed swiftly from side to side, then suddenly stiffened.

"Watch out, Baas," Jim warned excitedly. "He is going to charge."

He thrust the rifle he was carrying toward his Baas. The Major took it and dropped on one knee.

Both men tensed, seemed to become as inanimate as the boulders which dotted the clearing and reflected the sun's rays.

SLOWLY, IN a movement absolutely free from jerks, as if the weapon was a part of his body, the Major's

rifle came up to his shoulder; the sights came into alignment; his index finger caressed the trigger.

Then the lion, a beast of temperament, relaxed and, ignoring the two men, turning his back on them, indolently stretched itself at full length, basking in the sun, washing its face. Its rasping *purrs* sounded like the exhaust of a steam engine.

"By Jove!" the Major exclaimed. The words and the tone seemed to create about him an environment more in keeping with his dudish attire than the wide, African veld. It conjured up visions of London's Rotten Row and Regent Street. There one would expect to see a man like the Major. But here—! Not even in her gentlest mood is South Africa kind to her precious elegants. And yet, it is wise to remember this: outward appearances count for very little and things are not always—almost never, in Africa— what they seem.

"By Jove!" the Major repeated. And now the personality his tone had suggested appeared only as a stalking horse behind which lurked a keen, active brain, just as his foppish clothes disguised a perfect physique. "By Jove! The old fellow is playin' just like a little kitten. I wonder what he'd do if I scratched him between the ears?"

He rose to his feet and took a tentative step forward.

"Baas!" the Hottentot exclaimed protestingly, fearing his Baas was going to attempt some greater folly.

The Major halted and looked back at Jim, smiling provocatively.

"PUT AN end to this folly, Baas," Jim pleaded. "All night that one—"Jim spat toward the lion—"kept us awake with his singing. In the dark before dawn he killed one of our mules and with difficulty we drove him off before he stampeded the rest. *Au-a!* He was so close to me that I could smell his stinking breath." The Hottentot's broad nostrils dilated at the remembrance of that charnel-house smell. He continued: "Since sunrise we have followed his spoor through thick bush and shoulder-high grass. And now, now that for the first time we have caught up with him in a place where the Baas can get a good shot, the Baas does nothing but play the fool like a maiden with a kid goat. Shoot, Baas, and let us get back to the outspan."

The Major reflectively stroked his firm, smooth-shaven chin.

"But why kill him, Jim? His death will not restore life to the mule he killed. And it is his life to kill. Look at him. See how the muscles ripple under his skin. See—"

"Baas! My eyes are blinded with fear. *Wo-we!* I know that with one blow of his paw he can smash in your skull as easily as you can smash an egg. I know that he can break the neck of a big bull—and I am no bull. I know that— *Au-a!* All that I know, you know. A lion! *Wo-we!* It is an evil beast. A hyena is his best friend. So shoot, Baas. Shoot before he remembers the power that is his."

"But I can't shoot a 'sitter'," the Major drawled in English. "It wouldn't be sporting." Actually he wanted to postpone the shooting until the last possible moment, would have liked, if possible, to avoid it altogether. But that, he knew, was impossible. Lions are vermin. The gamekiller of today may prey on pack animals tomorrow; may become a man-eater within the year!

The Major sighed. The big, tawny cat was so graceful playing there in the sunlight.

"Make him charge, Jim," he said in the vernacular.

"That is easy, Baas," said Jim and danced a wild fandango, shouting insults at the lion, misnaming it, crediting it with mixed and base parentage, accusing it of mean, cowardly crimes.

THE BEAST ceased its kittenish play and looked contemptuously toward its puny derider, yawning magnificently. But the yawn ended in a vicious snapping of its jaws. For a moment it hesitated, seemed to be on the point of moving majestically away from the place. Then, as if stung by a particularly slurring insult, it wheeled and, facing the men, crouched belly down, snarling defiance, its tail waving to and fro.

Suddenly, with the swiftness of an arrow shot from a bow, it leaped into its charge and came forward, head down, tail up, at an incredible speed. Its coughing growls echoed across the veld.

Again the Major's rifle came up to his shoulder and he waited coolly for the last possible moment before pressing the trigger which would send a heavy bullet crashing into the lion's skull; a shot which would end the lion's devastating charge in a lifeless sprawl, carried by the very impetus of its rush to the hunter's feet.

It was a matter of seconds—the Major's finger contracted about the trigger—instead of a report there was only a harmless *click!* The cartridge in the chamber was either a used one or a dud! With lightning swiftness the Major worked the bolt and fired again. Again failure. The experienced hunter had failed, had acted like the greenest of greenhorns! He had failed to open his magazine "cut-off!"

Jim ran to the left, shouting, gesticulating, hoping to divert the lion from his course and so give his Baas time to rectify his carelessness.

The cut-off open, the Major worked the bolt again, but before he could fire a native dressed in the uniform of the Rhodesian Native Police staggered out into the clearing from the bush on the right.

And, at the last moment, when a spring would have carried him on top of the Major, the lion swerved toward the newcomer, skidding with the suddenness of its check.

Recovering swiftly, it sprang, roaring, open-mouthed at the native.

The Major's first shot entered behind the shoulder when the lion was at the highest point of its spring; his second crashed through the tawny one's skull just as he collided with the native, sending him to the ground.

Man and beast rolled over and over, hidden in a cloud of dust.

JIM AND the Major ran forward, the latter in the fore, ready for another shot. Through the swirls of dust they saw the lion crawl a few paces toward the shelter of the bush. He roared once, choked as the blood poured out of his mouth, stiffened convulsively, and then was very still.

"By Jove!" the Major muttered as he and Jim bent over the stranger. "I've lived a lifetime in five seconds!"

"Death was very near us then, Baas. I do not think we will play games with a lion again. If this man had not come out of the bush—*Au-a!* His coming saved the Baas' life. Is he hurt, Baas?"

"Badly, Jim. But it was not the lion who did it. Look!"

He had gently cut the native's clothing from him and pointed to a long, deep wound in the man's groin. It was crudely plugged with a wad of leaves.

"An assegai made that wound, Baas" Jim said, "and not very long ago! *Wo-we!* He must have lost much blood. Will he live, Baas?"

The Major shook his head.

"The wonder is that he lived till now, Jim. Death entered with the assegai that made that wound. I wonder where he came from and what is the story back of this?"

He moistened the man's lips with water from his flask.

The wounded man opened his eyes; his lips moved. The Major bent lower to hear his whisperings.

"Go quickly to my *inkosi*—the white policeman," the man said. "He keeps guard over an evil one—he is weak with fever—he—"

"Do not talk, warrior," the Major interrupted gently. "First we will tend your wound, and then—"

The native made an impatient gesture with his hand.

"Nay, listen to me. I must talk whilst strength is with me. My *inkosi* sent me to you for help—we saw your cook fire last night at sundown. The servants of the man my *inkosi* watches waylaid me. There was a fight." He smiled grimly. "They are not so many now as before. But, still, they were too many for me. They left me, thinking me dead. In the blackness of the night I awoke from the sleep which is like death and, first plugging the hole to stop the blood—it was flowing fast, faster than I could run—I came on that my *inkosi's* orders might be obeyed."

He closed his eyes. His pulse was feeble; he seemed to have fallen into the coma which precedes death.

THE MAJOR looked inquiringly at Jim and the Hottentot took from the bunch of charms which hung about his neck a quill containing medicine concocted by a witchdoctor. Most of its ingredients were filth, but—and this the Major knew—it also contained, obtained from the seeds of a Kaffir Orange, strychnine. Jim mixed it with some water and poured it into the native's mouth, stroking his throat to induce swallowing action.

They waited anxiously. Presently the wounded man stirred fitfully and opened his eyes.

"Why haven't you gone to my *inkosi?*" he demanded.

"Where is he? How shall we find him?" the Major asked gently. "Speak quickly before life runs away."

The native nodded understandingly. A challenging gleam came into his eyes and quickly faded.

"It was after yesterday's sunset that I left my *inkosi's* outspan—and I traveled fast until the evil ones waylaid me— Travel fast to the north until you sight a kopje crowned by one withered tree. You cannot miss it.

"There, near the bank of the river which skirts the kopje's base, you will find my *inkosi's* camp. Hurry, hurry! You should be there before, before—" His voice faltered. The drug was losing its hold on him; his strength was fast ebbing away. With an effort, he continued, "You will be there before—" He stared up into the fathomless blue of the sky; the molten glare of the sun did not dazzle his eyes. *"Au-a!* A cloud hides the sun. Where is it?"

"It is high noon, warrior," the Major replied gravely. "You cannot see it because the Spirits veil your eyes. They wait for you."

"*Wo-we!* Am I so near an end?" He chuckled softly, "It is a good time to die—when the sun is high. Go now. Do not wait for my Snake to pass." To the native the snake was a symbol of the soul. "I am a Matabele! I am not afraid to die. Go now and you will be at my *inkosi's* camp before sunset. Tell him my body failed me, not my spirit. He will understand. He is a man."

"And you, too, you are a man, warrior," the Major commended.

Again a gleam flashed into the man's eyes, as, with a last sudden surge of strength he sat erect.

"*Bulala!* Kill!" He shouted hoarsely. Then: "I am a Matabele, I am not afraid to die."

And, with the war-cry of his people still trembling on his lips, he fell back. Once he shuddered as if he were shaking free his soul, then he was very still.

"A good way to die, Jim."

"A man's way, Baas. And now, what?"

"We will protect his body from the bush scavengers, Jim, and then go to keep faith with the warrior's spirit."

FOR A little while they worked silently, covering the man's body with boulders, making it as secure as they could from the ravages of hyenas and vultures.

"But the Baas does not intend to go in search of the warrior's *inkosi?*" Jim said when, their task completed, they sat down to rest on the carcase of the dead lion.

"Truly, Jim," the Major replied gravely.

"But he is a policeman, Baas. He will put handcuffs on us and the end of it all will be—"

"We cannot look to the ending, Jim. A man is ill, needing our help. Another man—truly he was a man—died that we might know of his *inkosi's* need. But for his coming I now might be dead. I give you back your own words. So we hasten back to the outspan and then trek north, looking for the camp of the warrior's *inkosi*. Come!"

He rose to his feet and stood looking down impatiently at the Hottentot.

"The Baas played a fool game with the lion," Jim grumbled, "and nearly met death. Now he goes seeking a policeman. What will the end be—"

He rose reluctantly and stood for a moment kicking the lion's carcase with his naked, horn-hard feet. Suddenly the scowl on his ugly face was chased away by a broad good-humored grin.

"Maybe, Baas," he continued with a chuckle, "all that happened here is an omen of what is to come. I think maybe something will come between you and the policeman, as the warrior came between you and the lion."

And then he set off at a run, taking a bee line through the bush for their camp. The Major, running easily, kept close to his heels.

Their progress was a silent one. Not a remarkable fact in the case of the Hottentot, to move silently through the bush was his birthright, as natural to him as to the wild creatures of the bush. But that the Major, a white man, booted, standing fully six feet and weighing over two hundred and twenty pounds, should move with equal craft, effortlessly, was something in the nature of a miracle. At least it was a clue to the man's ability, to his absorption of the lore of the bush.

SIX HOURS they had followed the spoor of the lion, zigzagging through the bush, doubling on their tracks. In less than two hours they were back at their outspan where they were greeted by the wandering native hunter they had left in charge of their trek animals.

Half an hour later—and during that half hour the Major had gained from the native what information he could of the land to the north—six mules were hitched to the light trek wagon. A shouted farewell to the native hunter, in whose care they had left the mate of the mule killed by the lion, a loud *cracking* of Jim's long driving whip, and the onward journey was commenced.

"And so, Baas," Jim commented dryly as the mules settled down to a steady, space destroying gallop, "we go to put our head in a lion's mouth. It may be all a trap."

"The warrior's wound was no lie, Jim."

"No. But can you say his story of how he came by it is no lie? Suppose the white man sent him with that tale he told of being sick, of guarding an evil man, of needing help—knowing that it was *you* to whom he sent the message, knowing—because you are the man you are—that you would go to his help, unsuspecting, and so make it easy to take you captive? Suppose—"

"I have already supposed all that, Jim."

"*Au-a*, Baas! Will you never get full wisdom. This what you now do—it is as: bad as if you again pelted a lion with stones to see if he would run from you."

The Major smiled.

"Take heart, Jim. I have learned my lesson. I'll not trifle with a lion again and, if one charges, I'll run. At least," he amended, "I'll not wait so long before firing, and I'll not again make the mistakes I made today."

And then for a long time the two men were silent.

THEY WERE so different outwardly; so much alike in their attitude toward life and their contempt for danger; the Eternal Boy was strong in each. In all the years they had been together, adventuring their lives in whatever play South Africa put before them, their mutual, unquestioning loyalty had never wavered; the reliance one placed in the other had never been falsified. The one was the complement of the other. They were friends, ignoring the color bar. But there was no mawkish sentiment or "my black brotherings" about the Major. Jim never presumed; on the contrary he was wont to debase himself more than the country's stern unwritten code, which governs relationship between black and white, demanded, lest men should criticize his Baas. Only when they were alone, on the veld, and his Baas threatened a too venturesome course did he assert his independence and planned, on his own initiative, ways and means whereby his Baas might be saved from the consequences of his rashness.

And so he planned now. His eyes gleamed as, reaching back into the covered rear of the wagon, his hand closed on a bundle of knobkerries and assegais.

"I think, Jim," the Major said with a chuckle, reading the Hottentot's thoughts, "there will be no need of killing. The warrior's tale was a true one."

"Maybe, Baas. But *your* weapon failed you twice today. There is no harm in seeing mine will not fail me."

He took an assegai from the bundle and examined it carefully to make sure the haft was free from flaws. Then he sharpened the broad blade, softly humming the "Song of the Spear" as he did so.

The Major shrugged his shoulders and once again let his thoughts take possession of him, driving mechanically, steering the mules around ant hills and thick patches of bush, making sweeping detours to avoid hole-pitted ground, but always returning to his former line after each detour.

He was thinking, rather bitterly, of the queer twist of fate which was speeding him to the rescue of a policeman whose sickness might be a ruse to trap him. The Major laughed at the irony of the situation. That he, the Major, badly wanted by the police just now on a charge of murder and highway robbery, should deputize for a policeman, had its humorous side.

FOR MANY years he had led a life of crime—if his I.D.B. adventures could be strictly labeled "crime"—and had been at constant warfare with South Africa's various police forces, yet he had always enlisted on the side of justice; his wit, his horsemanship, his knowledge of the veld and its people, his innate uprightness, had always been thrown in the scale on the side of the underdog. So that, actually, his warfare with the police was a friendly matching of wits, with the best of fellowship on both sides. They both played the game fairly.

Occasionally a corrupt police officer, or one seeking promotion by a smart capture, had attempted to "trap" the Major into buying diamonds illicitly. It had always seemed so easy; he looked such a silly ass. But invariably such traps had always closed upon the trapper, to the great mirth of those who knew the Major's real worth and his abhorrence of anything approaching uncleanliness.

So, now, despite this charge which now hung over him, despite the hue and cry after him, despite the police circulars which advertised him as "Wanted for murder," offering a reward for his apprehension, men who knew him shook their heads sagely and told each other, "You can't tell me the Major's guilty of anything like that. Don't care what evidence the police have got. Bet you all I've got he'll be able to clear himself."

And if a doubter would object, "Well, if he's innocent, why did he make such a hasty get-away. He didn't even take his tent. And how do you account for the fact that the stolen stones were found in his tent?" the answer would be, "No doubt he's got a good reason for leaving as he did. We'll know when he thinks it time for us to know. An' about them diamonds they found—that's proof enough for me he ain't guilty. He's *slim*, the Major is, he's no man's fool. If you ask me, somebody else planted those diamonds there after he had gone, or maybe he left them so's to draw suspicion on himself. Yeh! That's it. He's shielding somebody."

And that *was* it.

THE MAJOR was shielding a woman who had shot a blackmailer. She was only a chance-met acquaintance; her record was far from savory. But she was a woman, in distress, and the Major acted. That was his way. Acted in such a manner that it would be extremely difficult, now, for him to prove his innocence.

So his thoughts were far from pleasant ones as he drove fast to give succor to a policeman who might be sick or who might be waiting, ambushed behind a rock, ready to arrest him.

"But it can't be that," he exclaimed aloud.

"The Baas said?" Jim asked, looking up from his spear sharpening.

"The native policeman's story was a true one, Jim," the Major explained in the vernacular. "The white policeman could not have got on our trail so quickly. Therefore the policeman who is ill did not know that it was to me he sent for help." He frowned thoughtfully. "But what is a

Rhodesian policeman doing here? We are two days' trek from the border, in the land of the Portuguese. He is out of his territory."

"*Au-a!* Who shall say where a white man's stride ends? And all between its beginning and its end—there is justice," Jim said sagely.

The Major nodded.

"Well put, Jim. This country of you black ones—*Wo-we!* It is overrun by whites. Their shadow falls across the land from the Cape to Broken Hills and beyond; from Mozambique to Walfisch Bay. But sometimes it is a shadow of oppression, Jim."

"Not a *white* man's shadow, Baas. In most places touched by the white man's stride, the shadow is lifted. Where it remains, death will always let in the sun again."

Jim smiled grimly and resumed his spear sharpening with renewed vigor.

The Major was silent, scanning the bush ahead, noting with satisfaction the kopje which loomed up against the sky; on the top of that kopje, its gnarled branches stretched out as if in supplication to the Great Spirits, was a stunted tree.

"We'll know soon," the Major muttered in English, "just how much truth there was in the warrior's tale." Then he mused for a while on the wide spreading influence, for good or bad, the white race had gained on the land of the dark-skinned children of the sun. The white man's stride, Jim dubbed it. It was an apt description.

THE SUN was setting when the Major halted his mules at a small stream which joyously gurgled along its rocky bed. The shadow of the tree-crowned kopje created an impression of eerie coldness.

The Major turned to speak to Jim who, a short time previously, had climbed into the rear of the wagon to get things ready for the night's outspan, he had said. But no Jim was to be seen. The Hottentot, with his bundle of assegais and knobkerries had dropped out of the wagon some time back and was now moving stealthily through the thick bush.

The Major chuckled.

"He's a suspicious blighter, is Jim. But he's barking up a wrong tree this time. And yet—I wonder? I think I must move with caution. Oh, quite. I may have to contend with the servants of the 'evil one' the native policeman fell foul of. Bally funny, come to think of it, that I should have overlooked the possibility of danger from that source. But, now I have thought of it—" He shrugged his shoulders. "Oh, well. There doesn't seem anything I can do, except keep my bally eyes wide open, until I've found the police laddie's camp. Funny he hasn't hailed me or something. Wonder where he is? Up stream or down?"

He stood up on the driver's seat and looked keenly about the veld.

To the west, a three hours' trek distant, he judged, he could see the smoke of many cook fires, marking the location of a native village. And, nearby, redly reflecting the sun's dying rays, was a tin roofed building—a store or a mission.

"Funny," he mused. "Wonder why the police chappie didn't go to the kraal and camp with the white folks there—at the store, or mission or whatever it is? Of course, he may have come down with fever when he was on his way; was too sick to trek. Or—Um! We'll have to look into this. Maybe he'd been there and was on his way back to headquarters with his prisoner—the Evil One, the native policeman called him. Sounds as if it might be the devil an' one can quite well imagine that the well known tailed gentleman would choose this spot as his, er, winter residence."

His searching scrutiny was now concentrated on the banks of the river. Presently he uttered a grunt of satisfaction, spying, some three or four hundred yards upstream, a faint coil of blue smoke which floated lazily into the still air.

He tightened his hold on the reins, called to the mules and, driving them over the river, turned them up toward the coil of smoke.

A few minutes later, rounding a chaotic jumble of rocks he patted the mules with a low, sustained whistle.

HERE WAS the white policeman's outspan, a neat, orderly camp. A small, one-man tent surrounded by a thorn stockade. Near the fire was a plentiful supply of firewood; a canvas water sack hung from a pole that, by evaporation, its contents might cool.

A well-ordered camp; nothing about it to suggest that there was need for caution except—

Except that midway between the tiny tent and the fire sprawled the body of a man. For a fleeting moment the Major thought he was asleep and was about to shout a boisterous greeting. But the words never found utterance. The stark, rigid pose of the man checked them at their inception.

Again the Major stood on the driver's seat in order to get a better view of the surrounding country. He saw no sign of life; the veld seemed to be untenanted. Nothing moved, there was no sound.

Quickly, then, he jumped down from the wagon and ran to the horribly still form and knelt down beside him, turning him gently over on his back.

His face was hideously contorted, as if death had been very painful.

He wore the uniform of the B.S.A.P. and in his left hand he clutched firmly a sheet of paper—it looked as if it had been torn from a large note book. The fingers if his right hand closed firmly on a pencil stub.

Both sides of the paper were covered with minute handwriting. Gently releasing it from the dead man's grip the Major sat down on a nearby boulder, hoping that the writing would give him a clue. In this he was disappointed. This leaf had formed part of the dead man's diary. Undoubtedly it told a lot, but, lacking the context, the Major found it as difficult to understand as an elaborate cipher.

It read:

"—*very suddenly. Later belligerent. Threatens suit for illegal arrest. Says I'm on Portuguese soil without warrant. Hope he tries to escape. Like to shoot him. Ought to be boiled alive.*

"*Monday: Coming down with fever. Got to make camp. P. jubilant. Know he expects a rescue.*

"*Later: Guffa tells me I've been delirious all day. Worried about prisoner. Common sense tells me to shoot him while I've the chance. Guffa can see a campfire to south. I'm going to send him for help.*

"*Guffa gone. Prisoner gagged and bound. I'm sitting on him. Sunset. Writing by fire-light. Got the shakes. Keep seeing and hearing things—Don't like killing a man in cold blood. But the prisoner's not a man. God! I ought to shoot him—now—before it is too late.*

"*Tuesday: Why didn't I shoot prisoner? He's not a prisoner any more. He's gone. I don't know how it happened. I don't know if it's really Tuesday. I may have been delirious two or three days. I'm very weak and alone. Guffa not back. I wonder. He's taken my rifle and revolver. I see men crawling about behind the rocks—I wish they'd rush me and get it over with. But I think this is his way of amusing himself. He's torturing me. He's the devil. Wonder what happened to Guffa? He's my only hope— The ring of warriors is closing in. An assegai just stuck in the ground beside me. I threw it back at them. What a fool! I should have killed myself with it. He just shouted that the warriors killed Guffa last night! I shouldn't have sent him. And that's my only hope gone. Dying, being tortured, even, wouldn't be so bad if there was somebody to take on this job I've bungled. But that's not possible. I stumbled on his rotten game by accident. He'll be more cautious after this. Not likely anybody else is going to have the luck I had, and he'll go on. A white man's—"*

"Now what is this," the Major commented thoughtfully. "Delirium or—?" He shrugged his shoulders. "At any rate, this doesn't really tell me anything. On the face of it, it looks as if this poor chap had arrested an out and out rotter. A white man, I should say, but that's not certain. After reading that, one would suppose there'd be signs of violence hereabouts. But there's not! And not a mark of a wound or anything on him. And yet—you know, I'm willing to gamble quite a lot that he didn't die of fever. Rather not. Then what? Fear?" He looked curiously at the dead man's distorted face. "One would almost say 'yes.' But Guffa was full of admiration for his *inkosi* so I think we must count fear out; unless it was a delirium inspired fear. That's possible."

HE BENT down again over the man, intent on turning his pockets inside out, hoping to find some further clue.

But, save for a few silver coins, the pockets were empty.

The Major looked keenly into the man's face, as if hoping to find there an answer to the things which puzzled him. Then he gently veiled the staring eyes, murmuring, "Old lad, if I knew what the job was I'd take it on for you. You didn't bungle it, either. The fever beat you."

He noticed a fleck of dried blood on the man's cheek and a tiny abrasion of the skin just above it.

He stared at it thoughtfully.

"That may mean something—or nothing."

He looked up at the sky. Sunset's afterglow was swiftly fading. Soon the veld would be blotted out by the night's curtain of darkness.

"Wish Jim'd come," he mused, "before it's too late to see to make camp."

He rose slowly to his feet and made a tentative step toward the mules and wagon as if intending to outspan. Then, with a shrug to his shoulders, he threw more wood on the fire and sat down again, near to the body of the policeman. He fumbled in the breast pocket of his tunic and, taking out his monocle, fixed it in his eye. Lighting a cigarette he smoked languidly, blowing smoke rings, looking absolutely alien in Africa's bizarre surroundings, amid the funereal gloom of a dying day; the menacing, formless shadow of the kopje; the silent, starkly pathetic form of the policeman and the flickering flames of the fire which seemed to be surrendering to the crushing pall of fast descending night, accentuating the vast emptiness of the veld.

NIGHT BIRDS called to each other, mournfully monotonous. Swarms of mosquitoes *pinged* their battle-cry against humanity, and, in the far distance, sounded the savage beat of tom-toms, the throbbing of Africa's barbaric heart.

Something *whirred* softly by the Major's face, brushing his cheek.

He put up his hand with an impatient gesture, thinking to brush away one of the soft, unclean insects of night.

Tat-tat-tat!

The soft pattering noises were made by some flying things knocking against his helmet. Absently he took it off and examined it in the firelight.

He threw himself at full length to the ground, crawling back out of the circle of light, sheltering behind a rock outcrop. His helmet he left on the end of a log of wood—it almost looked as if a man were lying there—and sticking into its crown were three tiny feathered darts.

He waited breathlessly, revolver in hand, listening intently for some noise that would indicate the location of his attackers.

Other darts feathered his helmet.

"Judging by the way they're decorating my bally helmet," he said, "I'm encompassed, as it were, on all sides. One must be very cautious, very! I imagine those arrows are beastly poisonous." Remembering, with a rush of panic, the feathery thing which had brushed his cheek, he rubbed the place vigorously. Then he laughed softly. "Mustn't be an old woman. That one didn't break the skin. The point didn't touch me. But that's what killed the policeman, of course.

"Wonder where Jim is? Hope they haven't got him. But I fancy not. He's a downy bird."

As he spoke he heard a dull thud sounding from the gloom behind him, then a pattering of naked feet.

Before he could turn to meet an unexpected attack Jim rushed past him, carrying something on his back, crying, "To the wagon, Baas. To the wagon before they charge."

THE MAJOR leaped to his feet and followed Jim's lead, stopping to pick up the body of the policeman, carrying it easily in his arms.

The wagon was moving. Jim had climbed into it and was swinging the mules around.

Hampered slightly by his burden the Major clambered in over the tail board.

"Safe, Jim?" he called.

"Ugh! Not yet, Baas," the Hottentot replied. "Take the reins, and hold tight."

He put the reins into the Major's hands and taking the long driving whip lashed the mules into a frenzied gallop.

Savage yells greeted this maneuver; black gesticulating shadows sprang up from behind the shelter of boulders; arrows pattered against the canvas hood of the wagon; assegais transfixed it.

The wagon bumped and rattled over the uneven, boulder strewn ground, threatening to capsize, but Jim lashed remorselessly, adding the threat of his voice to the cutting lash of his whip.

Over the river they passed, and on, with no slackening of pace.

"Enough, Jim," the Major cried, bracing his feet, hauling on the reins.

"It is not enough, Baas," Jim replied in a grim voice. "To linger here is to die."

His whip rose and fell, rose and fell, sounding like rifle fire.

SNORTING WITH terror of the lash the mules galloped headlong through the fast gathering darkness. The wagon careened madly from side to side; thorn bushes tore ragged holes in its canvas top.

The yelling of the natives sounded very faint now, finally died away entirely.

"This is folly, Jim!" the Major said sternly at length. "Put away the whip and help me check the mules before they break their necks, and ours. Quickly," he concluded sharply, for Jim was still using the whip and shouting to the mules like one gone berserk.

When the Major reiterated his command, the Hottentot answered like a man awakening from a nightmare, "Yah, Baas! I hear—I obey."

With fumbling hands he put the big whip into its rests, muttering vaguely to himself, staring fixedly straight before him as if he could see beyond the veil of night which surrounded them.

Suddenly, with a hoarse warning shout, he snatched the reins from the Major's hands and, by exercising almost superhuman strength, swung the mules sharply to the right.

The wagon tilted dangerously on two wheels as it followed the sudden change of direction; sparks flew upward as the iron shod wheels skidded on a hard rock surface.

A hundred feet further on and Jim succeeded in bringing the mules to a halt, and they stood panting, their hides wet with foamy sweat, their bellies drawn up.

"Has the madness passed, Jim," the Major asked quietly, "or do you plan more wild doings?"

Under cover of lighting a cigarette, he held a match so that its flame lit up Jim's face. He whistled softly. Beads of sweat rolled down Jim's cheek; his eyes were dilated; his nostrils quivered.

The match burned down to the Major's fingers and Jim laughed, a harsh, strained laugh.

The Major smoked a few minutes in silence. Then, "If you are not mad, Jim, what is the answer to all this? Your desire to escape from the poison-arrow folk I can understand, though I wondered that fear should ride you so hard. But why this last? Why take the reins from me? Why turn them so suddenly that—"

Jim's chuckle interrupted him; the Hottentot had completely regained his self-control.

"Listen, Baas," he said, "and then judge if I am mad."

AND NOW the Major heard the rippling, gurgling sound of water flowing over rocks. It seemed to come up from a great depth. As understanding came to him he said simply, "It is a deep *donga*, Jim?"

"Yah, Baas. I think, perhaps, it is made by that river we crossed back there. It has worn its way deep down through the earth. Another spear's throw and we should have been over the top of the bank. No, I am not mad."

"Truly, not, Jim. This is another count to you."

"We do not count such things, you and I, Baas. Today to me; tomorrow to you. And it is my folly at the beginning which made the rest necessary. There was no need to have driven so fast. But I was afraid, Baas. When I saw those evil ones back there shooting arrows—then I knew fear. A man with an assegai, or six men with assegais, I do not fear; if I am so killed, it will be a clean death. But to die of a scratch, a wound no larger than the prick of a bee! *Au-a!* I would run far to avoid that."

He climbed into the rear of the wagon and lighted a hurricane lantern.

His soft *click* of annoyance brought the Major to him and they both stood looking down at the burden Jim had carried on his back when he made his dart for the wagon.

It was a native, naked save for his loin cloth. The stark rigidness of his limbs and the hideous contortion of his face seemed to give him a kinship, a death kinship, with the policeman.

"He was very close to you, Baas—he had an arrow ready on his bow, when I jumped on him," Jim said in a dull voice. "I hit him on the head with a knobkerry, not very hard, only hard enough to make him sleep for a little while. Then I picked him up and carried him on my back to the wagon. I meant, later, to ask him a few questions."

"He's already answered them, Jim," the Major replied gravely.

"Aye. But do you understand his answer, Baas?"

As Jim spoke he turned the dead native over. The skin of the man's naked back was punctured by small wounds; a feathered arrow hung in the man's loin cloth.

This Jim too, gingerly examined, then wrapped it up carefully in a piece of canvas.

"I have never heard, Baas," he said slowly as he turned the man over again on his back, "of a poison which kills so quickly. And, Baas, do you notice this dead one's teeth? Cannibals file their teeth that way. Does that tell you anything?"

For a little while both men were silent.

THE BEAT of tom-toms at the kraal sounded louder, more bestial. The yells of the natives who had attacked them sounded again. Evidently the natives were following the spoor of the wagon.

With a muttered exclamation Jim extinguished the lantern and went to the driver's seat.

"We must get away from here, Baas," he said, taking up the reins.

The Major joined him on the driver's seat and, taking the reins from him, swung the mules around and drove slowly away.

"Keep your eyes open, Jim," he said. "I do not want to drive into the *donga*."

"Where does the Baas go?" the Hottentot gasped.

"To the kraal of the drums, Jim," the Major said sternly. "I've taken upon myself the errand of the policeman who is dead. So—keep your eyes open; I drive fast. Keep your eyes open."

"*Au-a!* What folly." Jim wailed as the Major urged his mules to a canter. "The Baas tells me to keep my eyes open, yet he goes to a place where they will be closed forever."

"So you think that too, eh, Jim?"

"Without a doubt, Baas, that kraal is the place of the men with arrows. The headman of that kraal sent them forth, and so—sharp left, Baas—and so we go to death. *Au-a!* We have faced death before, and if for a little while we can dodge the 'birds' these evil ones let fly, we will first send many to prepare a place for us. Mind the ant-hill, Baas!"

This warning came almost too late, the wagon tilted dangerously but, by clever handling of the mules the Major rectified the tilt and the drive through the night's abysmal darkness continued.

It was a nerve-racking ordeal even for these two whose familiarity with danger and superb physical well being had made them almost impervious to nerves. Again and again Jim's shouted warnings gave the Major the proper cue and that man's powerful wrists swung the mules around the threatened danger.

IT WAS an hour later, when the drums sounded very near and the blackness ahead was shot with the yellow gleam of fires, that the Major, acting on a sudden thought, reined in the mules to an abrupt halt.

"Light the lantern, Jim," he said and, when that order was obeyed, continued. "Where is the arrow?"

Carefully Jim unwrapped it and handed it to his Baas, watching anxiously, for a horrible death waited on its needle-sharp point.

"It is a very small thing to be so evil, Jim," the Major said. "Give me a cork."

Wonderingly Jim gave him a large cork from an empty water bottle, and the Major pierced his shirt, where it bulged loose at the waist, with the point of the arrow, driving the poisoned point deep into the cork which he held inside his shirt. Then he carefully broke off most of the feathered shaft of the arrow, but left enough to show, so that it looked as if it had been broken off in an impatient attempt to pull it out.

"Careful, Baas. *Wo-we.* It looks as if it is sticking into you."

"And so it is meant to look, Jim."

"But why, Baas? Why play with death?"

The Major shrugged his shoulders.

"I don't know, Jim. The thought came to me."

He put out the light, climbed back into the driver's seat and the trek was resumed.

Half an hour later—and by this time the multitude of stars enabled the Major to see well enough to avoid the large obstacles—they came to a vast open space. It was level and entirely free from bush growth.

The kraal they were seeking was in plain sight, the beehive shaped huts silhouetted against the yellow glare of the fires.

The throbbing tom-toms broke the stillness of the night air into mad-dancing waves which broke upon the ear drums. Wild songs and wilder laughter accompanied the drumming.

"It must be a big beer drink, Baas," Jim said, and licked his lips. Jim was a thirsty soul.

THE MAJOR did not reply. He was looking for the residence of the white man, endeavoring to locate the tin-roofed building which had reflected the rays of sunset. Presently he saw it, a long, bungalow type of house some distance to the right of the kraal. He drove slowly toward it. As they neared it seemed as if the drumming lessened in volume and the shouting died down. They could see men running from hut to hut; one or two left the kraal and sped to the tin-roofed bungalow.

As they drew rein in front of the place, lights appeared in the window of the bungalow and several natives sprang to the heads of the mules, loudly expressing their readiness to help the strangers outspan and make camp for the night.

"Softly, softly," the Major shouted, "we do not outspan until we know we are welcome. Where is the white man who lives here? Why has he not come, to greet me?" Another native came running up into the beam of light which poured from the window. A filthy looking individual wearing a fantastic head dress which almost covered his face. A cloak of lion skins fell from his shoulders to his knees. What little of his body showed was daubed with white ash-paint.

He held a curved, blood stained knife in his hand.

"I will see where the master is," he shouted and his voice was shrill, metallic-sounding. He went to the door of the bungalow and pounded on it.

It opened and a native woman appeared. She wore a long white shapeless garment of the type affected by mission converts. They exchanged a whispered conversation then the man came back to the wagon, walking with the affected, mincing step of a dandy.

"The master bathes," he said. "He asks that you go in. Your servant and the mules will be taken care of."

The Major hesitated, puzzled yet unable to say what puzzled him.

"Come!" the man repeated impatiently.

The Major shook himself like one awakening from a deep sleep.

"Guard well, Jim," he said in a low voice, then climbed down from the wagon and walked briskly toward the bungalow, followed by the bizarrely clad native.

JUST AS he entered the bungalow, Jim called out, "Take care, Baas. A white man's stride—"

The door closed behind him with a bang and the Major found himself in a well furnished room.

The floor was carpeted with skins. Curios and trophies of the hunt decorated the walls. At the far end of the room was a well filled book case, near it a chair and reading lamp.

The white gowned woman told him to seat himself and noiselessly withdrew. A door closed behind her with the sharp click of a spring lock.

"I wonder," the Major mused as he roamed idly about the room. "I wonder what Jim's shouted warning meant? Was the old lad trying to be sarcastic? Telling me that, in taking up the policeman's job, the white man's stride, I'm begging for trouble? Of course, poking one's nose into things which don't concern one, is always asking for trouble. But this affair *does* concern me, most decidedly. Wonder what Jim meant?"

He shrugged his shoulders and sat down in the chair near the book case.

"Interesting lot of books the dear old bungalow owner has. Wish I had time to dip into them. He's got every book dealing with natives that's ever been published. I should say. The man must be a walking mine of information. Wish he'd hurry up. I'm anxious to see him.

"Well. I'm bally glad he's clean! I mean, if he takes all this time to have a bath he must be a clean chappie. Or—he must have been very dirty!" And at that thought he clapped his hands softly together.

"Why, of course," he murmured. "*That* was what Jim meant."

He polished his monocle briskly with a white silk handkerchief, and fixed it in his eye. With his white but very firm and capable hands he smoothed back his jet black hair, then lighted a cigarette and smoked with every outward show of enjoyment.

FOR A moment his fingers toyed with the arrow shaft, then he relaxed, lounging back in his chair. But the fingers of his right hand were close to his revolver, which he had thrust down between the side of the chair and the cushioned seat.

Presently the door opened and a man clad in gaily striped pajamas and ornate dressing gown entered. His hair was shaved close to his head, giving him a strangely infantile appearance. He was of medium height and tending to a flabby softness. A mild innocuous sort of man, one would have said; but his eyes had a cold fanatical glare in them; his lips were thin and tightly compressed.

"I apologize for keeping you waiting," he said suavely as the Major rose to greet him. "But my nightly bath has become almost a religious rite with me." He laughed softly. "One gets so filthy after the heat and sweat of the day's toil."

"Exactly," the Major murmured. "I quite understand, my dear fellow. Consider the laddies who—er—handle pitch. I should think no amount of washing would get the dirt off them. My name, by the way, is Aubrey St. John Major. But I'm generally called the Major."

The other started.

"I've heard of you, Major," he said slowly, glancing narrowly at his visitor. "My name's Dodd. I'm a trader and amuse myself investigating native customs. A man must have a hobby."

"Rather," the Major agreed enthusiastically. "Of course there's a danger in riding a hobby. It might—er—throw the rider and the rider becomes ridden, if you know what I mean."

"I don't!" Dodd replied sharply. "Have you had *skoff*?"

As he spoke he moved restlessly about the room. Once he halted with a muttered curse and, bending down, pulled a tack out of his naked foot.

"That's bally interesting," observed the Major. "I should have cursed long and loudly if I'd run a tack into *my* foot. But there you are. That's what I meant about riding a hobby too hard. I should imagine from a purely—er—superficial, bird's eye view, as it were, of the soles of your feet, that you've been walking shoeless so long that your bally feet are as calloused and as dead to feeling as—a—er—nigger's. You see—"

A SNARL interrupted him. Dodd's eyes were hate filled. It was only by a palpable effort that he controlled himself sufficiently to say, "I asked you if you wanted *skoff.*"

"My belly is filled," the Major replied in the vernacular. "I only want to sleep."

"Sleep is always desirable," Dodd answered easily, also in the vernacular. "It is—" He broke off abruptly. Then snapped in English, "What the hell are you talking nigger dialect for?"

"Just an experiment, dear old Dodd. Just wanted to see how far your hobby was riding you."

Dodd ignored this.

"What are you doing in this district, Major?"

"Running from the police, dear heart. I'm wanted for murder."

"If you behave yourself, you'll find this a soft place to hide. We are not bothered by patrols."

"That's good of you, Dodd. 'Pon my soul it is. But, as I was saying, I was running from the police and—just my bally luck—I ran into one back there a way. At the Lone Tree Kop, as a matter of fact."

"Did he try to arrest you? He couldn't legally, you know. You're on Portuguese territory."

The Major nodded.

"I know. But these police laddies are blind to boundaries when they are on the trail of justice. I mean, the white man's stride goes over a boundary just as if it weren't there."

"White man's stride?" Dodd said questioningly.

"Exactly. It's an important factor. Hard to conceal; difficult to ignore."

"So the policeman tried to arrest you, eh?"

"No." The Major's voice was very grave.

"The poor devil was dead."

"Fever?"

"No. An arrow."

Dodd sat down in a chair opposite the Major.

"An arrow? I don't understand."

"Can't say I do, either. He held this in his hand."

The Major took from his pocket the paper he had taken from the policeman and handed it to Dodd.

That man read it thoroughly and handed it back to the Major with the comment, "Sounds as if he were delirious."

"What I thought," the Major admitted. "Then I thought: Supposing it were true? Then there must be some devil loose around here. And so I decided to take on the trooper's job. Carry on his stride, as it were. But there's nothing to go on, is there? Well, anyway, almost coincident with my arriving at that decision I was attacked by natives. Arrows simply crowded the air, dear lad, and we—Jim and I—only just managed to escape by the skin of our teeth."

"And you say the policeman was killed by an arrow?"

"Well—I didn't see a wound or anything," the Major stammered. "I just surmised that."

DODD CROSSED his legs and pursed his lips thoughtfully. "I wouldn't be surprised to learn that you killed the trooper, Major. And—"

"Oh, I didn't, I assure you!"

Dodd waved his hand.

"And if you didn't, I was going to add, then he got what he asked for from the natives. I told him when he was here—the fool didn't know he'd crossed the border—not to monkey with the women at the kraal. He refused to pay any heed to my warning. And so—the white man's stride faltered. Just the same, I must talk to my people in the morning. I can't have them taking the law into their hands this way."

"What nice chatty manners your people have," the Major commented lightly.

There was silence for a little while during which the two men covertly scrutinized each other. Both were very much on the alert; both affected a careless nonchalance.

But, whereas the Major was chiefly interested in Dodd's face, attempting to read the expression in his eyes, Dodd scrutinized the Major from the top of his well groomed head to the toes of his highly polished, brown riding boots.

His wandering eyes focused at length on a point just above the Major's belt. He was staring at the broken arrow fixed in the Major's shirt.

"You say," he said slowly, "they fired arrows at you?"

"Hundreds, thousands. 'Pon my soul they did."

"And you weren't hit?"

The Major shook his head.

"No. We were bally lucky. Made a dash for the wagon and were on our way before you could say Jack Robinson."

He leaned back in his chair stretching and yawning.

"Yes, we were bally lucky," he continued, his hands clasped behind his head. "Jim—the Hottentot you know—tells me these arrows were tipped with a deadly poison. One little prick and you hear golden harps, an' all that sort of thing."

Dodd nodded.

"Yes. You were very lucky."

He leaned forward in his chair, staring hard at the arrow. It looked as if it had caught in the Major's shirt; hung there as if about to drop.

"My dear man," the Major exclaimed self consciously, "is there anything wrong with my bally belt? The way you stare at—"

"Don't move—don't move a muscle," Dodd said in a low, tense voice. "You've been luckier than you suppose. There's an arrow sticking in the fold of your shirt, I'll pull it out. Don't you move. It might prick you. And there's no antidote."

WITH FEAR dilated eyes, his hands now gripping the arms of his chair, the Major glanced down, flinching as his eyes focussed on the arrow.

"Hurry up, then," he gasped. "Take the bally thing out. *Eugh!* It's making me feel sick."

Dodd laughed softly and rising from his chair crossed over to the Major.

For a moment the two men's eyes met. Then the Major's right hand dropped to the butt of his revolver which was hidden in his chair. At the same moment Dodd's hand closed on the arrow shaft.

Laughing harshly, insanely, he jabbed the arrow forward, against the Major's ribs, then sprang back.

"You fool!" the Major exclaimed angrily. "You fool!" he repeated, and there was cold fear in his voice. "You've pricked me with the poisoned point. And you meant to! Why? Why?"

Frantically he tore open his shirt, pulled out the arrow—Dodd did not see the cork—and threw it from him with the disgust with which a man treats a snake.

Dodd sat down again in his chair, laughing softly.

"There's no antidote," he said titteringly, silencing the Major's appeals for help. "There's no antidote for the poison that tips my people's arrows. I ought to know. I prepare it for them. In five minutes—no, I'll give you ten, you're a strong man—you'll be dead. Already it's beginning to burn. Can't you feel it."

"God, yes!" the Major roared.

He struggled to rise, but failed. The muscles of his face were strained.

"It's acting quicker than I thought," Dodd remarked, observing the symptoms with professional interest. "Death follows a rapid form of paralysis."

THE MAJOR mouthed inarticulately; his outstretched legs shook violently; his whole body seemed racked with a painful convulsion; his face was hideously contorted. One eye was half closed but the other, propped open by the monocle, glared dolefully.

"Why did you do it?" he managed to gasp, articulating with difficulty.

"Because you've come butting your nose into things that don't concern you. You're not the first I've treated this way. You won't be the last. Trooper Jenkins—" he laughed sarcastically— "was very clever. He found out a great deal. He professed to be horrified at my mode of life. If he'd been content to let it go at that, he might be alive now. But perhaps not. He followed my people over the border because they'd raided a small kraal for our sacrifices. He called me a dirty, bloody cannibal—the fool! He didn't have the brains to appreciate the symbolism of our feasts." Dodd lapsed now into the vernacular. His face twitched spasmodically, his eyes moved constantly and were lighted by an inner madness.

"In blood is life. We kill to live!"

Words tumbled out of his mouth in a hideous recital of blasphemies and of deeds as black as hell.

"You're mad—stark, staring mad!"

At the sound of the Major's cold voice, Dodd shivered as if suddenly doused with cold water. And he looked dully at the Major, who had risen from his chair, looked in fear at the revolver in the Major's hands.

"So you were shamming?" he said meekly. The madness had left him, limp and submissive.

"Exactly. My God, Dodd! What a filthy beast you are! And I'd have never suspected you except—of course you were the nigger in the lion skin and mask. Your walk gave you away. It was a white man's stride. I wondered at the time. But it was Jim who gave me the clue. And even then there was nothing to go on. If a man wants to turn a white kaffir that's his own look out. But you—

"I fancy, Dodd, you're not a white kaffir in the accepted sense. But you're something infinitely worse. You've handled pitch and defiled your soul.

"Now call out to your natives and tell them to send my servant in here, alone. Tell them to inspan my mules, then go to the kraal. All of them, the men and women. And don't say anything else. If you do I shall fire. And, let me tell you," he concluded grimly, "I hope you do."

DODD HESITATED a moment, then shouted the orders the Major had given him. And there seemed to be relief in his voice.

A few minutes later the door opened and Jim entered, expressions of fear and relief struggling for mastery of his face.

"*Au-a*, Baas!" he exclaimed. "The things I have heard. And so you have caught the evil one?"

"Yes, Jim. Tie him up."

Jim quickly obeyed and, in a few minutes, bound hand and foot, Dodd was lying a helpless heap on the ground.

"Let us go now, Baas," Jim urged, "before this evil one's servants return."

"In a little while, Jim. But first I must find things which will make the tale I tell to the police a tale they can believe."

"And you take this one to the police, Baas? *Wo-we!* Kill him! That is justice. Why go to the police? As well pelt a lion with stones."

"Nevertheless it must be done, Jim. Watch him. I go now to the other rooms."

The Major took one of the lamps and explored the rest of the place.

FIFTEEN MINUTES later, grave of face, laden with a lion skin robe, several note books and a bottle containing a green viscous liquid, he returned to the room.

"Have you the things you wanted, Baas," Jim asked.

The Major nodded.

"I have here," he said, "proof of great evil. All that he did was written down. His punishment will be death."

"He has already received that punishment, Baas."

The Major looked down at Dodd, noting the stiffened limbs and pain contorted face.

"Did you kill him, Jim?" he asked sternly.

"Nay, Baas. Three times he rolled over and I thought nothing of it. Again he rolled—and then I saw what was in his mind. But I was too late. There was an arrow on the floor—the Baas threw it there?" The Major nodded and Jim continued, "Before I could stop him, Baas, he had rolled on to the arrow. He laughed once, softly, Baas. And then—I watched him die. *Wo-we!* I do not want to die that way. And dying that way he paid, I think, for the evil he had done."

"If one death can pay for many, Jim. Now let us go."

They went outside and, finding the mules inspanned, climbed up into the wagon where the Major carefully stowed away the things he had taken from the bungalow.

At the kraal the tom-toms were beating a monotonous nerve racking rhythm; the yells of the dancers sounded bestial.

"Something I had forgotten, Jim," said the Major, and jumping down from the wagon ran into the bungalow.

A few minutes later he again emerged and, taking the reins from Jim, drove off at a fast pace.

They had only gone a mile or two when Jim, who was looking back, exclaimed:

"The bungalow is on fire, Baas."

"I know it, Jim. I set it. And, unless the wind has changed sparks will blow on to the huts of the kraal."

"It has not changed, Baas," Jim exclaimed gleefully. "Before long they will catch fire; they will be utterly destroyed."

"And so," the Major commented, "the building of a new kraal will keep them from evil. By the time the building is finished I will lead the police here that the evil doers may be punished."

"And the Baas still intends to do that?"

"Truly, Jim. Having undertaken the white man's stride we must see to it that it does not end in mid-air."

HALF AN HOUR'S WALK

WE ASKED Pat Greene to tell us something about the phrase "White Man's Stride" and the story of that name in this issue. Here is what he says:

"The phrase 'White Man's Stride' refers to an old time custom of measuring off farms by a process of striding; half an hour's walk in each direction from the centre was the regular extent of the farm. In Barrow's 'Travels' published 1801, one reads:

" 'If a farmer is supposed to have put his baaken, or stake, or land mark, a little too near to that of his neighbor the Feld Wagt-meester or peace officer of the division is called in by the latter to pace the distance, for which he gets three dollars.'

"And in a book by Bains, published in 1887:

" 'Not many years ago their—the Boers'—own surveyor general was mobbed for using a theodolite instead of striding off the distance like the Feld Wagt-meester of the good old times.'

"The phrase has also been applied to the extension of the white man's dominion in South Africa, and it struck me as peculiarly apt title for a 'Major' story.

"The lion passage which opens the story is not one bit far-fetched. The big cats are notoriously temperamental, specially the males. I say temperamental, but possibly cowardly would be a more correct term to use. On one occasion, quite unarmed, I chased a good sized male cub through thick bush.

I will admit I thought I was chasing a wild dog. I felt very white and foolish when my 'boy' caught me up and pointed out the truth. But there you are. I chased a lion and undoubtedly Mrs. Lion was knocking around somewhere in the immediate vicinity, and nothing happened. Just the same, I would not do it again!"

BLACK GOODS

THE BELL-TENT and the canvas-topped wagon, silhouetted against the gray clouds which masked the red glory of Africa's westing sun, looked incongruously bizarre in the vast expanse of billowing, treeless veld. Fantastically, they looked like derelict ships on a turbulent sea.

A stallion, coal black, and arrogant in his consciousness of breeding, grazed fastidiously near-by; occasionally he looked up with contempt at the twelve, butter-fat mules which kept him company.

A fire burned midway between the tent and the wagon; a fire fed with "kaffir coal," dried dung being almost the only fuel in certain treeless districts of South Africa.

A Hottentot who squatted near the fire was polishing a pair of brown riding boots with an intentness which suggested that nothing else in the world mattered.

But occasionally he looked up at his Baas, the Major, who was seated in a deck chair just outside the tent, frowning thoughtfully over a letter he held in his hands.

Jim, the Hottentot, was worried by that frown and angry at the cause of it. He felt that the "talking paper" was an evil charm.

"Jim," the Major said, looking whimsically at the Hottentot, "there is no evil in this." He fluttered the paper in the air.

"*Wo-we!*" Jim exploded, startled by the manner in which the Major had read his thoughts. "But if it is not evil, why do your brows knit together when you look at it? *Au-a!* Every night since the transport rider gave it to you, and that was two weeks ago, you have looked at it and scowled as you scowl now."

"I frown, Jim, because I am not sure what course to take, that is all. We have been trekking now for many months, avoiding the *dorps*. And, now the season of rains is at hand, I wonder shall we remain wanderers, hunting, prospecting, avoiding places where white men gather, or shall we go back to the *dorp?*"

"Why question, Baas? What have the *dorps* to offer to compare with this?" The Hottentot's gesture embraced the far reaching veld.

"The rains are coming, Jim. Trekking will be hard, and very lonely. Whereas, if we go to the *dorps*—"

"Baas," Jim interrupted, "what care we for the rains or loneliness? Here, I say, we can live as men should live. Whereas in the *dorps*—" He spat contempt. "Besides," he added, "in the *dorps* my Baas is in danger. The police would take him and lock him up in *trunk.*"

The Major laughed, and again turned to his letter. It read:

"Dear Major,
    "I don't know how to thank you, so maybe I'd better not try. When you took my crime on your shoulders you did a big thing. Only, God knows it wasn't a crime to kill Jake Monkton, the blackmailing hound. But the law wouldn't look at it that way.

And they'd have arrested me on suspicion if it hadn't 'a' been that you fixed it to look as if you'd done it. God knows why you should do a thing like that for me; for a woman you hardly ever have seen. But you did, God bless you.

"At first, when I'd heard what you'd done, I was going to lay low and say nothing. I told myself that you could take care of yourself and that you probably did what you did for some private reason of your own. And when I heard folks talking about you, saying you were too clever for the police to catch you, there didn't seem any point in my confessing anyway. There's nobody really believes you did it, not even the police, though they're out to get you because of the evidence. So your good name isn't dirtied: My God—when they know the truth your name'll shine brighter than ever.

"But I wasn't satisfied. I kept thinking of what might happen. Suppose I died suddenly—I ain't got long to live, even if I'm very careful, the doctor says six months at the most—an' you was arrested: Why they'd hang you. So I confessed to Father Joyce. He's got my confession all sealed up and in a safe place with instructions for it to be forwarded to the proper quarters after my death, or before should you be convicted. And even then I wasn't satisfied quite. So I'm writing this to you so that you'll know it's safe for you to come back if you want to; so you can show it if any *up-country* policeman tried to arrest you.

Elizabeth Hansen."

The signature of Father Joyce, a deservedly popular prelate, followed a P.S. in his copper plate script, which read:

"Major, you're a broth of a boy. I am sending this by an old friend, who's riding transport up-country, who can be trusted. Hope you meet each other."

He put the letter down again on his knees and after fumbling absent-mindedly in the pockets of his tunic coat produced a monocle which he screwed into his right eye.

"By Jove!" he muttered in English— and his drawling words, appearance and gesture belonged to a stage door Johnny, not to the veld-rover, the expert hunter he actually was. "The old bean must be soft. The—er—profusive gratitude of Mrs. Hansen—not to mention the dear old Padre's pat on the back—must have gone to my head. After all, I've done nothing; much prefer loafing about here with Jim, seeing things, to pretending to be civilized in the towns.

"And so I'm goin' to do what I ought to have done when I first received this bally letter. And I hope the dear lady cheats her bally doctor an' lives many years. I'll steer clear of arrest if it's within bounds of the well-known possibilities. At least, I'm willing to gamble they won't catch me within six months, eh, what Jim?"

"Golly, no, yes, Baas," the Hottentot replied after a moment's grave consideration.

"EXACTLY, JIM," bantered the Major. " 'No, yes!' A most masterly answer." Then his mood changed and leaning forward he said seriously in the vernacular, "Jim, in all the years we have been together we have always played whatever game came into our hands. We have hunted where no other man has set foot, we have 'poached' ivory for the game's fun, and dealt in 'stones' in ways not proper in the eyes of the men who make the white man's laws. We have been accused of all manner of evil, but are guilty of none: For years the police have tried to trap us, yet have been our friends. *Au-a!* Where could we go and not find friends. But now—" he hesitated—"now men are seeking me with anger in their hearts; the police are no longer my friends. They accuse me of breaking the white man's strongest law. They say I have killed a man. And the law says: 'A life for a life.'"

Jim moved uneasily.

"And what is all this to me, Baas? If you killed a man, doubtless you had cause. That is no matter. And before they catch you, they have Jim to deal with."

As he concluded Jim sprang to his feet and walked swiftly up and down, beating his barrel-like chest with his clenched fists, his eyes flashing fire, as if challenging the whole world.

The Major watched him, shading his eyes with his hand, but Jim, turning suddenly, saw that his Baas was smiling.

"Au-a, Baas!" he said sheepishly. "You make a mock of me."

"Not exactly, Jim. I wanted to hear you say what you have said. It gives me a prop to lean on."

"But you *knew* the prop was there, Baas."

"A man knows the sun is in the sky, Jim, but it comforts him to look up and see it. And so—" he rose to his feet and walked slowly toward the fire; he overtopped the Hottentot by head and shoulders, yet, because of his perfect proportions, seemed not so very tall—"and so—" he lapsed into his soft, English drawl again—"I will burn my bridges behind me."

As he spoke, he dropped his letter into the fire.

"The Baas means?" Jim questioned, greatly relieved as he saw the "talking paper," burst into flames.

"That the *dorps* are forbidden us, Jim. That, for a woman's sake, we seek the solitude and avoid the company of men."

"Then for once," Jim retorted with the easy cynicism of a four times married man, "I can thank the spirits for having made woman."

IT WAS an hour later.

The Major was smoking a cigarette watching the changing glory in the west. The clouds parted as the sun neared its setting, and now their edges were tipped with its blood-red glow.

The Major half rose, intending to seek shelter from swarms of mosquitoes and other flying pests under the mosquito netting which surrounded his bed, then decided to wait until the sun dropped below the horizon and the afterglow had faded from the sky.

The clouds piled up again, and, rolling across the sky, blotted out all light. The darkness was as sudden as if a dense velvet curtain had been drawn between day and night.

The Major rose from his chair.

"We must light some smudge fires for the animals' sake, Jim," he said.

The northern horizon was illuminated spasmodically by flashes of lightning and dull rumbles of thunder reverberated across the veld.

"If it would rain," Jim grumbled, "it would wash away these pests. But it only talks like an old woman."

"The rains will come soon enough, Jim," the Major said.

Something stung on the Major's cheek. He felt a sharp stabbing pain, as if he had been pricked with a red hot needle.

He put up his hand swiftly, instinctively.

When he took it away again he held an insect between thumb and forefinger.

Rising, he went over to the fire and examined it by the light of the flickering flames. It was little larger than a common house fly. Its color was a dull gray, relieved by bars of a faint pinkish tinge.

The Major's face was grave.

"I'm very much afraid," he muttered, "that this is our nasty little pal *glossina morsitans*. It doesn't deserve such a pretty name. I should just call it 'death and damnation' an' let it go at that. *Oh-e*, Jim!"

The Hottentot came running at his call and squatted down beside him.

"What is it, Baas?"

"What is this?" The Major showed the insect to Jim.

The Hottentot looked at it and his face fell.

"Au-a! To think that this should come to us, Baas. It is *'ntsentse-a-tsetse':* It is the fly-flea of death."

The two men stared at each other, consternation in their looks.

Then said Jim, springing to his feet, "Let us trek, Baas. Maybe we can get away from these dealers of death before the animals are 'stuck.'"

In less than half an hour the mules were inspanned, the wagon packed, the horse tethered to the rear of the wagon.

"Ready, Baas," Jim called.

"Ready, Jim."

The long whip slammed. *"Juk!"* Jim shouted and the mules broke into a frenzied canter, leaving the field to a number of crimson-banded flies whose swift moving wings beat a chant of victory.

CHAPTER II

IT WAS three days later and nearing the hour of sunset.

The veld was encompassed with a blackness almost rivaling that of night; and that blackness had cloaked the veld ever since the rising of yesterday's sun. The rains had started and the whole world seemed to be a dreary waste of waters. It came down from the low lying clouds so rapidly and with such force as to present an almost solid sheet of water; it leveled the coarse veld grass and turned the once iron-hard soil of the veld into a quaking bog.

Heads down, their bodies bent to the force of the storm, the Major and Jim struggled desperately forward, heading for the kopje which loomed up through the curtain of rain before them. They hoped to find there some sort of shelter: a cave, or, at least, a friendly boulder under which they could crouch and get respite from the storm's buffettings.

Both men were almost spent. Since yesterday morning they had fought against the storm; last night they had spent crouched miserably under a crude shelter of thorn bush and ate the last of their scanty supply of food. All this day they had fought forward, hoping that chance would lead them to a kaffir kraal or to a white man's homestead. They were both drenched to the skin and plastered from head to foot with mud.

"*Wo-we,* Baas!" Jim exclaimed lugubriously, his teeth chattering with the cold. "That this should happen to us! Soon I shall be washed into the ground like mud."

The darkness deepened. The kopje was no longer visible. It seemed as if it had melted before the combined attacks of rain and darkness. But they kept on.

Presently Jim sagged forward and hung limp on the Major's arm.

The fever had taken him suddenly, and badly. Natives rarely suffer from malaria—but when they do, it is serious; they seem to have no constitution to combat it.

"Jim!" the Major called. "Wake up! Fight! You must not sleep. The sickness is nothing. It will pass. It—"

"It is death, Baas," Jim groaned. "All this day I have been fighting against it. And now I can fight no longer. I do not want to fight. Let me stay here. You go on."

"This would seem a bally hopeless situation," the Major murmured. "Even if everything were in our favor, I'd have the deuce an' all of a job getting Jim over an attack of fever. As it is— Oh, well, talking that way is conceding defeat! An' we won't do that!"

He picked Jim up, slung him on his back, tied his hands together so that his own hands could be free and groped his way forward.

After a while, lurching painfully, bent nearly double under the load he was carrying, he came to a halt, conscious of murmuring water beneath him.

HE STRAIGHTENED and endeavored to see through the blackness.

He could see nothing; he had vague fancies of wandering through an eternal, rain swept night, Jim's weight increasing with every forward step.

There came now a temporary lull in the storm, but the noise of swirling water increased.

And then suddenly, telling himself that his brain must have been water-logged not to have realized it before, the Major knew that he was standing on the bank of a river—

knew that the river, already swollen by torrential rains, ran between him and the makeshift refuge of the kopje.

He groaned with despair. Even in daylight the fording of the flooded river would have been hedged with peril. In the blackness of night and hampered by Jim, the dangers were multiplied a thousandfold.

He squatted native fashion on his haunches, Jim still on his back, and stared thoughtfully before him into the darkness, wondering what was to be gained by venturing the crossing; wondering if the scant promise of shelter the kopje offered was sufficient reward for the unknown dangers of the swirling river.

He had decided against the crossing, had decided to wait where he was in the hope that in the gray light of another day a better way would be shown him.

And then a yellow blob of light gleamed faintly ahead. He rubbed his eyes and looked again. It was still there, it was not imagination, no optical delusion. It was fixed, constant.

He rose to his feet and shouted, but the rising wind drove the words back into his throat, and, like an obligato to the wind's howl, the voice of the river deepened.

There was no question in the Major's mind now. Beyond the river was a safe haven, warmth, light, medicine for Jim. And the river must be crossed tonight, now. It was probably still fordable, was not yet "down." But every moment wasted now increased the danger; any moment the hill waters might come down with a rush, sweeping everything before them, filling the banks, bearing bone smashing trees on their turbulent surface.

It might be that the headwaters were already down. In that case death was the only end to the venture. But death was sure for Jim, if they waited here. And so—

The Major went cautiously on hands and knees, groping before him, until, at a point almost opposite the yellow blob of light, he thought he detected a road—actually deep cart-tracks filled with water.

He stood erect then, endeavoring to fix a course in his mind, knowing that once he got down to the surface of the river his guiding light would be out of sight and the current would tend to wash him off the course.

The wind dropped suddenly, and the rain descended again with redoubled force. The light disappeared, hidden by the curtain of rain.

Breathing hard, the Major went down the steep road to the ford. Water, icy cold, lapped presently about his ankles. He had come to the river's edge. He took a cautious step forward. Another step, another and another. He could feel the current tugging at his knees.

He went on, very slowly, shuffling, not daring to lift his feet from the bed of the river, fearing, should he do so, he would be washed off his balance.

THE WATER was up to his waist; the rain beat upon him as if in malignant partnership with the river. He could see nothing, and Jim, moaning fitfully in the fever's delirium, hung from him, weighing him down.

He stumbled over a rock and fell face forward in the flood and only regained his feet with much difficulty, falling again and floundering helplessly several times before he finally won complete balance.

Another pace forward, then he halted, in the grip of a panic. The force of the current was now on his left side. Before it had been on his right. He must have turned round during his flounderings and was going now in the wrong direction, was now retracing his steps. But was that it? Or was this a fluke current, a back eddy?

He considered thoughtfully; then turned about, going even more cautiously now, not sure yet that the direction was right. But the water deepening, it was now up to his arm pits, convinced him at last that he was right.

Each forward step was a struggle. He swayed like a fragile reed.

Jim moaned continuously, and once, fighting desperately against some fever phantom, almost throttled his Baas, almost pulled him off his balance.

The waters deepened yet more, was up to the Major's chin. Occasional wavelets spilled into his mouth, and his feet were raised off the bed of the river.

"I'll have to swim for it," he muttered ruefully, "an' that'll be bally hell. I'll be washed out of my course and won't know where I am if I do make land. 'Pon my soul I believe we'd have been better off waiting on the bank. If the clouds would break and the stars shine a chappy could see what he was doing. As it is, I may be walking downstream toward a waterfall. There might be crocs floating down."

Way up stream he heard a dull booming sound which drowned the lash of rain and the rippling gurgle of the river.

Frantically, he increased his speed, throwing all caution to the winds, stumbling, floundering, fighting against the current. It seemed as if steel talons were clutching him, trying to trip him.

The water shallowed suddenly, was now only to his knees, and he halted a moment to ease this laboring lungs. He inhaled with long, labored gulps and felt horribly nauseated.

Jim was shivering again now and, his fever temperature lowered, was almost fully conscious, sensing vaguely the big thing his Baas was doing.

"Let me down, Baas," he pleaded. "I can walk. And you—*Wo-we!* You are no pack mule. I—" then he lost grip of himself again and talked of past adventures he and his Baas had met together, of bushfires, lions, evil white men and black.

The booming noise sounded nearer, was approaching with express speed. The water, even in this short time he had halted, had risen almost up to the Major's waist.

AGAIN PANIC drove him on and he did not stop again until his feet slipped in the mud of the bank and he knew that he had made the crossing. Bent double he groped about with outstretched hands until he located deep ruts and knew that he was on the road leading up from the river. He followed it a few paces, then collapsed, ready to cry with relief.

The booming noise sounded very near now. A rushing wave of water surged up the roadway, lapped about the Major's body. And, retreating sullenly, dragged him a few paces with it. It was as if the river, like a mighty octopus, had sent out an exploring tentacle to retrieve the prey which it had so hardly won from it.

The Major forced himself to his feet and ran desperately up the treacherous road. The universe seemed to be filled with shriekings of angry waters as the hell flood swept down stream, a devastating battering ram rushing pell mell through the darkness, sweeping everything before it.

The river was "down" in full flood. It would be impassable for days, maybe weeks, to come. He had been just in time.

Wave after wave swept up the gully of the road. The last one lapped about the feet of the Major, speeding him on.

At length he came with his burden to the level ground on the top of the bank and he could see, very near, the yellow oblong blob of light. The sight of it revived him and he ran jerkily toward it, shouting hoarsely.

Another larger blob of light appeared just to the right of the first. A door opened. He could hear men's voices, guttural, harsh, raised in excited discussion.

Other lights appeared, lights which swung to and fro, up and down. Men were hastening to meet him, carrying hurricane lanterns.

They caught hold of him, holding him up. One took Jim off his back.

The Major laughed.

What was the man saying who supported him?

"Who are you, *roinek?* Who sent you to spy on us? Speak quick or I'll blow your brains out!"

And then the Major's laugh changed into an hysterical giggle.

"You can't old dears," he tittered. "That's where I do you one in the eye. You can't blow my brains out: I haven't any. Can prove it: I've just crossed that bally river."

For a moment the lights were multiplied into millions. Then they went out together and the Major was lost in the merciful darkness of oblivion.

THE MEN, there were three of them, wrangled violently; the one who had been supporting the Hotten-tot let him slide from his hold into the rain-spitted mud.

"It is best," said one in the uncouth speech of the back veld Boers, "that we throw them into the river. And there's an end of them—spy or no spy. They're *voet gangers* and everybody knows *voet gangers* are poor men." The speaker referred to "foot-goers."

"Alamopsticks!" growled a second, who was supporting the Major. "I think Hans is right. Throw them in the river and there's an end to it. Take up the nigger, Hans, and we'll do it. And quicker the better say I. I am already to the skin wet."

"Wait." It was the third man speaking, and the other two growled impatiently. "I am thinking that it would be best to hasten slowly. Suppose this fool *roinek* is a spy, we have nothing hidden, nothing hidden that a man can find. So why kill? Let him live. Let us treat him well, let us show him all there is to see. *Almighty!* By seeming to show him everything it will be all the easier to hide what we want to hide. And then, as I say, if he is a spy, he will go back and report to whoever sent him that there is nothing evil at Tante du Toit's place and her three nephews are good young men—not?"

"There is sense in what you say, Paul. But if they're not spies—what then? They are *voet gangers*. They cannot pay their way and all through the rains they'll be with us. The Tante will not like that."

"It may be," said the man Paul, "that the *roinek* is rich and only lost. But if he cannot pay, then he shall work. Almighty! How he shall work!"

The three laughed at the thought.

A shrill discordant voice, charged with suspicion, sobered them.

"You three dunderheads! Why are you so long? It is the *sjambok* you need. Return quickly, and bring what you have found."

They sprang apart like children, guilt-conscious, discovered by a scolding school-dame.

"Ja! We are coming, Tante," Paul shouted. "But the thing we found is *verdoemte* heavy." He laughed, but was instantly silenced by the shrewish scolding voice.

"Almighty!" he swore under his breath. " 'Yes, Tante,'" and 'No, Tante' I say to her as if I were a little boy!"

He took the Major up in his arms and walked swiftly with him toward the light.

The other two followed, their booted feet making loud *kler-oshing,* sucking noises in the deep mud.

They had almost reached the crudely constructed house when Paul remembered Jim.

"Go back for him, Hans," he said.

"Almighty! Why should I? Long enough I have stood out in this rain. He's only a *verdoemte* black."

"He may be useful—after we have trained him. Besides, Tante will be angry if she knows we have left him out there to die. 'Black goods' mean money. Take him to the black quarters. They'll cure him."

Hans grumbled, but returned for Jim, whilst Paul, carrying the Major, and Jacob entered the house.

THE MAJOR was dreamily conscious of an inward warmth and a sense of well being. His whole body glowed and he relaxed contentedly.

Someone raised his head and liquid was poured into his mouth.

He wanted to open his eyes, but they felt still as if they were sealed by heavy weights. His head was lowered again. Someone expertly, but with hard, horny palmed hands, was massaging him expertly. The soft *flick-flick* was hypnotic.

He heard a dull muttering of voices, coming to his ears, it seemed, through walls of felt.

The *flick-flick* of the massaging hands ceased.

There was a period of absolute emptiness, and then—
he thought for a moment he was still floundering in the
river—icy cold water was dashed into his face.

The weights were released from his eyelids and he sat up,
spluttering noisily; dazzled by the glare of a lamp, confused
by the roar of laughter.

He was in a large, filth littered room, lying on a pile of
skins before a fire. An old, repulsive-looking native woman
knelt beside him, regarding him with the satisfaction of a
doctor who had worked a cure.

"Thank you, Mother," the Major said in the vernacular,
and then gazed beyond her, puzzled by his surroundings.
And then he saw three men seated on rough hewn chairs
and remembered. They were whispering together, laughing rudely.

"That will do," a voice said sharply. "Go, black one. Hold
your tongues, you fools!"

The native woman cringed, rose to her feet and hobbled
out of the room. The three men separated, and ceased
laughing.

"Jim—where is Jim?" the Major questioned anxiously,
looking at the three men, wondering at their colossal size
and the fact that they showed such fear at a woman's voice,
if it was a woman who had ordered them to be silent. He
meant to turn presently and see. But not yet, his faculties
were not quite back to normal and something warned him
that he would need to be fully alert before he matched wits
with the owner of that voice.

He repeated his question in the *taal*.

"Jim, my Hottentot, where is he?"

One of the men answered.

"He is safe. He is with his kind. The woman who cured
you says he has the fever, but will live."

"Ah!" The news brought its modicum of healing power and the Major sat up, pulling the skins about him. "I must thank you, *Mynheers*. I—"

"Paul, Hans, Jacob—" the harsh voice broke upon the Major's expressions of gratitude, silencing him— "why do you all sit there like stupid asses! Get to bed and do not listen at the door or you shall taste the *sjambok!*"

Like chidden children the three brawny giants rose. A moment later the door closed behind them.

"And now, Englisher," continued the voice, "we will talk."

THE MAJOR did not move or respond to the invitation. His keen eyes carefully scrutinized that part of the room which was in his range of vision. It told him nothing. It was the bare, crudely furnished room of a back-veld Boer. The floor and walls were of *dhaga*, the roof was of thatch—nothing to tell a story or to create an atmosphere for the owner of the voice.

It broke in now on his thoughts:

"You wonder who I am and what I am. Turn and look, Englisher. Look at Tante du Toit. Perhaps, yes, you will wish to *opsit* with her, Mister Whiteskin."

The Major winced at her laughter.

He hitched around slowly and saw, seated in a chair where the full glare of the lamp fell on her face, a monstrously fat woman whose face had no suggestion of the good humor which custom associates with fatness. Humor was there, true! But an evil, malignant humor. Her eyes expressed that, otherwise she was expressionless. A shapeless monstrosity.

The thought passed through the Major's mind that even in the soft days of early childhood she must have been hideous. And now that she was old, work-stained, sin-stained, her ugliness was beyond belief. He felt sorry for her.

"You have been very kind, Tante du Toit. I am very grateful. I—"

"Words—always words from you Rednecks," she interrupted. "And words are not trade goods," she laughed. "But go on: give me more words. Praise my beauty! Exclaim in wonder that I should be nearly eighty, yet so slim and beautiful! *Ach sis!* I know you Englisher fools give away words. But me! I tell you, *ma-an,* that yesterday I was not born. No, nor yet the day before.

"And now you are wondering many things, many things. Maybe you shall be told them. But first, like a long-nosed judge I will be, I will ask you questions and you shall answer. But do not lie, Englisher, not even about the littlest thing! My memory is very long. *So-a!* What is your name?"

"Aubrey St. John Major.

She repeated the name thoughtfully; her eyes, normally almost hidden by her balloon fat cheeks, vanished entirely in her effort of concentration.

She relaxed again; her eyes regarded him keenly.

"It is a dude's name," she commented easily. "But you are no dude. No. I, Tante du Toit, can judge men. I say you are stronger than Hans or Jacob. Maybe you are stronger than Paul. Surely you are quicker; a brain controls *your* muscles. I must match you against Paul some day, if I decide to let you live."

She smiled ghoulishly; her chair creaked with the mirth which shook her.

"Have you heard of me, or my nephews, *roinek?*"

"No!"

"Then why did you come seeking me?"

"I came for shelter, Tante. Shelter for the Hottentot. He had fever."

"And it was for the Hottentot you crossed the river, in the dark?"

"Perhaps for myself, too."

"That sounds truer. For yourself, of course. Whoever heard of a man doing what you did for a nigger?"

"Maybe you have not met many men, Tante," the Major replied easily.

SHE SCOWLED forbiddingly. "I have met too many men. I have forgotten them. They do not forget me. *Ach sis,* no! Now tell me how you came here on foot, no money, nothing. But first—*Ach sis!* You are hungry—not?"

"Very hungry, Tante du Toit."

"Of course, yes. So, wait, Paul!" She raised her voice in a deafening shout.

The door opened and Paul stood there in the rain, yawning, rubbing his eyes.

"You called, Tante?"

"Truly. Come in and shut the door, Fool! Do you not see that the rain is pouring in and the wind blows the fire about the room. Get food for the Englisher."

"*Ja,* Tante."

Paul moved awkwardly about the room, muttering under his breath. From behind a curtained arras he brought a large, smoke-blackened kettle containing soup stock. He put this on the fire. Then, giving the Major a wooden bowl and a pewter spoon, he growled, "Help yourself when it is hot, Englisher."

"Thank you," the Major said and looked at him curiously.

The big Dutchman reminded the Major of some fabled giant, but a giant not yet fully matured. His face was covered with a black, downy beard which suggested uncleanliness rather than masculine vigor. A tattered felt hat was drawn down low over his eyes, but the Major guessed that his forehead was narrow, receding. His ears were enormous and stood out from his head; his big hands—the fingers moved continuously—hung down almost to his knees. Altogether, the Major thought, a very unprepossessing specimen, and undoubtedly strong. He wondered if it would be possible to hurt him.

"That is all, Paul," the woman said. "You go now."

"*Ja,* Tante." Paul moved toward the door.

"And Paul—" he looked inquiringly round at her after-thought—"it was foolish of you to come so quickly when I called. Almost I was ready to think that you were listening at the door. Truly. I suspected—of course unjustly—" she laughed—"that you had not gone to bed as I ordered. And that suspicion led to another: that Hans and Jacob were listening with you. Now go. But do nothing to arouse my suspicions again. That would be very foolish, not?"

"Yes, Tante," Paul stammered and hastened to the door.

He passed out, for a moment the fury of the night entered the room again, then the door closed.

The Major thought he heard furtive whispering outside the door, then panic-stricken footsteps *sloshing* through the mud. Then silence!

Savory smells from the kettle recalled him to the present needs and he filled his bowl with the thick, steaming buck stew and ate slowly, relishing every mouthful, knowing the danger of over-eating following a period of fasting.

THE BOWL empty he sighed with satisfaction and looked up at the woman, aware that her eyes were upon him. He felt foolishly self-conscious of his position.

She was so evidently in command of the situation. Sitting there on the floor with only a skin for covering, looking up at her great bulk, the Major felt that his thoughts were as exposed to her as was his body. Whether by accident or design—he suspected the latter—she had staged the coming discussion so that, psychologically, he was at an immense disadvantage. The thought flashed through his mind, "I feel like a bally worm on a dissecting table. If I had a cigarette, or my monocle, I'd feel more like a man. Wonder where my clothes are?"

He looked around the room, searching for them.

The woman laughed. She seemed to have read his thoughts.

"You should not feel bashful, Englisher. Almighty! I am no simpering girl. And I have lived. In the morning you shall have your clothes. Now you shall tell me about yourself: How you came to this place? Why you are on foot? Why you had nothing in your pockets, no money, only that trash."

She gestured toward the table, and the Major, raising himself slightly, saw that on it was his revolver in its holster and the trifles which had been in his pockets—a muddied handkerchief, cigarette case, match box, a clasp knife, and his monocle.

Gathering his skin rug closely about him he rose to his feet and moved swiftly to the table. He snatched up the monocle and cigarette case and the next moment was sitting down again beside the fire.

The few cigarettes in the case were a wet, soggy mess. He put them carefully on the hearth to dry. The monocle he polished on the skin rug and then, fixing it in his eye, looked up inquiringly at the woman. The glittering piece of glass seemed to have entirely dressed him, restored his self assurance. The woman ceased to dominate the situation. Realizing this, she laughed uneasily.

"It is well for you, Englisher," she said, "that you did not try to take up your little popgun. That would have been the end of you. This would have scattered your bones and blood over the floor."

This, which she now showed him, was a sawed-off shotgun. She had been holding it on her lap, hidden from sight by the bulge of her voluminous skirts. The Major considered that in some part it accounted for the instant obedience rendered her by the three men. When within its range it would be suicidal not to obey!

"And now," she continued, "take that window from your eye, for it masks truth, and talk."

The Major obeyed with a mocking flourish.

"And where shall I begin, Tante? With the hour of my birth? It was foretold then that I should cross water in the blackness of the night and fall under the domination of a not-thin Boer good-wife. With—"

THE ROOM shook with her gargantuan mirth. Then she scowled. "You make fun of me, dog," she threatened, "and you will die with that mock on your lips."

"Excuse, Tante. I did not mean harm. So now I will tell you what you want to hear. Three days ago I had a wagon, well-loaded, twelve mules and a stallion horse—a king of horses!" The Major was silent for a moment. His black horse, Satan, had been a well tried friend.

The woman cleared her throat with a harsh, impatient cough and he continued, "We were on a hunting trip, the Hottentot and I, trekking north. We were out-spanned on the flats to the south of here. The tsetse fly appeared. We inspanned hastily and fled to escape it. But it was too late. All the animals were 'stuck' and the next day they died."

Again he paused.

"*Ja,*" the woman commented easily. "The fly is a good servant of the blacks and of us Boers. It keeps this country from being over-run by *verdoemte roineks.* But go on. You would say next that your wagon was 'stuck' by the fly also and it died!" Her sarcasm was loaded with her surfeit of fat.

"No. Not that. But lightning struck it.

The Hottentot and I were far away at the time, burying the horse, which I could not leave for the hyenas; he was a friend; and when we got to the wagon it was a pile of ashes, nothing left. That is all. Without food, empty handed, we hurried from the place hoping to find a kraal or—or a homestead such as this.

"The rains came. All day yesterday and today we trekked through the rain. This afternoon we saw the kopje which must be near here. We headed for it. The darkness came. We reached the river, I saw the light of the homestead. And because the Hottentot had fever, I crossed the river seeking hospitality—and found it. That is all, Tante du Toit. I thank you."

He bowed mockingly, replacing his monocle, and helped himself to another bowl of stew.

"I am very hungry," he said apologetically, "and this is very good."

Not until the bowl was empty did he look up, wondering why she made no comment.

Her thick lips then parted in a high chuckling laugh, she shook from head to foot. But her hands clutched the arms of her wooden chair with a firm grip and her black, beady eyes did not smile; they glittered evilly.

HE PICKED up one of the cigarettes, dry now but discolored, and lighted it, apparently quite at ease; actually, a little overawed by this amazing woman.

"So you've told me all, eh, Englisher?" she said suddenly. "But I am not satisfied. I want to know more. I will believe that you crossed the river for your black goods' sake. Almighty, yes. And your name—*ach!* Men call you the Major, not? I have heard much of you. It may be we will be friends. But first I want to hear of the things you have not told me."

The Major stared at her through the shifting cloud of cigarette smoke.

"But there is not much I have not told you, Tante."

"And still you play with me," the woman laughed. "So listen: I will tell you. I have another nephew. *Ach sis!* He is not like the three fools you have seen. He is almighty *slim*, he has brains. He keeps a kaffir canteen near the big dorp. He grows rich selling rum to the *verdoemte* blacks. He grows rich, Jan does. And he's a good boy. He comes to see his old Tante very often. An' last time he came he brought a policeman with him. A fair-haired *yonker* who simpered like a girl. And Jan showed him all about the place and the other nephews took him hunting and made much of him. And I dressed in a dress made of velvet Jan gave me. I put shoes on my feet and spoke softly. I was just like a mother to that little policeman, so that he went away full of love for me."

She laughed and the Major shuddered slightly.

"So he went away saying he would deny all the evil things that had been whispered about Tante du Toit and her good little nephews. If he had been clever and discovered things, I think he would have died. His horse would have stumbled when he crossed the ford. It has happened!

And there are crocodiles. Almighty, yes! *So-a!* While he was here he showed me a police paper. It had a picture on it of a white man who wore a glass in his eye. And it told much about the white man and his Hottentot servant, Jim. It said five hundred pounds would be given to who told the police where that Major *ma-an* and his nigger would be found. The Major had killed a man. That is why the police are willing to pay so much for him. But so have I, but they haven't put a price on me. Almighty, no!

"And the little fair-headed *yonker* told me to be on the look-out because the Major was a very dangerous *ma-an*, and he might come this way." She paused a moment before adding significantly, "And he has come this way."

The Major picked up another cigarette, looked in annoyance at its mud stained covering, and lighted it.

"Ah!" he exclaimed, expelling a cloud of smoke.

THE WOMAN sagely nodded. "Myself, I suspected when the children first brought you in. But I was not sure until you put that glass thing in your eye. I am glad that you have sense and do not deny that you are the man. I do not like contradictions; it arouses my anger. And when I am angry, I kill."

The Major found that easy to believe, but he made no comment.

"Also," she continued easily, "it would hurt me to kill you. You are very valuable. Five hundred pounds is a lot of money."

"A lot of money, and so easily earned," the Major drawled.

"Truly," she agreed with a dry chuckle. "But not yet am I sure that I want to earn it. No. Listen, Englisher. You and your Hottentot shall stay here with Tante du Toit. If a

policeman comes, you shall hide behind my skirts. I think
we should be friends. *Ach!* I can help you, and you, maybe,
can help me. Now sleep."

"But where, Tante?"

"On the skins by the fire, fool. Or out in the rain. What
do I care?"

The Major shrugged his shoulders and burrowed down
in the skin rugs. But sleep was far from him; his active
brain endeavored to find some explanation of this strange
menage, and tried to solve the mystery presented by Tante
du Toit's enigmatic self.

The lamp burned low. Presently it went out, smelling
vilely, and the room was in darkness save for the flickering
light of the fire.

Outside the rain descended with unabated force, the
wind howled, the river boomed between its rocky banks.
But in the room all was very still, so still that the *tickling*
of a cheap clock sounded loud.

Twice—the second time was in the gray hour of breaking day—the Major, thinking himself alone, looked around
the room.

Each time his eyes were drawn to the chair, behind him.

The woman was still sitting there, motionless, like some
grotesque sculpture.

IT WAS two days later.

The clouds had parted and had retreated sullenly to the
distant horizon where they waited ominously for the sun's
setting and the evening breeze which would gather them
once more to the attack.

But now the sun shone with added force, as if its temporary eclipse had enabled it to recuperate lost powers, and
the rain soaked veld was veiled in heat mist. The grasses,

a luscious green, slowly straightened; almost perceptibly, the mud hardened.

The Major, who was sitting on the river bank, watching the yellow, swirling flood waters, swore emphatically.

"What is it, Baas?" Jim asked. The Hottentot, still a little weak from the fever, was lying in the full glare of the sun, drinking strength from the life-giving rays.

"The river has not gone down, Jim. It is, instead, higher than yesterday. The stake I drove to mark its height is now almost covered."

"What matter, Baas?" Jim asked languidly.

"I like not this place, Jim."

"And I do not like it either, Baas. So let us go."

The Major looked at him, a whimsical smile on his face.

"And even if we could cross, Jim, how far could you walk?"

"Not so far, Baas. I am a weak thing today. But tomorrow—besides, Baas, there are horses and mules and wagons at this place. We could borrow."

"It will be hard to borrow what they will not lend, Jim."

"Then we'll take without asking, Baas."

The Major shook his head.

"If that could be done, we would not be here now. But they watch too closely, Jim. I am very valuable to them. At least—" he smiled grimly—"Five hundred pounds. Otherwise, I do not think we would now be alive."

"Au-a!" Jim exclaimed. "Is that the way things go? Then we must go on foot, Baas."

"If the river had dropped we might try, Jim." He shrugged his shoulders, moodily staring at the turbulent flood. "It will not be easy to get away, Jim. They keep a close watch at the ford."

He turned back then and looked at the homestead. On top of a rubbish pile in front of the house, her skirts billowing about her, sat the Tante du Toit.

"She's cold, viciously cold, like a snake, in spite of her bloated body," the Major muttered.

And, as if in answer, as if she could possibly have heard him, she waved her hand derisively, shouting, "The good old Tante watches very carefully, *kinderkins,* to see that her little ones do not get their feet wet."

The Major turned again to Jim.

"You heard, Jim. She watches all the time. I do not think she ever sleeps. And we have no guns, no food, and you are still weak. No. Until the ford is safe, we are prisoners."

"*Tch!*" Jim exclaimed impatiently. "This is not like you, Baas. One road is closed, but there are others, many others; either up the river, or down the river, or back yonder away from the river."

THE MAJOR laughed shortly. "There is no other road, Jim," he said. "We are caught in a trap. Look!"

With a piece of wood he drew a crude map on the ground.

"See, Jim," he explained. "Here the river sweeps round in a big bend. At the middle of this big bend is the ford. Here is the homestead; here the kopje; here the kraal and here—cutting off all escape to the north—is a great ravine, so deep, its sides so steep, that I think even in the dry season it would be impossible to cross; anyway now the overflow of the river rushes through it with force strong enough to carry a boulder on its surface for a spear's length. We are penned in all around. And so—"

He shrugged his shoulders again.

The Hottentot looked wonderingly at his Baas. Never before had he known him so despondent, so lacking in optimism. It seemed as if the Baas's courage and wit had been lost, or that it had never been real, but only a veneer, an outer covering which he had donned with the dudish attire he was wont to wear when times were good.

There was nothing of the dude about him now, his clothes were ragged; his hair long, unkempt; a beard— ugly in its infancy—blurred the contours of his face and gave him the appearance of a back-veld Boer. But worst of all was the expression in his eyes, whereas they had been indicative of a man of keen wit and buoyant health, indicative of superlative courage, they now held a hint of resignation.

"Baas!" Jim exclaimed, pityingly.

"I know Jim," the Major replied, understanding that the Hottentot realized what a change there was in him. "It is that woman, the Tante du Toit. She is evil, Jim. I feel that her spirit is crushing me. *Wo-we!* At night I sleep in the room and she—she does not sleep, but sits in a chair looking down on me. I cannot escape her. She—"

"Oh, *tula*, Baas," Jim interrupted angrily, disguising his sadness. "You talk like a foolish maiden. That you should let a woman, even an evil one like that fat one, crush you! What folly! Baas, tell me, have you ever seen a goat trying to get out of a *scherm?* He tries to butt down the poles, or to squeeze through where there is no room. And, failing, he gets frightened and tries still harder. And so he does not see the opening where he could easily get out; neither does he remember that no harm will come to him even if he does remain."

"You mean, Jim," the Major questioned.

"That you are trying so hard to run from the woman, Baas that you are creating fear of her. *Wo-we!* She is only a woman, though fat enough for four. And her menfolk, they are only men."

"But very strong, Jim. And I have no guns."

"You have, or had, Baas, a brain, which they have not. *Au-a*, Baas! You have thought only of their strength. Have they no weakness?"

"Hi, *roinek*," it was the woman's voice, shrill, insistent. "Come here!"

"Do not go, Baas." Jim pleaded. "Are you a dog?"

The Major straightened himself. He fumbled in the pocket of his ragged tunic.

"Come quickly, when I call," the woman shouted now, angry impatience in her voice, "or must I send my nephews to get you?"

"Baas, stay," Jim implored.

The Major shook his head, "Coming Tante," he replied and turned slowly away. When he looked back at Jim his monocle glistened in his eye.

"I go, Jim," he said, grinning reassuringly, "to discover her weakness."

SHE WAS hideously repulsive in the garish light of the sun. Her pink scalp, showing hideously through her scant gray hair, reminded the Major of a vulture's obscene baldness.

She eyed the Major closely, suspiciously.

"I called you twice, *roinek*. You heard me the first time, yes?"

He nodded, his eyes fixed on the shotgun she held. He had never seen her without that.

"Then why did you not come?" she continued.

"I had much to say to the Hottentot," the Major replied easily. "And he gave me advice. It was good advice."

She scowled, wondering at his new-found poise.

"You are a fool, *roinek*. All *roineks* are fools. They treat their black goods as if they were well favored by the Almighty. There is only one way to treat kaffirs."

"And that is, Tante?"

"Like cur dogs, *roinek*. Thrash them. They are all lazy, so beat them for their laziness; they are all thieves, beat them for that; if they had the guts, they'd rise against us, so beat them for the desire they possess; if they had the wisdom, they would desert, so beat them because they are fools!"

She laughed, then suddenly sobered, and her flaccid lips for a moment were compressed in a cruel hard line. Almost immediately they parted again and, with her fatness, helped to give her face a lying expression of good fellowship.

"The *sjambok, roinek,*" she continued with a greedy smack of her lips, "that's the only kindness a nigger understands. And that is the way your nigger—he is mine now—will start the morrow. Almighty! I will give the order. And you shall be there. Better, you shall yourself *sjambok* him! How does that please you?"

"Amazingly. Only, good Tante, Jim is valuable. If he is beaten too hardly, and dies, a good driver will be lost you. Also, think, the police will give you money for him as well as for me."

"True," she murmured, "I had almost forgotten that. But, Almighty, a nigger's hide is very tough."

She laughed at the Major's expression of disgust.

"I think I know now," he said irrelevantly.

"Know what, *roinek?*"

"What your weakness is. You are afraid of natives."

She cackled derisively.

"Almighty, *roinek!* You make me laugh too much. As if a good Boer woman was ever afraid of a nigger.

"Listen. I will tell you something. When I was a little girl I fought the blacks by the side of my father and my brothers. All Boer women did so, and we beat them though they outnumbered us a thousand to one. We were not afraid, no. Then you *roineks* spilled yourselves over the land with your *verdoemte slim* ways and your soft talk of peace between the whites and the blacks. *Ach!* You said there must be no more slaves. Your fool preachers told the blacks they were as good as whites, forgetting the Almighty had created them to serve us! Because of that talk the black devils got out of hand.

"They killed without fear of punishment. All my kin were killed—my children and my husbands. Only the three nephews are left to me.

"And now I pay back; I make them suffer for all they have made me suffer. Here, *roinek,* in this place, there is no law but my law. My law is the old Boer law: And that law, *roinek,* you will find in the Good Book. An eye for an eye; a tooth for a tooth. I exact that payment—and interest.

"Also—" she laughed merrily—"I grow rich."

HE WAS silent for a moment, conscious of a feeling of pity for her. After all she had suffered much and, her mind, through brooding on her losses, was undoubtedly unhinged. But the feeling of pity was followed by one of revulsion. She was essentially evil. If she had lost her kith and kin at the hand of the natives, that loss had served simply as a spur to her innate savagery.

"You said, Tante," he began, feeling his way carefully, "that I might be of help to you. How?"

She rocked back and forth, her bare feet thudding into the dirt with each forward movement.

Presently the rocking ceased.

"Listen, *roinek*," she said. "You have seen all there is to be seen in this place of mine. Does nothing strike you strange?"

"Many things," he answered promptly. "But chiefly two."

"Name them," she commanded.

"The first, that your nephews should go in such fear of you—"

"I brought them up," she interrupted. "They have never been away from here. They have always obeyed. They always will. And what is the second thing?"

"That there should be so many natives here, nearly all men, and of different tribes."

At that she laughed.

"The beer I make brings them here from the mines. And once they're here they have to pay me all they have—aye, and give me labor besides—before I let them die. Truly, *roinek*, I am very kind. I give them good beer, I give them huts to sleep in and food to fill their bellies. I treat them in the good old way, much work and the lash by way of thanks. And then—*ja*. I am very soft—I let them die."

She commenced her rocking again.

"And how can I help you, Tante?" the Major asked, looking at her, wondering if he could spring on her and snatch the shotgun away, but deciding not to make the attempt, for failure would mean the end of everything.

"I had thought," Tante du Toit said slowly, "that it might be possible for a man like you to waylay natives on their way to the mines and bring them here. They pass very close, within a forenoon's trek. Then, later, when we had taught them things, you could take them to the mines and receive the pay."

"No, Tante," the Major said slowly. "That I could not do; men would recognize me and then—"

He drew his finger across his throat and around his neck, suggesting hanging.

"Fool! They would not recognize you. Even now, if you took that glass thing from your eye, men would think you one of us."

"And suppose, Tante, I did not return?"

She laughed.

"You will. I shall keep your nigger here, and—besides, I shall have told my other nephew all about you so that, if you try to play any fool tricks on me, he will tell the police, and, *so-a*, what say you?"

"What will I get out of it if I go in with you?"

"I give you a roof over your head, food, drink, tobacco, and shelter you behind my skirts from the eye of the police. Am I not generous? Is it a bargain?"

"*Ja vachtig!*" said the Major, adding in English, "A most hellish one."

SHE LOOKED at him as if she meant to question him further, but at that moment a native came from the cook hut and beat upon a piece of iron bar suspended by a rope from a tree. It was the primitive gong and, in answer to its jangling summons, the three nephews approached at a heavy footed run.

The old woman smiled sardonically, remarking, "That is the sum total of their wisdom. They are ruled through the belly. Well, we too must eat."

With much puffing and grunting, disdaining the Major's proffered hand of assistance, she scrambled to her feet.

She motioned to the Major to precede her. Simpering, "And so I follow a man. I am lost to shame!"

She waddled closely behind him and her monstrous shadow, projected before her, completely engulfing the Major's, looked like the shadow of an obese fiend from the nethermost hell.

IT WAS late afternoon of that same day. The sun had dropped behind the kopje. The clouds, mustering again to the attack, added to the sombreness of a passing day.

The Major looked at the huddled mass of natives who had gathered on a level space at the base of the kopje.

They all looked cowed, unfed, but he sensed that a sullen resentment possessed them all. A resentment which, fanned just a little, would burst into open revolt.

They numbered, he estimated, at least two hundred, but the advantage numbers might have given them was nullified by the fact that they were from many districts, many tribes. Old hates, traditional enmities, proved stronger than the need to present an unbroken front against a common foe. Distrust, mutual self suspicion broke them up into groups making their subjugation so much easier. The Major knew that a white man by playing one group off against the other, favoring now this one, now that, could impose his own will upon them with impunity—so long as he did not step too far. Even a worm will turn under sufficient provocation.

Anxiously, the Major looked for Jim amongst the natives, alarmed because he could not see him.

Then he smiled with relief. That blanketed man in the rear, the man who moved about continuously, whispering first to this native, then to that, going back and forth, courier like, between opposing parties, that was Jim!

The Major wondered at his industry, concluding finally that it was connected with a beer drink which was to be held that night.

The Major turned to the woman. She was seated in her big chair, facing the natives.

Dressed in a black satin dress, her feet shod, a flower trimmed bonnet on her head, one might have thought at a first casual distant glance, that here was a fat, motherly Boer *vrouw*, dressed in her best in honor of a minister's visit or waiting to be driven to Nachtmaal. But the impression would have been a fleeting one. Her facial expression gave the lie to her sedate dress her eyes glinted cruelly; her gnarled hands closed firmly on her shotgun. She was a personification of everything evil.

The Major gestured toward the natives.

"Tante," he said, "their hate for you and yours is like a river during the rains, welling up between the banks. Some day, when all the hill waters come down together, it will overflow its banks, and—"

"You are afraid, *roinek*. You would urge me to talk softly to my black goods! Almighty! There is only one way to treat them—" she laughed harshly—"and you shall see that way. You know why we have come here?"

"To see a beer drink dance, and—" he hesitated—"to *krink* a wagon."

She nodded.

"That is true. But you have put the last first. First the punishment and then the reward."

"I can see," he said slowly, "that the beer drink might be a reward—if the beer is good."

"It is very good," she interrupted smacking her lips. "I myself make it. And I put much gin into it."

The Major nodded thoughtfully.

"That, of course, is really a punishment. It takes away their strength and they sleep forgetting their manhood. But tell me, what punishment is there in *krinking* a wagon?"

"Is it possible you do not know, *roinek?*" she blinked in amazement. "Then a great treat is in store for you. Have you never heard of a nigger being *krinked?* No? Soon you shall see. Look! Here come my three nephews—with the wagon."

AS SHE spoke a large trek wagon, drawn by a span of oxen, appeared round the base of the kopje. Walking by the side of it were the three big men—Paul, Hans and Jacob. Each carried *sjamboks* which they flicked continually. All reeled slightly in their gait and talked and laughed loudly.

Evidently they had been drinking.

"They shall be punished for that. *Ja vrachtig!*" the Major heard the woman mutter.

He wondered at the low murmur which now broke out from the natives; it drowned the noisy clatter of the wheels.

The woman shrilled an angry imprecation. The murmurs ceased, the three men were silent and as the wagon came to a groaning halt, not far from where the woman was sitting, there was no sound.

Quickly the oxen were outspanned and then the three Boers advanced toward the natives making the air resound with the cracking of their *sjamboks*.

The natives did not move, but watched with sullen intentness. The Major was conscious, for a moment, only of four hundred staring fear-filled eyes.

Suddenly the three Boers leaped forward. There was a short sharp scuffle, then they backed slowly toward the wagon each holding a squirming native in his grip.

The Major heard a sigh of relief go up from the others and saw that the air of tension, of suspense, had vanished. They joked and laughed together. It was as if they had been reprieved, had been granted another day in which to live. And tonight there was beer and dancing.

The Major moved away from the woman, close to the wagon.

The Boers were arguing as they bound the arms and legs of the three natives.

Presently they came to an agreement. They separated, and two, coming to where the woman was, squatted on the ground nearby.

"Paul always takes the best," Jacob grumbled. "He *krinks* first. And he has taken my nigger—the rascal who dared to raise his hand against me yesterday. It is not right."

"Paul is older than you, Jacob. It is his right. So no more grumbling unless you want a taste of *sjambok stroop*. Watch Paul now."

That man had picked up one of the natives, a powerfully formed Matabele, and propping him up against the near hind wheel of the wagon he lashed his head and shoulders to the wheel about half down. That done to his satisfaction, and he was very deliberate in his movements, he tied the native's feet to the near front wheel.

Then he turned and grinned at the Major.

"Do you want to *krink* him, *roinek?*" he asked.

The Major shook his head. He still did not understand what was intended.

HE THOUGHT the native was going to be *sjamboked*. Indeed, Paul now gave the luckless man several drawing cuts, and he was schooling himself to witness that without interference. He realized that, to interfere now, would mean his own death. Not that that of itself influenced him, but, by living, he hoped to put an end to all this. First he must gain complete confidence of Tante du Toit. And to gain that confidence, he must be prepared to simulate a cruelty equalling her own. If need be, he too would thrash.

"Do you want to *krink* him?" Paul asked again.

The Major started. Then, "If you are afraid to, I will," he said softly, and took a step forward.

Paul laughed. "Afraid?" he jeered, "Watch!"

He went to the wagon pole, raised it and walked with it, slowly, toward the off-side.

As the front wheels turned the native's body tensed: a moan of pain burst from his lips.

And then the Major understood what was meant by *krinking.* The native was on a rack as devilishly cruel as any of the inquisition, The further over the pole was pushed, the further out of alignment was the front wheel with the rear wheel. The native, his feet tied to the front wheel and his head and shoulders to the rear wheel, was being stretched.

Paul halted, put down the pole and looked around with a grin on his face, shouting some ribald remark to his aunt and brothers.

Then, deliberately, he spat on his hands, and took up the pole again, leaning his weight upon it.

The Major lost all self-restraint. In the face of such inhuman torture he lost sight of the bigger aspect. All the evil of Tante du Toit and her unnatural kinsmen, all the sufferings of the natives, was personified by this one act, by the agony this one native was suffering.

With a hoarse cry of rage he sprang forward.

Paul, warned by cries from his aunt and brothers dropped the pole and turned with a snarl to meet the Major's attack.

He towered above the Major's six feet; the width of his shoulders indicated an ox-like strength, and, as he stood there, slightly stooping, his big hairy hands stretched out before him, his feet wide spread, he looked a colossus, looked as firm and immovable as a rock of granite.

The Major stopped short just beyond the reach of those outstretched hands.

Paul, mistaking the action for fear, lurched forward. The Major, swiftly sidestepping, evaded the rush and countered with a smashing right which landed on the side of the Dutchman's jaw, caught him off his balance and sent him sidewise to the ground.

A SHOUT of wonder and glee went up from the natives. Hans and Jacob, swearing wrathfully, would have rushed to their brother's rescue. But Tante du Toit restrained them. Saying, "First let us see what Paul can do. He is not hurt. Afterwards you shall have your turn. And then we will *krink* the *roinek*."

And now Paul had regained his feet, bellowing with rage, and rushed blindly forward, covering his face with his arms, exposing his body to the Major's hammer-like blows, cursing with pain as each blow sank into the softness of his body, but willing to take all that and more if he could only come to grips.

He forced the Major back and back.

"Stand still and fight like a man, *roinek!*" he snarled.

"Aye, stand still, *roinek!*" the old woman shouted. "Stand still and let Paul cuddle you!"

The natives surged forward. This combat was awakening their old fighting instinct. They straightened themselves, the cowed look disappeared from their eyes.

Still the Major retreated, sidestepping whenever Paul's rush was too fast to suit his purpose, slapping the big man in the back as he blundered by.

But presently Paul saw the sense of the advice his brothers shouted continually and stood his ground, waiting for the Major to come within reach of his arms. He was badly winded. The Major's blows had taken toll of his vitality.

"Come nearer, *roinek*," he panted hoarsely as he pivoted awkwardly so that he could keep the dancing Major before him.

"Certainly! Close enough?"

"Almighty!" Paul roared, for with the words the Major darted swiftly in and out, and landed flush on the Boer's nose, drawing blood. And again Paul rushed, arms swinging wildly, breathing noisily. Again the Major retreated, warily, getting in punishing blows whenever the chance presented itself.

He fought coolly, intent on punishing the big man as much as possible, at the same time trying to evolve a plan to be followed when the fight was over. Weaponless, he knew that he could not hope to compete with the other two men. His only chance was to appeal to the natives—and it was the natives' only chance. If they rallied to his support, the rest would be easy. And yet, he felt that he could not appeal to the natives, could not lead them against people of his own color. It was too much like a betrayal of race.

His retreat brought him very close to Tante du Toit. She was leaning forward in her chair, her chin resting on her hands, gloatingly following every movement of the fight.

The shotgun was resting across her knees.

And then the Major laughed gaily. The way was clear now, and he no longer retreated, but stood firmly, jeering.

THE LAUGH and the Major's new tactics puzzled the big Boer. He came to a confused halt and peered suspiciously at his opponent. His hands hung loosely by his side, his head thrust forward.

Swiftly the Major leaped forward, his hands working in and out like pistons. The Dutchman staggered, his slow witted brain unable to formulate a plan to meet the vicious attack. Blood streamed from his nose and from his cut lips; one eye was almost closed. And he was doing nothing to defend himself—he could not think.

"Cuddle him, Paul," the woman screamed.

"Almighty, yes!" he gasped, and grinned hideously. But his arms were slow in reacting to his brain's command and when they did it was too late.

The Major danced lightly out of reach.

There was a loud shout of triumph from the du Toits; a loud groan of dismay from the natives. For the Major, in his backward leap tripped, staggered backward, his arms weaving wildly in an attempt to recover his balance, and finally fell, on his back, at Tante du Toil's feet.

"Now, Paul!" the du Toits cried, and the big fellow lurched forward, sure of victory now, determined to make the *roinek* pay for all the punishing, flesh-bruising blows.

And then he stopped, and stared in open mouthed wonder. Fear came into his eyes. The woman screamed curses; the other two du Toits dropped to the ground, sheltering behind a rock. The natives shouted with glee.

For the Major was on his feet and in his hands he held the shotgun which he had snatched from the Tante du

Toit's lap. He was standing a little to the right and behind her, menacing her with the gun.

"This, Tante du Toit," he said slowly so that all could hear, "this is the end of all the evil you have worked. Tell your nephews to stand up, their hands above their heads, their backs toward us. Tell them!"

She looked around, flinched at the sight of the gun which was aimed at her, then slumped back in her chair, sullen, her eyes furtively glancing at the crowd of natives, estimating their temper.

The three men swiftly obeyed the Major's orders; fear evidently possessed them.

"Ropes," the Major now called for, addressing the natives. "Ropes and stout hearts who will bind these evil ones."

A NUMBER of natives came eagerly forward. From the wagon they took some ropes and advanced cautiously toward the Boers.

"If you try to resist," the Major warned the du Toits, "your aunt will die."

The woman seemed to lean still further back in her chair.

"Do not move, children!" she cried imploringly. "Do as the *roinek* says."

At that moment she seemed very old: Her fatness, her stupendous bulk seemed to melt away from her, leaving bare her mean, shriveled soul.

The natives—her black goods—were surging forward, hate in their eyes, triumphant in their anticipation of vengeance.

The Major looked for Jim, he needed the Hottentot's support.

Presently he saw him, wrestling with two natives, one of whom had a hand over the Hottentot's mouth, stifling him.

Before the Major could act Jim broke away from his assailants, and—

"Baas—behind you! Quick!" Jim shouted warningly.

A heavy weight struck the Major on the head and he dropped in a senseless heap to the ground.

CONSCIOUSNESS RETURNED tardily. He was aware first of a confused din; loud piercing shouts, the *cracking* of whips and boisterous, mocking laughter. He felt that he was suspended in mid air. His head ached; his feet were numb.

He shuddered at a sudden, sharp cutting pain across the shoulders, he gasped for breath when water was thrown violently into his face.

Opening his eyes he looked into the mocking face of Tante du Toit. She was sitting on the ground; in one hand she held a *sjambok;* in the other a gourd of muddy water.

He wondered that his face should be on a level with hers, yet he was lying down and she was sitting up!

He tried to move, but failed, and winced at the pain it caused him—a strangling sensation.

And then he realized and relaxed, as much as he could. He was tied to the wagon wheels, as the native had been tied.

The woman laughed. The three men who stood behind her mocked him. To their right, huddled together, were the natives.

"You see, *roinek*," Tante du Toit said complacently, "we know how to treat black goods. They love us. They would not see us manhandled by you. So, now we shall *krink* you.

And then—"she laughed—"we will deal with these black ones."

The Major was silent. There was nothing he could say or do now. He had failed. And this was a hellish way to die.

He wondered where Jim was. He'd like to say good-by to the Hottentot. They had done so much together.

The woman, as if answering his thoughts, said, "The Hottentot! *Ach!* He is going to *krink* you. He begged that he might in order to be avenged on the years you have ill-used him. He waits now, with the pole in his hands, for permission to begin."

"Ah!" The Major breathed softly and sent out a silent message to Jim, realizing that the Hottentot meant to do the deed swiftly and save his Baas from prolonged torture.

"But first," continued the woman, "You shall see once again how we treat our black goods. It will be a good sight for your eyes. It will give you strength to endure the torture. So—to them, children! Give the black devils a taste of the *sjambok.*"

Obeying her gladly, the three Boers rushed at the natives, shouting oaths, thrashing indiscriminately.

The Major watched, grieved that the natives should submit so tamely.

"Be men, be warriors," he shouted, and repeated his objurgations in several dialects. He pleaded with them, he commanded. He stung their pride, reminded them of their fighting ancestors. Using all his knowledge of their involved psychology, he whipped up their courage.

The woman scrambled to her feet: She endeavored to shout the Major down. But it was too late!

The cries of pain had given way to yells of anger. At last, tribal hates were forgotten and the natives closed in on the three white men.

Jim ran to release his Baas, stopped, and, sensing Tante's motives, endeavored to trip the woman as she waddled past him. She barely eluded him, and, picking up the pole, pushed upon it.

The Major's body stiffened; then a merciful darkness engulfed him.

And at that moment the last red tinge of sunset's after glow faded from the sky. The clouds closed in and the rain recommenced.

THE MAJOR wearily opened his eyes.

His throat burned, his head ached. Seeing that he was in the big room, lying on skin rugs in front of the fire, he groaned aloud, thinking of the torture and evil he was fated to witness, believing that the du Toits had succeeded in obtaining control of the natives.

He sat up and looked about the place. He was alone and, on the table near him, where the lamp light shone on it, was his revolver.

Moving cautiously, cursing softly because his limbs felt so weak, he retrieved his gun, saw that it was loaded, then sighed with relief. He felt he could face any situation now.

He walked slowly toward the door and opened it and stood there wondering at the red glare which lighted the rain-drenched sky.

He heard footsteps, a man running. He tensed; his fingers on the trigger.

And then Jim came running up the path of light which shone through the open door. The Hottentot grinned happily, and panted as he neared, "It is all right, Baas!"

"But what is happening, Jim? What has happened?" the Major asked.

Jim led him back into the room then shut and bolted the door.

"Baas," he exclaimed, "they are fools, those black ones. When you had conquered, when freedom was assured them, some Fingo cowards, thinking to gain much favor and wealth, crept up on you from behind. And when you dropped—with a knobkerrie they struck you, Baas—then the courage of the others went from them. And nothing I could do would rouse them. *Wo-we!* They released the three white men and did all the woman commanded. *Wo-we!* She was all evil."

"Was, Jim?"

"Aye—was, Baas. I will tell you all in order. After they tied you to the wheel, Baas, the fat woman made a mistake, Baas. She told her men folk to *sjambok* the black ones, and they did, Baas, sparing none. You saw that!"

The Major nodded.

"And there, I say, Baas, they made their mistake. They thrashed Zulu, Mashonas, Basuta and Fingo. They vowed to *krink* them all. Yet even so, nothing would have happened had not you talked to the black ones. You woke them up. *Au-a!* Never have you talked better. And so the black ones fought for their manhood's sake, realizing, at last, they were all meant for death, that there was hope for none. You saw them turn upon the white men, Baas."

"Yes, Jim. And I saw the woman get up and rush past you. Then I saw no more."

JIM MADE a wry face. "I nearly failed, Baas. But, *au-a!* That woman was mad. She had the pole in her hand, Baas, and was turning the wheel. I could not stop her. She was a mountain. It was the Fingo who felled her—the Fingo who had before felled you."

Jim paused.

"Go on, Jim."

"There is no more, Baas. I cut you loose and carried you here."

"And then left me. Why, Jim?"

"To see justice done, Baas."

"You mean, Jim?"

"Baas, you would not approve. But it is too late now for you to stop them, so I can tell you. They killed the Boer folk, Baas."

"The men *and* the woman, Jim?"

"Yah, Baas. The men and the woman. It was just."

There was a pause.

"Most just, Jim—but very terrible," the Major finally agreed. "And now, Jim?"

"They dance round the huts they have put to flames and drink the beer prepared for them. Tomorrow they will have aching heads, Baas, but you will be able to reason with them."

The Major nodded and was very thoughtful.

The river would not be fordable for many days. He and Jim were penned on this "island" with a horde of natives, drunk with freedom, their blood lust whetted by the killing of the four Boers.

He was faced with a hard task. He had to control tribal hates, to restore respect for and confidence in white men. Now—he could hear their wild yells—they were savages, void of all restraint.

But in the morning, "Yes, Jim," he said confidently, "I will be able to reason with them."

A BOER
MATRIARCH

PAT GREENE tells us of an old woman like the one in "Black Goods." He also explains his attitude toward the Boers in general.

"*Zwart-goed,* or 'black goods,' is a phrase in common use among the Dutch Boers and applied by them to their native servants. The phrase has come down from the old slave owning days and is used contemptuously. The Tante du Toit of the story must not be taken as a typical representative of the Boer womanhood. Quite the contrary, in fact. But there is, or rather was, such a woman. At least I have drunk black muddy coffee at the homestead of a woman who was capable of the cruelties I have attributed to Tante du Toit. She simply lacked the opportunity to be fully as bad. My visit to her was as a result of a complaint received at police headquarters of her ill-treatment of native laborers. She was very old, very fat, and very evil. I don't think that she had undressed for months or washed for ages, but her personality was a dominating one, and my visit was a pure waste of time. She could not speak English, I could not speak Dutch and her gray-bearded son was a slow-witted oaf—or he might have been very cunning. He could only say 'yes' and 'no' and used them indiscriminately. This woman I afterward learned had had several husbands and had fought through many native wars. In a sense, she was rather magnificent.

"I do want to stress this point: although Boers often figure as villains in the 'Major' stories, or if not villains, then fools, it must not be supposed that I consider all Boers fools and villains. That is not so. Quite the contrary, in fact. Several of my best friends were Boers. And, with very few exceptions, the Boer farmers I met when on patrol were splendid folk.

"One other point: the torture described in the story was, in the early '80s, a fairly common treatment of insubordinate natives. It is described fully in Glairmonte's *The Africander*, published 1896. And so was evidently in vogue then. I quote from the book: 'He showed us great weals in his dirty skin where he had been thrashed with the *sjambok*. He further stated that on the previous day they *krinked* him—'"

GRADED

CAPTAIN VAN Eyck of the Mounted Police tugged at his black, pointed beard and looked at the ragged man who stood easily before him, a mixture of affection, admiration and doubtful indecision in his mild brown eyes.

Then he looked out through the open door of the office hut where, in a clearing bathed in yellow sunlight, sat a horde of natives, men of many tribes, watchful, silent.

They were, for the most part, naked, disclosing gaunt, food starved bodies, scored with scars of many brutal *sjambokings*. They looked fixedly toward the hut, and their eyes, focussing on the raggedly dressed man, suggested something of a dog's devotion for a just, understanding master.

A Hottentot, gaunt like the rest of the natives, squatted on his haunches just outside the office hut.

"It's incredible," the captain muttered. "And the marvel of it is it's true. Of course it's true. One doesn't question the Major's word."

In louder voice he continued, tentatively addressing the man before him.

"If you would only let me report the matter officially—"

"Neither officially or privately, dear old lad," the other replied. "You gave me your word of honor about that, you know."

His speech, an affected drawl, seemed oddly incongruous; did not belong to the tattered, dust stained clothes, unshaven face and general unkempt appearance. Indeed his speech and the monocle—even if it was cracked—which he wore in his eye belonged to a brainless fop, not to a man who looked like a sundowner, one of those "Weary Willies" who tramp across the African veld, from homestead to homestead, risking many perils, laboring hard in order to avoid labor.

"You gave me your word about that," he repeated.

The captain shook his head regretfully.

"I know. And I'll keep it. Just the same, you're a fool, Major. Any man's a fool to hide his light under a bushel. And in your case now— Look here, if the truth of this affair were reported officially, it would count heavily in your favor when, should you be arrested, you come up for trial."

The ragged man considered this for a moment. Then: "But I've done nothing. Really I haven't."

Captain Van Eyck laughed.

"Done nothing! Of course you've done nothing!" he scoffed in kindly, sarcastic tones. "You've only freed those niggers out there from death—from worse than death. Your modesty is a little overwhelming, Major, at times. It is a form of conceit, I think."

THE OTHER stiffened, squared his powerful shoulders, and for a moment looked his full height. Immediately the mood passed and he seemed again, for all his rags and dishevelled beard, an inane, spineless individual.

"No," he said quietly. "It is not conceit. I did nothing. It was all Jim."

As he spoke this name the Hottentot leaped to his feet and entered the hut.

"The Baas called?" he said.

"No, Jim," the Major replied in the vernacular. "The name was used in talk. That is all."

"Your Baas was saying," explained the policeman, "that in this affair he did nothing, you everything!"

The Hottentot laughed.

"That was always my Baas' way," he said. "He runs from praise as fast as a bashful maiden runs from an overzealous lover. But we know what he is and what he does."

The Hottentot's face glowed and its ugliness seemed to melt away. Looking at him, one was now conscious of the fine spirit which dwelt in his immensely powerful frame.

"Shall I tell you all that my Baas did, in order to save those dogs?" he continued. *"Au-a!* They were mad at the time! Having killed, the blood lust was still upon them. But he cured their heat. *Wo-we!* That is a story which must be told."

"No, Jim. Get outside and hold on to your tongue with both hands before it wags you into trouble."

Jim grinned as he obeyed, muttering, "Just the same, I *shall* tell the story some day."

"Splendid fellow, Jim," the Major commented softly. "He's saved my life a dozen and one times. He's—he's a white man."

Captain Van Eyck nodded. He knew all about Jim, the Hottentot.

"There's no false color about you, either, Major," he said. He knew all about that man, too. "But what are you going to do now?"

"Dashed if I know, old bean. Work for a living, I'm afraid—or join the police."

"Wish you had years ago. It's too late now. And are you really as broke as you appear?"

"QUITE. LOST everything. The fly killed my horse and mules. And my wagons with all the provisions went up in flames. Funny, though, how things like that turn out for the best. If it hadn't been for my misfortunes, I'd never have struck the du Toit's place or have been able to help those chappies out of a nasty hole. A very nasty hole! What are you going to do with 'em?"

"Send those who want to, back to work in the mines. And ship the others to their kraals. I'll feed 'em all up, first, though."

The Major sighed with relief. "That takes a load off my shoulders. Jim and I can go on our lonely way rejoicing."

"And where are you going?"

"Personal inclination would take me up-country, far from the crowded haunts of men and all that. But—" he shrugged his shoulders and his white, even teeth flashed in

a deprecating smile—"that's impossible. I can't go ahunt-
ing, lacking the few essentials—sheets and pillow cases and
what not. Besides, I have no guns. And so, I am afraid—"
he sighed heavily, theatrically— "I'll have to return to the
busy hives of—er—industry, and investigate, as it were,
the diamond field. Some of the dealers are beastly careless, and so—"

His voice trailed off into silence.

"You mean you're going to recommence I.D.B. operations?"

"You mustn't take my—er—little operations so
confoundedly seriously."

"Why shouldn't I? You're notoriously the cleverest
I.D.B. in the country."

"Ah! Now you're dealing in rumor, and she is such a
lying jade. A few diamonds may have passed through my
hands—"

"A lot have!"

"Doubtless you are right. But, nevertheless, I have
never—oh, well, hardly ever!—been guilty of any unethi-
cal act. *Bent* a law, maybe, yes. But that is all."

Van Eyck nodded.

"I know that, Major. We all know that. Otherwise, I
think, your career would have been ended long ago. We've
leant over backward in our desire to give you a square deal."

"Yes—bally sporting lot your chaps are. A few exceptions, of course. But then a few black sheep are bound to
creep in. One or two, you know, have been so beastly blind
to good form that they have tried to trap me."

"And we know what happened to them," Van Eyck
commented.

THE MAJOR waved his hands, dismissing the matter, yet he could not refrain from a low chuckle as there flashed swiftly through his mind memories of attempts of ambitious police troopers, misled by his asinine inanities, to trap him into illegally buying diamonds.

"Well, I must be on my way," he smiled. "Must set about earning a little money. Need so many things. Toodle-oo!"

He turned to leave but halted and stared incredulously at the other's stern command.

"Wait! You can't go like that!"

"But I can, dear old fellow. There's the open door. What's to hinder me?"

He laughed softly at the policeman's meaning gesture toward the revolver which, serving as a paper weight, was on the desk.

"Oh, well, of course," he drawled. "If you're going to be that sort of Johnny!"

The police captain cleared his throat with a nervous, rasping cough. Then, slowly, reluctantly, his eyes fixed on the Major's face, he said, "There's a warrant put for your arrest, Major."

"Rippin'!" chortled the monocled one. "That, as it were, sets a seal on my efficiency. It also provides me with an object in life. I have been suspect so many times—"

"But—" the captain interrupted swiftly and his tone was grave—"never before of murder."

"No, that's true," the Major agreed. And now his voice, too, was grave. "I suppose," he continued, "that the police have a complete case against me?"

"A very complete case. I'll admit that it rests entirely on circumstantial evidence, but there is not a weak link in the chain, and—"

"Ah!" the Major softly interrupted. "I'm glad to get your expert opinion on that. I took the deuce an' all of a lot of trouble to forge that chain of evidence. You understand of course, that the word 'forge' has several meanings? But, pardon: you were saying?"

Van Eyck shrugged his shoulders.

"I think you will find it very difficult, if not impossible, to break the chain you have forged. Any jury, hearing the evidence, would bring in a verdict of guilty, and you would hang."

"An uncomfortable way to die," the Major commented.

"Very," Van Eyck agreed dryly. "Well?"

"Is it well?"

"I'm afraid not, Major. I'm afraid I cannot let you go. I must hold you for trial."

"That would be most unfortunate, old chap," the Major said hurriedly, earnestly. "You must let me go. There are reasons—"

"There would be. Now, despite the evidence, because I know you, I do not believe you guilty of murder. You would not shoot a man in the back. You—oh, never mind the rest! You are not guilty of murder, are you?"

"Oh no, word of honor an' all that."

"And you can prove your innocence?"

"If I had to—yes."

"Then why not submit to arrest, go up for trial and get this nasty affair ended?"

THE MAJOR considered this thoughtfully.

"Can't do it," he said finally. "There are reasons, very strong and sufficient reasons, why I must not be arrested and tried."

"Yet you come here, risking arrest. You might have stayed out there—" the captain's gesture indicated the vast veld which surrounded the camp—"and never have been found. You walk into the lion's den. You have no right to suppose the lion will let you go."

"I had to bring the native chappies to a place of safety. And there are several ways of escaping from a lion's den."

"As for instance?" But for all his easy sarcasm, Captain Van Eyck tensed visibly. His right hand closed upon the butt of his revolver and his eyes were fixed upon the Major's face. He regretted that he was temporarily alone at the post save for two or three native constables.

He had no doubt that, should the Major appeal to those natives who waited so patiently outside, they would respond and would rescue him, at the risk of death, from arrest. The Major had a way with natives; understood them better than any living white man. Besides, he had just delivered them from a slavery that was worse than death. Still, he felt reasonably sure that the Major would not appeal to the natives.

The Major had taken his monocle from his eye and was examining it ruefully.

"Pity it's cracked," he murmured. "And I haven't another with me. You don't happen to have one? No, of course not. Well, I must polish this to the best of my ability. One has to be so very careful though. I've a patent powder here, somewhere, which polishes splendidly."

As he spoke he was fumbling in the pockets of his ragged tunic.

"Ah, here it is." He exhibited a small package which he opened carefully.

"All one has to do," he continued, "is to cover the lens with this powder—so. And then—mind your eyes—blow!"

His breath scattered the powder like a thin coil of smoke toward the policeman.

THAT MAN'S hand reached forward again for his revolver, but never reached it. Instead, he was shaken by a succession of devastating sneezes which rendered him incapable of action. When the paroxysms had passed, leaving him physically weak, tears rolling down his cheeks from reddened, inflamed eyes, the Major was covering him with the revolver.

"I said 'God bless you!' every time you sneezed," the Major said. "And I do hope you acted on my warning and closed your eyes. Native snuff is so bally powerful! And now—well, the door is open, I have the key—" he waved the revolver—"and there is nothing, I think, to detain me any longer. But, before I go, I want your word that you will not attempt to follow me until say, twenty-four hours have passed."

"And if I refuse?"

"That would be awkward, very. I might shoot you—but that would be murder, wouldn't it? No, I couldn't do that. So I'm afraid I would be compelled to take you along with me. Yes, that would be splendid. I'd like that. I hope you will refuse."

"I won't," Van Eyck snapped. "I'll give you my word, Major, not to attempt to follow you for twenty-four hours. But after that, I shall come after you myself."

"Splendid!" the Major murmured. "Absolutely splendid. So here's to our next meeting."

"I wouldn't be too cheerful about it, Major," Van Eyck growled. "It'll end in your being put on trial for murder."

The Major looked grave.

"I'd forgotten that. And so, dear lad, it would be better if you did not try to catch me. Really. There are reasons why I must *not* be tried. I shall resist arrest. You are a little disgruntled now, of course. Probably your eyes smart a little. And your pride, what? It was such a simple trick. Oh, well! Now I must go. Twenty-four hours is a short start—and you will be mounted. But the veld is wide. So—toodle-oo!"

As he spoke he put down the revolver on the desk and the next moment had left the hut.

Captain Van Eyck heard him speak to the natives, bidding them farewell, assuring them that they were to be well treated. He heard the natives' affectionate reply. Then there was a great silence.

An hour passed swiftly and for the greater part of the time Captain Van Eyck had stared blankly before him, tugging at his pointed beard.

Then, with a harsh exclamation of self reproof at his thoughtless stupidity, he whistled shrilly and, to the native policeman who came in response to his signal, gave a series of curt orders.

When the man withdrew to carry them out, Captain Van Eyck hastily wrote a short note enclosed it in an envelope, then went outside and questioned the natives. They answered him willingly on all points until he questioned them about the direction the Major had taken and his probable destination. And those questions were met with blank looks and silence.

AN HOUR later the native constable, riding a sturdy horse, and leading a well laden pack mule, reported himself to Van Eyck.

To him the captain gave final instructions, gave him the letter he had written, and sent him off to pick up the trail of the Major.

That evening a native runner brought Captain Van Eyck word from headquarters that his application for long leave had been granted and that Lieutenant Greenacre was on his way to take over charge of the post.

The messenger informed him, answering the captain's questions, that Lieutenant Greenacre was barely a day's trek away and would, in all probability arrive before tomorrow's sundown.

But when Lieutenant Greenacre did arrive, *three* days later, Captain Van Eyck was not there to welcome him: Instead, a native constable handed him a letter.

Lieutenant Greenacre read it hastily, all but the concluding paragraph, for it contained much detailed information in regard to the routine of the post, disposition of men and so forth. All *that* the Lieutenant meant to read and digest very thoroughly after he had bathed and *skoffed*.

But the last paragraph:

> *"I'm going to spend my leave—all of it if necessary—hunting the Major. He's been seen in this neighborhood. In fact, he's sort of challenged me to catch him and the chase ought to be good sport. I only hope I can head him off and prevent him from seeking sanctuary in German territory. Of course I don't put much faith in this charge of murder that's against him. But he's wanted badly, and it ought to be a feather in my cap if I catch him. Wish me 'good hunting!' I'm after Royal Game."*

"By God, you are, sir," Greenacre chortlingly commented as he finished the letter. "And, if you only knew it, it's highly protected."

Then he burst into a fit of uproarious laughter. The captain's letter was evidently mirth-provoking.

He sobered suddenly and questioned the wondering native constable as to the time of the captain's departure and the route he followed.

"I suppose," Greenacre finally concluded, failing to get satisfactory information, "that I ought to send a messenger after him. But he's got too big a start and it's doubtful if a runner would catch up with him. Oh well—!"

ABOUT THIS time Captain Van Eyck arrived at a small kraal where he intended to pass the night. He was off-saddling his pack mules when the grease smeared headman timidly approached him, handed him a dirty piece of paper and quickly retreated.

Opening it, Van Eyck read:

> "I'm surprised at you—really I am. I thought you were a bally sportsman and counted on a clear twenty-four hour's start. Instead of which, you send one of your native trekkers after me within an hour or two of my departure. It's not playing the game—really. For a long time I wouldn't believe he was after me, but when, yesterday, Jim pointed out that we were still being followed, I arranged with Jamba, the headman here, to detain your sleuth hound. I hope they treated him tenderly.
>
> "Under the circumstances, I do not care to see you again. Hence this note; I might get angry if I stopped to welcome you.
>
> The Major.

Captain Van Eyck groaned, then swore irritably. His face flushed.

"Oh, hell!" he muttered. "That's too bad. Now I've *got* to catch him. I can't have him thinking me guilty of playing a dirty game like that. *O-he!* Jamba!"

He raised his voice in an imperious shout and the head-man shuffled slowly into view.

"You call me, *inkosi?*" he asked in a tone of incredulity.

"Yes—you!" snapped Van Eyck. "The white man who gave you this—where is he?"

Jamba grinned.

"Who knows, *inkosi*. Like the wind he came; like the wind he went. He, and the Hottentot who was with him, stayed long enough to do me a service, then they went."

"What was that service?"

"They cured my son of sickness. The witch doctor who lives in the hills had failed, but this white man, he succeeded. *Au-a!* But all witch doctors are alike. Their fees are high."

Van Eyck grinned.

"And what was the fee?"

"A mule, some mealie meal and a goat. A big fee—but the goat had died of a sickness. A big fee, and I am very poor. The *inkosi* will get back my mule for me?"

"THE INKOSI will not. Your son was cured, you say. Is not your son of more value than a mule, a little mealie meal and a goat—" the captain spluttered—"which had died of a sickness?"

"Truly," Jamba agreed. "I had almost forgotten."

Van Eyck continued, "Where is the black policeman you hold?"

Jamba looked at him in amazement.

"You know that there is such an one?"

"Yes. All things are known to me. Why did you hold him prisoner?"

"If the *inkosi* knows all things he knows why."

"Aye. I know," Van Eyck interrupted testily. "I ask to see if you tell the truth. So, speak."

"It is part of the wonder working that the white man performed when he cured my son. He said that a black policeman would come soon after he left, riding a horse and leading a mule. He said that we must take that man prisoner and hold him until you came. *Au-a!* He said that if we failed in this, his wonder working would be of no avail and my son would die.

"He said the black one would say many foolish things and threaten us. And so he did. But we were to shut our ears to it. And so we did.

"I said to him that, when you came, you would punish us for having held your man. So he made a charm to protect us. It is that which you hold in your hand. That is all, *inkosi*."

"And where went this white charm-maker when he left you?"

"I do not know, *inkosi*. Like the wind he came, like the wind he went."

"Is that part of the charm he made?" Van Eyck asked dryly. "That your eyes be closed to his coming and going?"

Jamba looked at him stolidly, uncomprehendingly.

"I do not understand," he said slowly. And Van Eyck realized that further questioning would be useless.

"Go send the black policeman to me," Van Eyck ordered curtly.

"I might have known!" he told himself. "The Major's well able to take care of himself. And with Jim—the combination is irresistible. They won't starve. Far from it. Before many days have passed I'm willing to gamble the Major'll be quite well equipped. And all honestly earned, at that. He's started well. But he'll find it harder to get guns and ammunition. He'll find it impossible to get a monocle."

Van Eyck laughed.

A NATIVE policeman came from the kraal, halted at the regulation distance and saluted smartly. But there was a sheepish expression on his face.

"Well?" Van Eyck questioned sharply.

"Au-a, inkosi! It is not well. I have been put to shame. I followed the white man and his Hottentot dog as you commanded, but I could not catch up with them. They were too cunning.

"I think they are devils, *inkosi.* They have put me to shame. I, who have boasted that no man can better follow spoor! I rarely saw them—and then at a great distance—but I think they could always see me.

"When I came to this kraal, I knew I was very near to them. Yet here I lost them entirely. That old fool Jamba made a prisoner of me. He would not let me go. He would not listen to me, saying I was a worker of evil magic. You will order a punishment for him, *inkosi?*"

"No—no punishment. You were not harmed? You were well fed? The horse and the pack mule are safe? Good."

"And tomorrow it is permitted that I take up the trail of those two?"

"No." Van Eyck grinned at the expression of relief which came into the native's eyes. "You will return to camp. I go on alone. But which direction, think you, are they heading?"

"West, *inkosi.* Undoubtedly west."

Van Eyck nodded.

"That is my thought, too." In English he added to himself: "And I'm going to follow them, German territory or no German territory. This is going to be a big game hunting with a vengeance!

"Help me outspan," he said to the native, and for a while the two men were silent.

Not until food was cooking on the red ashes of a fire did the captain speak again.

"Where," he asked, "is the paper I gave you?"

The native policeman handed him the note.

Van Eyck opened it slowly and, a light of merriment dancing in his eyes, read:

> *"Dear Major:*
>
> *I'm sending this fellow after you. The horse, mule and provisions I hope you will accept as a present, or at least a loan.*
>
> *I'll be after them when the twenty-four hours are up, so you'd better not loiter on the way!*
>
> *I ought to have thought of this before, but better late than never.*
>
> *Yours,*
>
> *Van Eyck."*

"Damn!" Van Eyck exclaimed. "And he thinks I played a dirty trick on him. Well, we'll clear up that misunderstanding when I've caught him."

Then he frowned and stared moodily into the flickering flames of the fire.

He shivered slightly. He felt that he had been suddenly endowed with second sight and saw, mirrored in the flames, the long, perilous trek before him. He sensed that he would experience all the dangers of the veld—hunger, thirst, savage beasts and savage men. Yet he would not swerve from the task he had set himself; he would not turn from the spoor of his quarry.

Gradually, a feeling of resentment crept into his reveries; a feeling of hatred toward the man he had vowed to capture. His earlier sporting attitude vanished and he cursed the Major and his will-o'-the-wisp-like wanderings.

A loud hiss, the pungent smell of steam commingling with wood smoke, recalled him to the present and he sprang forward to rescue the coffee pot.

As he commenced his evening meal he laughed at his glum forebodings and tried to forget his unjust annoyance toward the Major.

"This," he assured himself, "is going to be a sporting event. No hitting below the belt."

He laughed again.

He reached out for a stick to throw on the fire. Something cold, clammy, squirmed under his touch. He heard an ominous hissing noise.

He looked down and saw a fat, bloated puff adder wriggling lethargically away.

Then the bitterness welled up again and, though he endeavored to fight it down as something unclean, something entirely foreign to his makeup, it still persisted. And later, even sleep brought him no freedom from it. He lived in his dreams through days of torment; he wandered across a desolate sun scorched desert, following footprints in the shifting sand; he crossed turbulent streams; he was attacked by pigmy bushmen—their weapons poisoned arrows; he was treed by lions; he experienced fever's delirium; and always before him, sensed but never seen, was a raggedly dressed man in whose right eye gleamed a badly cracked monocle!

NORTH, SOUTH and east stretched mile after weary mile of dazzlingly white sand, barren, waterless. To the west, sparkling in the sunlight, the Atlantic heaved monotonously and seemed to convey some portion of its movement to the land.

A few birds circled listlessly overhead; here and there, the sand bore the footprints of jackals and brown hyenas which lived solely on the harvest of fish which were strewn on the beach, left there by each receding tide.

Two men moved slowly over the waste, heading for the sea.

They waded through the loose, ankle deep sand, climbing up over steep sided sand dunes, walking with a queer shuffling gait, the gait of *zand trappers,* of men who were experienced desert travelers.

Both men carried small packs on their backs, both seemed at the end of their resources.

"I can go very little further, Baas," said Jim, the Hottentot. "My strength has almost gone from me."

His face was drawn and haggard looking. The blackness of his skin was veiled by a thick coating of dust. The Major looked at him anxiously.

"Only a little further, Jim," he croaked encouragingly. "It cannot be much further. Look! There is the island." He pointed seaward where a small, rocky island was visible. It was swarming with seals and penguins. "Soon we will come to the hut we were told of."

"Maybe, Baas. But I can see nothing but sand. I can smell nothing else nor taste anything. *Au-a!* This is a fool game we have played—running, when there is no need to run, from one white man. *Au-a.* A foolish game."

THEY WERE silent a little while, the only sounds the pounding of waves on the shore, a barking and quacking from the island and the crunch of their feet in the loose sand.

"A fool's game, Jim," the Major agreed presently, "but there is much merit in it. Unarmed, provisionless, we set out on this quest. Like cattle, we fed off the country—"

"And what feeding," Jim groaningly interrupted. "There is a great emptiness between my backbone and my ribs. And I am thirsty, Baas." He looked longingly at the sea. "If it were only permitted to drink."

"That way, madness waits, Jim."

Again they were silent, moving like shadows over the sand's whiteness.

Jim stumbled and slipped to the ground, sighing deeply. The Major bent anxiously over him.

"Come, Jim," he said sternly. "This is not a man's way—to give up—"

"As well here and now, Baas, as to climb up and down sand hills until death trips me."

The Major sat down beside him. "We will rest awhile, Jim," he said.

"And then what, Baas?"

"Go on, of course. Maybe the hut the Boer hunter told us of is just beyond this dune."

Jim grimaced.

"You have said that, Baas, many times since yesterday's sunrise." He closed his eyes, continuing dreamily: "The end does not matter, Baas. Death ends all things. Only—*Au-a*. This is no place for men to die. Hyenas will pick our bones. And men who have lived as we have lived, deserve a better fate."

"You would rather a lion picked your bones, Jim?" the Major bantered. "But what matter when the end is the same?"

"It is more seemly, Baas," Jim said simply.

"Let us eat, Jim. It will give you courage."

The Major opened his pack—it was little more than a blanket roll—and took from it a strip of biltong. He broke off a piece for Jim, telling him to chew it slowly.

"If I could sleep a little while, Baas," the Hottentot suggested presently. "I might find strength."

The Major glanced at the sun, it was directly overhead.

"Sleep then," he said slowly.

"And you, too, Baas?"

The Major hesitated.

"Yes. But first I will climb to the top of the dune. It is a very high one. I may see the hut from the top."

"You have said that so many times, Baas. You—"

Jim's sentence ended in a deep, resonant snore.

The Major rose to his feet and looked down at the prostrate Hottentot.

"POOR OLD Jim," he muttered. "He might have lived at his kraal like a chief, instead, he elected to follow me; and now, after these many years, I can do nothing better for him than to bring him to this waste of desolation to die. It's a poor return for years of faithful service and loyal comradeship. Oh, well. We've played the game an' life's been very full. I don't think Jim has any *real* regrets."

And as if in answer, the Hottentot murmured in his sleep.

"Golly, damme, no! If I don't see you, hullo!"

The Major chuckled softly: Jim's English was always amusing.

"That's the spirit, old lad," he murmured and climbed slowly up the side of the dune, taking great care where he

set his feet in order not to start a "slide" which might inter-
rupt the Hottentot's sleep.

To a superficial observer, the Major looked to be at the
end of his tether. His eyes were sunk deep into their sockets
and black ringed; his beard made his cheeks look gaunt and
hollow, hiding the firm lines of his chin; his clothes were
crudely mended; holes gaped in his *veld shoen*. His shoulders were stooped, his head bent forward; his movements
were almost lethargic.

But an experienced observer would have discounted
these surface indications of exhaustion and appraised the
man's enormous reserve power.

Actually the long trek he had undertaken with Jim,
the Hottentot, had been a game, a searching test of his
strength and bush lore. They had crossed the Kalahari
desert, unarmed, without equipment, save for the little they
had picked up here and there from grateful natives and big
hearted, if poverty stricken, nomadic Boer farmers.

At one time they had been so rich that they boasted
the ownership of four pack mules and a cumbersome,
muzzle loading elephant gun. But now, at the end of a
three months' trek they were as destitute as they had been
on the day they left Van Eyck's headquarters.

And Van Eyck? The knowledge that he was following
had added spice to the Major's game, had turned the labo-
rious trek into a gigantic game of hide-and-seek. Van Eyck
had made a strop for the Major's keen wits.

SOMETIMES PURSUED and pursuer
had been in sight of each other; once they had camped
on opposite sides of a river in full flood. They shouted to
each other, and, although the roar of the waters drowned
their voices, there had been no question of the meaning of

Captain Van Eyck's gestures or of the Major's. Surrender had been demanded and derisively refused.

Van Eyck had fired then and the shot had passed through the Major's helmet.

The Major and Jim had not waited for morning to resume their trek, but had left in the darkness of the night. African rivers are uncertain; they fall as suddenly as they rise. In two or three hours a raging flood becomes a thin trickle in the middle of a wide sandy bed.

But four days passed before Van Eyck was able to follow the Major's spoor again. Two weeks elapsed before he again sighted his quarry, and they were then only black specks distorted by the desert's mirage.

Afterward he had come within shooting range on several occasions and had, each time, emptied his magazine at the Major and Jim.

The Major pondered over that now as he mounted the dune.

"I wonder," he mused, as he had done many times these past weeks, "what's made the old lad so vindictive? I think he started the chase as a game. But the bush plays queer tricks with a man's mind—specially when he's alone with no one on whom to vent his spleen when it needs venting! An' maybe Van Eyck's taking this business really seriously.

"Maybe he thinks I'm really a murderer!

"Perhaps I should have told him why I could not submit to arrest. Told him that the only way I could prove my innocence was by proving a woman guilty. But no! I think not."

He was moving very cautiously now. Nearing the crest of the dune he took every care not to show himself against the sky line. In such a desolate, man-deserted spot his caution seemed a ludicrously futile precaution.

The slope of the dune was here very gentle; he crawled forward on hands and knees. When he was within a few feet of the top he lay down at full length and wriggled forward until his outstretched hands could reach the crest of the dune.

There he halted and looked back over the way he had traveled, seeing nothing but miles of glaring sand, curiously shaped dunes, salt pans which held out false hopes of water and the wide crack, snaking its way toward the sea, which centuries ago had been a mighty river.

HE LOOKED seaward. A faint cloud of smoke on the horizon, where a coaster rolled violently, seemed to add to the loneliness of the land.

"If it comes to that," the Major muttered, "we can light a beacon fire up here an' play at bein' shipwrecked mariners! There's plenty of driftwood." The beach was littered with it for miles. "And—" he looked across at the island, which seemed larger from this height and so crowded with seals and sea-fowl that they jostled each other when they moved—"a chappy might swim out there and gather eggs an' what not for food. A bally monstrously monotonous menu; but it would serve, An' it 'ud be no end of a lark playin' Robinson Crusoe. Jim would make a first class Man Friday. Oh, rather!"

He looked down to where the Hottentot sprawled, fast asleep.

"And now to view the land ahead," he continued. "An' what a gamble. What will I see? More dunes, a continuation of this bally desolation, or—"

He raised himself cautiously until his eyes were just above the level of the crest of the dune.

And then he almost gave vent to a wild shout of relief for, in plain sight, midway between this dune and the next, was the hut which the chance met Boer farmer had advised him to head for. It was, the Boer had said, a shelter hut built by sealers who kept in it a store of provisions and water.

The Boer had never seen it himself, had only heard of it, and his directions had been very vague; so vague, that the odds against the Major and Jim finding it were enormous.

But here it was. They had found it when their need was greatest. And, somewhere near to it—again this was a rumor passed on by the Boer farmer—was a pebbly cove strewn with colored stones.

The Major did not scoff at that rumor. He knew that there was generally some foundation for the wild yarns which come out of Africa. So, even if he failed to find a beach strewn with diamonds, he counted on finding a few "stones," enough, at least, to purchase a passage to Cape Town for himself and Jim on the first sealing boat which called—and enough to purchase a complete outfit, specially a monocle!

Yet he did not move, gave no audible sign of elation at finding the hut.

Instead, exhibiting the caution born of vast experience, he watched the actions of the three men who were seated under a tarpaulin sun shelter stretched from the roof of the hut to four stout posts.

They were playing cards and, although too far distant for the Major to see their facial expressions, he gathered, from their gesticulations, that the game was an amicable one.

Occasionally a murmur of voices reached him.

HE SAW one man rise to his feet and help himself to a drink from a water bag which hung on one of the posts.

Returning, he passed behind one of the others whose face was toward the Major.

Something flashed in the sunlight as the man raised his hand. It swept down in a sweeping parabola, a glistening arc of light which was extinguished as it entered the body of the unsuspecting card player.

He pitched forward on his face and was very still.

The Major's face was stern and it was with difficulty that he restrained himself from leaping to his feet and rushing down to confront the murderer. But he knew that such a course would be suicidal. He was unarmed, they could kill him as easily as they had killed the poor devil whom they had so treacherously disposed of. And he wasted no time in vain regrets. Even had he announced his presence on first sighting the men, he would have only delayed the murder; would, in all probability, he conjectured, have been murdered, too.

As it was, he was alive, and swore himself in as deputy officer of vengeance, at the same time withholding final judgment until he had seen and talked with the men. He crouched still lower and watched.

The two men had callously turned over the dead body and one was rifling the pockets whilst the other cleaned his knife in the sand.

Then they lifted the dead man and carried him to the foot of the dune opposite the one from which the Major watched, and, getting shovels from the hut, used them so cleverly that presently they started a "slide" and the body of the victim was buried many feet deep in sand, yet the appearance of the dune remained unchanged.

They returned to the hut, laughing, the Major thought, and sat down again under the sun shelter.

"Wonder what it's all about? Wish I wasn't so bally help-less. I fancy gunplay'll be absolutely necessary before this game's finished. An' I haven't a gun!"

IT WAS characteristic of the man that he refused to allow his sane judgment to be swept aside by the cold-blooded murder he had just witnessed. Neither did he comment on the strange weaving of Fate which had taken him to the top of the dune in time to see the murder. Coincidence plays a much bigger part in life than is generally supposed. Otherwise still fewer crimes would be detected, still fewer criminals punished.

Specially is that true of crimes committed in the barren, desolate corners of the world. Specially is that true of Africa.

The Major backed slowly down the dune, rejoined Jim and sat cross-legged beside the Hottentot, frowning thoughtfully. An hour, two hours passed. The sun dropped slightly but showed no lessening of its scorching power.

An errant breeze endowed the dunes with life, changing their contours. The air was filled with particles of sand.

Suddenly the wind ceased and the air precipitated its load of sand.

"Jim!" the Major said softly.

The Hottentot opened his eyes, yawned and stretched himself.

"Yah, Baas? Is it time to trek?" He looked up at the sun. *"Au-a!* And I have slept that long! What did you see from the top of the dune, Baas?"

"The hut, Jim. And three men. And I saw one of the three die."

"So, Baas?"

"Yah. He was killed by a knife thrust, Jim."

"In anger, Baas?"

The Major shook his head.

"The blow was struck from behind, Jim. The reason was hidden from me."

"Men kill that way from fear, or for a woman, or for greed, Baas."

The Major nodded.

"I think this time, Jim, it was greed. That we will find out. Come! The hut is just round this dune."

He started to move off, intending to circle the dune's base, but stopped at Jim's emphatic gesture of dissent.

"Well!" the Major questioned.

"Does the Baas want the men to know that he saw?"

"No. We have only just come to this place, Jim. We are lost—hungry—thirsty—"

"Then let us go this way, Baas. Lost men climb always to high places in order to search out the land ahead."

As he spoke Jim started to climb the dune and the Major quickly followed him.

WILD YELLS awoke Snape and Morson, replacing their pleasant day dreams of wealth easily acquired with visions of an outraged Justice.

They leaped to their feet and looked wildly about them, their hands resting on revolver butts.

For a moment they saw nothing save the welter of sand dunes, distorted by heat mirages. Then, the moment's panic of awakening leaving them, and, having focused their gaze in the direction of the shouts, they saw two tiny black figures capering wildly, waving, on the top of the mountainous dune which faced them.

Snape and Morson looked at each other inquiringly, and each saw fear mirrored in the other's eyes.

"Do you think they saw anything?" Snape asked. His voice was crisp, metallic.

"If they did-— We'll soon find out. Then we'll know how to deal with them! A slit in the throat to help 'em breath easier!" Morson's voice was like a man's well under the influence of drink. He spoke slowly; his articulation was thick and indistinct.

"It might be best to kill 'em without stopping to find out what they know, Snape said.

Morson grinned fatuously. He looked like a fat, overgrown and vicious child.

"Alright," he agreed. "I'll get my popgun. They're in good rifle range. Just the same—" his face clouded with regret—"I like working with a knife best. I can see 'em die then."

Snape looked at Morson irritably and, gripping his arm, stopped him from going into the shack for a rifle.

"You stay here," he said. "There isn't going to be any killing—yet. And not with a rifle any time. Makes too much noise."

"Nobody to hear," Morson grumbled.

Snape licked his thin lips, it was not a nervous act. Indeed there was something infinitely cruel in its suggestion and as loathsome as a snake's darting tongue.

"You never know," he said slowly, "what's the other side of a dune. Suppose them fellows—" he gestured toward the two figures silhouetted blackly against the yellow glare of sand—"have got friends hanging about! We've got to be careful. And you—" a note of passionate anger manifested itself in his voice—"you keep your mouth shut. You're too fond of talking about killing; you're too fond of killing, for that matter. It goes to your head an' makes you drunk. Do you hear?"

"I ain't deaf," Morson grumbled. "And as for the killing, I only do what you tell me."

THEY BOTH fell silent then, watching the actions of the two men who were descending the dune and whose shouts still disturbed the brooding solitude of the place.

"One's a nigger," Snape commented presently and laughed as the newcomers, in their haste to reach the hut, stumbled and, pitching forward, rolled down the lower slope of the dune.

"They're lost, that's what," continued Snape, checking Morson's guffaws. "Come on, let's go an' meet them. They'll think it funny if we don't."

IT WAS half an hour later.

The Major, sighing with satisfaction, announced that he could eat no more.

"If I only had a cigarette," he added, "everything 'ud be lovely."

Snape handed him one, watching him covertly as he lighted it and puffed contentedly.

"By Jove!" the Major drawled. "I can't begin to tell you what a bally relief it is to see you two laddies. We've been wandering for weeks, Jim and I. Half starved, most of the time, with absolutely no idea where we were. Hence my little—er—hysterical fit of weeping when we first arrived. I never expected to find a hut and white men here. I had visions of trekking along the coast until we reached Walfisch Bay. But, somehow, I don't think we would have lived to get there. We were almost at the end of our tether; specially Jim. I had to carry him part of the way today." He looked at Morson, who at that moment entered the hut. "He's all right, isn't he?"

"God, yes; he's sleeping now. But he'll have a belly ache bye an' bye. He's eaten enough for ten people."

Morson, the Major concluded, was only Snape's echo; a slow witted, unmoral man entirely under Snape's influence; ready to kill at a word. He realized that, though Morson was the actual murderer, he was no more blameworthy than the knife he had used. He, Morson, was merely an instrument in Snape's hand, just as the knife had been an instrument in Morson's hand.

So, although the Major was on guard against Morson, Snape was his chief concern. And that man's slim figure, well-shaped head and white, effeminate looking hands interested him immensely.

"Just who are you, and where do you come from? And why?" Snape asked. He was evidently puzzled by the Major. That man's poise and cultured drawl made such a striking contrast with his disreputable appearance.

"My name's Aubrey St. John Major—generally called 'the Major.' I've come out of the nowhere—the Transvaal, to be more precise—via the Kalahari. A beastly thirsty spot. Give you my word."

"And you made that trek without equipment, unarmed?"

"Oh, absolutely. When the law pursueth, a man's apt to be somewhat precipitous in his actions. Fear of a rope— er—necktie, lent wings to my feet, I assure you."

Snape thoughtfully digested this.

"So they want you for murder, eh?" he said slowly.

The Major nodded.

"Yes: But there are reasons—give you my word—"

SNAPE LAUGHED coldly. "There are always reasons. I take it you headed across country thinking you'd be safe in German territory? Is that it?"

The Major nodded.

"You won't give me up, will you?" he pleaded.

"No. Why should I? Instead, I'm willing to help you. At least I'll advise you to keep away from Walfisch Bay."

"Why?"

"Because it's British Territory, you fool. It's the one little bit of red in this German Colony."

The Major's face fell.

"Really? You mean that? But of course you do. Then what can I do? I planned to hide up there, under an alias, of course. As a matter of fact, I'd mailed—er-money to myself there. What can I do?"

"You can get to Swarkopond. There's a German settlement there."

"But my money? It's a considerable sum. It—"

Snape's eyes gleamed avariciously.

"I'll get for you, if you give me particulars, when I go into Walfisch Bay."

The Major's face beamed happily.

"That's bally decent of you. But, really! I don't like to think of you taking risks for a perfect stranger."

"Risks? What do you mean?" Snape asked sharply.

"Well—er—" the Major stammered, "we're all, as it were, tarred with the same brush, aren't we? I mean—" he floundered desperately, apparently confused by Snape's cold stare—"here you two chappies are, miles from civilization, you must be hiding from the police too."

"You're wrong," Snape rasped. "We came up here on a fool's errand, with two other men. They fooled us with a wild story of a beach pebbled with diamonds. We pooled our money and hired a sealing cutter to bring us up here. And I'll be damned glad when it comes back for us."

"Then you haven't found any diamonds?" the Major commented.

"Not a fragment of one," Snape snarled. "And it's hotter than hell here; the water tastes like bilge—it's stored in barrels which held whale oil. The flour's full of weevils, and the canned food stinks like rat poison."

THE MAJOR nodded. "I noticed all that, but I was hungry and thirsty. When do you expect the cutter to come back for you?"

"She's overdue now," Snape frowned.

"They have bad storms off this coast, I believe," the Major said. "Spring up suddenly. It 'ud be bally awkward if she foundered. What? I don't suppose you told anyone else your destination?"

"No: Course not. We didn't want a 'rush' camping on our diamond claims." He laughed harshly. "Diamonds! There's not a trace of diamonds in this God forsaken spot."

"Do you know anything about them?" the Major asked. "I mean—I've heard that inexperienced diggers chuck away valuable 'stones' an' hang on to others that weren't worth anything."

"I know all there is to know about diamonds," Snape growled. "So does Morson, here. But the other two—" he laughed. "What you say is right about them. Look what one of 'em brought in the other day. He was excited as if he'd found another 'Star of Africa!'"

As he spoke Snape placed an eight-sided crystal on the packing case.

The Major picked it up and examined it casually.

"I should have said," he remarked gaily handing the crystal back to Snape, "that it was a diamond. But, then, I know absolutely nothing about stones. They're just dirty pebbles, that's all."

Snape smiled.

"That's all this one is," he said and carelessly tossed the stone to Morson.

"He's collecting them to take home to his kids," he explained.

The Major looked idly about the hut, noting its crude furnishings and the ship-like bunks built along the sides.

He did not want to meet Snape's eyes for a moment, realizing that, for all Snape's friendliness, he, the Major, was under suspicion.

THE CRYSTAL he had been shown and which Snape, who boasted of his knowledge of diamonds, pronounced to be worthless was really a flawless diamond. He wondered if Snape had accepted his profession of ignorance!

Snape's next words reassured him.

"Can your nigger cook?"

"He can make a ten-year-old goat taste like Spring lamb," the Major replied reassuringly.

"Then he can earn his keep that way. An' yours too. When the cutter comes, we'll see if we can't arrange to take you as far as Swarkobond."

"That's bally decent of you," the Major gushed.

Snape waved his hands.

"White men must stick together. I don't know who you killed or why. Probably you were justified. But I'm forgetting all about it. Wish you hadn't told me. I'm going to treat you just as I would any white man who got lost like you were. I'm no police officer and as long as you act square with me, why the rest doesn't matter."

"That's bally decent of you," the Major said again. "Now if you can only lend me a razor an' what not, I'll be as happy as a sand lark. I don't suppose," he added wistfully, "that you have a change of—er—raiment, and a monocle."

Morson laughed derisively.

"A blooming dude—that's what he is. A monocle he wants. Sweet mamma's pet!"

"Shut up, Morson," Snape growled. And to the Major, "I reckon we can fix you up somehow. Bland—he's a six-footer like you—brought along a uniform case packed with duds. Help yourself. I don't think he'll object."

Snape scowled at Morson, silencing that man's inane tittering.

"Where is he?" the Major questioned. "I—er—don't like taking a man's clothes without permission. If you know what I mean."

"He won't object. Take my word for it." Snape said. "God knows where he is, went off at sun-up this morning. Said he was going to explore along the coast. It's a wonder you didn't run into him." He eyed the Major sharply. "You didn't, did you?"

"Oh, dear me no. I should have told you, of course. Besides—"

Snape grunted.

"It's easy to miss a man, at that," he said. "You pass one side of the dune and him the other. And there you are. Oh well! They'll both be back tonight or tomorrow. Bland and Graves—that's the other partner."

"Did they go together?"

"No, Bland went north, and Graves south. The fools. They still think there's diamonds about somewhere."

"Maybe there are," the Major exclaimed enthusiastically. "You'll let me help you search, won't you? Or, perhaps, you'd rather I didn't—er—butt in."

"Look all you want," Snape said dryly. "Only, what you find, if you find any, belongs to me. That's fair enough."

"Oh quite," the Major agreed.

IT WAS a new Major who greeted the morrow's sunrise. A Major rejuvenated by a vigorous swim amongst the rollers which pounded on the sandy beach. A clean shaven Major dressed in close fitting white ducks. Snape had been astounded that Bland's clothing proved a little too tight for the Major.

He looked the perfect nincompoop, his cracked monocle intensifying the vacuous facial expression he affected to mask the activities of his brain.

He was seated now on the sand, his back against a rock, watching Jim. The Hottentot was catching crabs in a shallow pool.

Morson and Snape were also on the beach, further from the sea. They were crawling along the sand, turning it over with knives.

"My word!" the Major exclaimed softly. "They look like a couple of water bugs. And of course they're looking for diamonds." He laughed. "Such an asinine tale they told me. Looking for *band-toms* for Morson to take home to his—er—kids! It is to laugh!" "Band-toms" was the miners' name for banded ironstone. "Oh well! I'm quite content that they should continue to think me a fool. Oh, rather. Really, it's a beastly ticklish situation and I don't enjoy consorting with murderers. Not at all What a beastly nightmare that laddie

Morson had last night! I'm no end glad I had decided to move my blankets outside. No fun in sharing a hut with a man who strops a knife in his sleep—if he was asleep! Eh what, Jim?"

The Hottentot looked up with a grin at the sound of his name.

"Golly damme yes, no, Baas!" he exclaimed breathlessly.

"Jim," the Major continued in the vernacular. "What do you think of those two?" He nodded toward Snape and Morson.

"They are both evil, Baas. But the little man is the worst. He feeds the evil that is in the other one. And yet—" Jim hesitated.

"And yet, Jim?" the Major prompted.

"I think, Baas, the little man is now afraid of the evil he created in the big one."

"EXACTLY, JIM," the Major ejaculated in English. Continuing: "And that explains a lot of things. It, as it were, makes the dark light.

"Now let me see.

"Of course I can't be quite sure of things until I've seen and sized up the other partner, Graves. But this, I imagine, is the way of things: The four pooled their money, as Snape said, and they came here looking for a beach covered with diamonds. Until yesterday morning they had no luck. Snape and Morson gave up searching, but the other two laddies determined to keep looking until the cutter returned.

"They went off yesterday morning—one going north, the other south. And I'm willing to bet my—er—borrowed sun helmet that Bland stumbled upon some diamonds almost directly an' he went back to the hut to tell Snape and

Morson, his partners. As soon as he'd told them everything they killed him. Snape doesn't mean to share the discovery with anyone. He's greedy. Wants it all to himself. Then he gets somewhat frightened, I think, of Morson, an' when we arrive on the scene, having seen or heard nothing as he thinks, he's quite content to let us live as a protection against Morson.

"A bally peculiar situation, if you ask me. Oh, very!

"I wonder what will happen when Mr. Graves appears on the scene. Will they tell him they've found the diamonds, or what? I think not. Neither do I think they're seriously searching for diamonds now. That's an empty gesture.

"Now where are they going?"

The two men, having reached the comparative shelter of a ridge of rocks had risen to their feet and were hastening along the beach to the north.

"Something tells me," the Major observed, "that they don't wish to be seen."

He rose languidly to his feet.

"Where do you go, Baas?"

"To follow those two, Jim. You will stay here."

"The Baas will be careful?" Jim pleaded. "They have guns, you are empty handed. Take care, Baas."

"Great care, Jim," the Major answered with a smile. "It might be well," he added, "for you to search the hut. Maybe you will find there a gun I can use."

"I have already looked, Baas. There is nothing save this." Jim exhibited a blunted carving knife.

"And that I cannot use, Jim. So I will be very careful."

He smiled reassuringly, his teeth flashing white in contrast to the deep tan of his cheeks, and moved off in the direction taken by the two men.

HIS STRIDE was easy, effortless. The way in which he leaped over pools, or clambered over jagged rocks, the perfection of his balance, denoted an athlete in the pink of condition. The way in which he utilized every scrap of cover, was a masterpiece of the art of tracking.

Rounding at length, a small jagged promontory he came to a halt behind a gigantic boulder.

Just beyond, the two men were down on hands and knees again, turning over the shallow layer of sand which covered the rocky ridge paralleling the shore line. Occasionally they pocketed something disclosed by their search; at such times they uttered grunts of satisfaction and were spurred to faster work.

The Major smiled knowingly. He had seen men in the feverish grip of diamond hunting many times.

And then, save that he noted subconsciously that neither man would permit the other to get behind him, he ignored the men and scrutinized the wide spread of beach.

The gravelly sand all about him was thick with diamond indications—agates, jasper, chalcedony and banded ironstone. He recalled the reports he had heard of diamonds being found in the Luderitzbucht sands, many miles to the south.

There the pebbles, smaller than those of the Vaal River Diggings, had been graded by the action of wind and water. So well graded, in fact, that acres of loose deposit looked as if they had been handworked by sieves. At the Vaal River Diggings, or at Kimberley, big and little stones are found together.

"Bally interesting," the Major murmured, "and, I think, proves a theory I've always held since hearing about the diamonds at Luderitzbucht. Now those diamonds must have come from the sea. Perhaps from a rich pipe somewhere at the bottom of the jolly old ocean, or from a big deposit washed down by the Vaal and Orange rivers during the course of ages. And they have been washed ashore by the prevailing northern currents, all properly graded.

"The smaller ones would beach first, at Luderitzbucht, say—and the bigger ones further north.

"Well, here we are! Undoubtedly that poor laddie, Bland, stumbled on a rich deposit—that stone Snape showed me was all of forty carats—and—"

He rose slowly to his feet, staring at a grotesque shadow which had suddenly appeared on the surface of the rock before him.

HE TURNED to face a gigantic, redheaded, redbearded fellow, who demanded roughly, "Just what's your little game? And before you reply—just look at this little truth seeker." He ponderously drew a revolver and levelled it at the Major's head.

"The beach is free, dear old carrots," the Major replied easily. "I was admiring the beautiful view and—er—the interesting antics of those two laddies yonder."

"You mean you were spying on my pals," Red Head growled.

"Oh!" The Major regarded him dubiously. "They're your pals, are they? Well, in that case, please don't show yourself, dear and honored, sir—let us sit down on the sand and have a quiet little chat. There's much you ought to know."

"My God, there is!" the other said. "You come with me."

He grabbed hold of the Major's arm and dragged him forward.

"Hi! Snape! Morson!" He shouted.

The other two sprang to their feet, guiltily. They came at a run toward the Major and his captor.

"If you'd only listen to me, dear sir," the Major began.

"Shut up!" Graves said with a curse.

The other two came to a panting halt.

"Glad you're back, Red," Snape said. "Any luck."

"No. Same old stuff. Plenty of 'indications,' but that's all. How about you?"

"Just the same. Morson's collected about a ton of *band-toms*. God! I'm sick of this place. Wish the cutter'ud come to take us off. Water's getting low an' the grub's rotten. Hell! When I think of the money I've lost on this venture—" He broke off suddenly, staring at the Major. "Say—who's your friend?"

"No friend of mine. Found him hiding behind the rock there watching you and Morson."

Snape's eyes narrowed.

"He needn't have hidden. We've got nothing to hide."

"Then you don't know him?"

Snape laughed.

"God, no. Never seen him before in my life. Where do you come from, and why?"

"Oh, I say," the Major protested feebly.

"Shut up!" Red growled, twisting the Major's arm. As that man subsided he continued, addressing Snape: "Hasn't Bland come back yet?"

Snape shook his head.

"No: We've been worrying about him. He took no grub and no water, as you know. Said he was only going to be gone a few hours."

The redheaded giant nodded.

"You didn't see him, did you?" He shook the Major.

"My word—no! Of course not."

"Then will you explain why you're wearing his clothes and his helmet?"

THE MAJOR looked keenly at Snape. He understood now why that man had appeared so friendly; why he had insisted on him wearing the murdered man's clothes and helmet.

This big redheaded man was evidently quick tempered, quick to jump to conclusions. It would be easy to persuade such a man that the Major had met Bland and murdered him.

Yes. Snape was clever. Once get it into Graves's head that the Major had murdered Bland, then he, Snape would be free from suspicion; would be asked no awkward questions. But Snape did not know that the Major had witnessed the murder and knew where the body was hidden.

That was the Major's ace in the hole, if he could live to use it. He had to concentrate now on *living;* therefore, this was not the time to tell what he knew. To speak of that now would sign his death warrant and Graves's.

So he exclaimed indignantly; "Why, Snape! Why do you lie like that? Tell the truth. Tell this big fellow how I came to the hut yesterday with my native servant. Lost, hungry and thirsty. And you gave me these clothes to wear in place of my own—"

He paused,unable to proceed in face of the mocking laughter of Snape and Morson.

"That's a hell of a yarn," Graves commented caustically. His hold tightened on the Major's arm. "What do you say, Snape! And you, Morson!"

"Never seen him before," Morson mumbled.

"What a question," Snape said. "What reason would we have for acting the way he said. It's my belief he murdered

Bland an' if you hadn't come on him unawares it's my belief he'd have murdered us too."

"It would have been so easy," the Major drawled sarcastically. "You see I am unarmed."

"That's true," Graves muttered dubiously. "I don't understand—"

"There's nothing to understand, Red," Snape said swiftly. "Bland was going to be here last night before sundown. He didn't come. He's not here yet. But here's this stranger. You caught him hiding behind a rock, watching us, God knows why. He's wearing Bland's helmet, clothes an'—by God! He's wearing the very *veld schoen* Bland wore yesterday morning when he left. I'd swear to that patch anywhere.

"That's conclusive enough anyway."

"Damned conclusive," Red Graves agreed.

"Let me get at the bloody murderer," Morson shouted, hopping around like an overgrown toad, flourishing his knife.

"Put a bullet through his brain," Snape urged, adding, "But no, that's too easy. Let's take him to Walfisch Bay and see that he's tried and gets his neck stretched."

SNAPE WAS wise. He knew that one murder does not, in the eye of the law, justify another. If they shot the Major there'd always be a danger of the case being reopened by some strange quirk of Fate. Chance might uncover the body of their victim and be the signal for a series of investigations which might have a nasty termination. But let the Major be tried, found guilty and hanged— then, if the body were found by some chance, the finder would say, "Ah! This must be the poor devil that Major chap killed," and the affair would end there.

"I reckon you're right," Graves said slowly. "If we kill him, somebody'ud be sure to say we killed poor old Bland too."

And the Major, realizing that his only hope for the present was to keep his mouth shut, did exactly that.

"Just the same," Graves continued, thoughtfully scratching his head. "I'd like to know what was the motive back of it. Why did this man kill Bland who was one of the best fellows that ever lived."

"That's easy," Snape said quickly. "Suppose Bland had found the diamonds we're looking for. There's your motive."

Graves nodded.

"Something in that." He yanked at the Major. "How about it?" he growled. "Where'd you see Bland? Why did you kill him?"

"I didn't kill him," the Major drawled. "An' it's silly you going off half-cocked like this."

"Aw, shut up!" Graves's fist crashed against the Major's jaw, rocking him. "You'll tell the truth or I'll beat hell out of you."

Again his fist swung, but this time the Major dodged and falling into a clinch smothered other blows.

Graves roaring with delight at the prospect of a fight, tossed his revolver to Snape and tried to break loose from the Major's desperate clinging grip.

And so loudly did he roar that he could not assimilate the information the Major was whispering in his ear. But presently a message penetrated into his brain. Relaxing his hold he stepped back and looking dubiously at the Major said, "What's that you was whispering?"

But the Major, conscious that the suspicions of Snape had been aroused and that that man had him covered, said vindictively, "Fight—you big lummox! Don't talk."

He punctuated his sentence with an upper cut which just missed Graves's chin.

The fight was on again; a battle of giants. But this was no slugging, wild swinging fight between two heavy weight novices, but a cold, calculating battle between two men who knew how and when to hit and who also knew how to avoid knock out blows.

THEIR FOOT work would have done credit to lightweights and yet they were economical in their movements, merely rolling their heads to a blow, when that was sufficient, rather than side stepping or leaping back. So that, although they had acres of firm, yellow sands for a battle ground, their movements were as confined as if they were pent in by ropes of a twenty foot ring.

The Major did all the attacking, endeavoring to go past Graves's guard and fall into another clinch. That, he thought, was the only way he could give the big redhead the information about Bland's murder. And that he found difficult to do.

Graves refused to clinch and stopped the Major's rushes with straight arm jabs: Jabs which hurt and bruised; jabs which closed up an eye and made the blood run freely.

They fought in silence; their condition so excellent that their breathing was scarcely above normal.

As he circled round, the Major saw Snape and Morson whispering together. He frowned thoughtfully, and, because his attention was distracted, ran into an uppercut which sent him down almost at the feet of the two men.

He rose swiftly, thrusting aside Morson who had bent over him, shaking his head.

For a moment he was forced to exhibit all his ability to avoid the punishment Graves seemed bent on giving him.

Gradually the effects of the blow wore off and he swiftly decided on a course of action which, he hoped, would check-mate the schemes of the two crooks.

When he had gone down Morson had bent over him and offered him a knife. The implication was obvious. They wanted him to kill Graves. And now, that plan of theirs having failed, Morson was moving to Graves's rear, a naked knife in his hand.

He was, the Major realized in a flash, going to stab Graves. It would be easy then to fasten that crime as well as the other—on the Major.

He retreated swiftly, head bent and guarded by upraised hands. Graves followed him, pressing him hard, getting in blow after blow.

Desperately the Major dodged to the right and left, hoping that Graves would see Morson and guess his intentions. But all to no purpose: Graves was, for the moment, a fighting machine, blind to everything but the task before him.

REELING LIKE a beaten man, the Major turned as if intending to run from the devastating shower of blows. He was facing the sneering, white-faced Snape now who, revolver held in relaxed grip, was watching the efforts of Morson to get within striking distance.

The Major rushed by him, snatched the revolver from his grip and pivoting swiftly, shouted, "Hands up!"

He saw Morson obey, stopping dead in his tracks, the knife dropping from his puffy hands, Snape, too, raised his hands above his head. But Graves rushed forward, cursing loudly, not one bit intimidated by the threat of the revolver in the Major's hand.

A rifle shot sounded.

The Major felt a hot burning pain in his shoulder. He jerked forward and his unguarded jaw stopped the full force of Graves's murderous upper cut.

He went down like a pole-axed bullock.

THE MAJOR returned slowly to consciousness, fighting his way desperately through horrible nightmarish fantasies, blinded by blood-flecked whirling shapes, deafened by a loud confused din like the breaking of heavy surf upon a rock girt shore.

He talked wildly and lived in those few minutes between unconsciousness and complete lucidity all that he had experienced during the past few weeks.

Then suddenly, the noises ceased, the visions vanished and he sat up, groaning at the pain of his head and the dull ache of his shoulder.

He was in one of the bunks in the hut. The smell of seal blubber and the fumes of the smoking oil lamp almost sickened him. Sitting beside him was Captain Van Eyck, looking haggard and completely worn out.

"Bally glad to see you, old horse," the Major drawled. "Congratulate you on your pertinacity an' all that. Quite the bulldog breed, eh, what? Get your man—even if you have to shoot him. But it was a rotten shot."

Van Eyck scowled.

"You'd be dead now, only Jim spoiled my aim."

"Oh! And where is Jim?"

"Handcuffed and gagged. He was violent and—"

"Ah!" the Major interrupted. "That's a pity. Did you give him a chance to talk before you gagged him?"

"No: Why should I?"

The Major sighed.

"You are such an impetuous laddie. And I'm disappointed in you, really I am."

Van Eyck flushed.

"You're thinking I didn't keep my word—that I took your trail before the twenty-four hours was up. Is that it?"

"Somewhat."

"Well, read this." Van Eyck handed him the letter he had written and entrusted to the native policeman to give the Major. The latter read it then chuckled softly.

"Oh, I say!" he murmured, "that puts the laugh on me and I owe you no end of apologies for the way I've been thinking of you. Just the same, I can't understand why you should turn so bally vindictive."

"I don't quite understand that myself, Major. Only—I was damned lonely. I've been through hell keeping to your trail."

The Major nodded thoughtfully.

"I think I understand. Every time something went wrong, even if a mosquito bit you, you thought that, but for me, you'd be living comfortably at your headquarters. And so, gradually, you got to the point when you blamed me for everything And that warped your judgment. That's it, isn't it?"

"Something like," Van Eyck said solemnly.

"JUST THE same," the Major continued, "it looks as if you'd exceeded your duty, old chap. This is German territory, you know. Officially you're of absolutely no importance."

"You'll find being in German territory won't help you, Major."

"You mean you have an extradition warrant?" the Major asked anxiously.

"This," Van Eyck said, patting his revolver, "is all the extradition warrant necessary."

The Major sighed. "You're not going to drag me back the way we came, old dear."

"No. No need to. I'm going to hand you over to the German authorities."

"But why?"

"Because," Van Eyck said heavily, "though I'm willing to believe you're not guilty of that other affair, there's all the proof in the world that you killed this poor devil of a prospector, Bland."

"My word!" the Major exclaimed softly. "I'd almost forgotten that. But do you really think so?"

"The evidence is conclusive."

"Damn the evidence. Do you really think I'm guilty of a cold-blooded, motiveless murder?"

"No," Van Eyck said reluctantly, "I don't. But the evidence—"

"Snape's word and Morson's word, against mine. That's all. Where are those chappies now?"

"Down on the beach; they've been collecting *band-toms* all day. And tonight they took some grub down there. Said they couldn't stomach eating anything near Bland's murderer."

"Ah! Squeamish laddies, aren't they? And Graves? Where's he?"

"Top of the big dune. He collected a pile of wood up there for a signal fire. Grub and water's running short and if the cutter doesn't come tomorrow—it's a week overdue, they say—we're in a hell of a mess."

The Major nodded, then said gravely, "Van Eyck, I want to tell you something important—"

"Wait a minute," Van Eyck interrupted hastily. "You're under arrest, and I warn you that anything you say may be used as evidence against you. Now go on."

The Major laughed softly.

"Word perfect!" he complimented. "Now listen: you've heard Snape's story, now you're going to listen to mine. Snape—" He stopped abruptly.

"Play up!" he continued hoarsely. "Play up! Only four more minutes to go!" He dropped back on the hard pillow, picking feverishly at the blanket, his eyes fixed on the roof of the hut. He raved like a man in delirium. The door opened suddenly, admitting Snape and Morson.

Morson laughed. "He's seeing things. He's delirious."

"I thought I heard you and him talking." Snape said to the policeman.

"And if you did," Van Eyck snapped, resenting the man's tone, "what of it?"

"PLENTY!" SNAPE said. "If he's got his sense back and able to talk, we want to know it. We want to know where he killed poor old Bland. We want to know where the diamonds are."

Morson chuckled inanely, Van Eyck sniffed contemptuously and the Major babbled of green fields and childhood's joys.

Said Van Eyck, "As a matter of fact I was talking to him, trying to calm him. Didn't do much good thought. Listen to him! Want to try your hand as a nurse?"

Van Eyck was not quite sure what motivated his present conduct. He would have denied the suggestion that he was actuated by the Major's command to "Play the game." Yet that was exactly what he was doing.

"I'll nurse the snake!" Snape snarled. "He deserves a knife in his guts. And that's what he'd get, if I had my way. The murdering—!"

"You'll keep your hands off him," Van Eyck said sharply. "He's my prisoner, and he's going to have a square trial."

Snape shrugged his shoulders.

"Suits me. My evidence and Morson's not to mention Graves's, will be enough to hang him high. For the matter of that, you'll have to appear as a witness. You saw him holding us up."

"What I'll have to say," Van Eyck retorted dryly, "will stand cross-examination. How about you and Morson?"

"Just what do you mean by that?" Snape demanded.

"Anything, or nothing. Only it's not so easy to prove a murder in court as you might think. And this fellow has brains."

Snape laughed.

"As many as Morson here, no more."

"I don't know about Morson. But the Major's one of the cleverest men that ever came from the diamond fields."

Snape started.

"You say he's a diamond man?" he asked incredulously.

"There's nothing he doesn't know about them."

SNAPE WAS silent for a moment. Then, with an effort: "But he's a murderer. You were after him for one he did in the Transvaal, you say. Now there's this business of poor old Bland. An' clever men don't commit murder."

"Exactly!" Van Eyck's tone was very curt. "They get other men to do their dirty work for them."

"An' just what do you mean by that?"

"Nothing, Snape. Just talking. Only I don't like your attitude."

"How the hell do you get that way?" Snape said angrily. "You've got no authority here—you're in German territory. Why," he continued with a burst of indignation, "for all we know you're in cahoots with the Major chap."

"I suppose that's why I shot him through the shoulder."

"Oh, that! Maybe you meant the shot for Graves and didn't shoot again because you'd given yourself away an' didn't have any chance—one man against three. Yes! How about it? You tell a wild yarn about tracking the Major across the Kalahari. But it's my belief you and him are partners."

Van Eyck laughed.

"You'll find out who I am when we get to Walfisch Bay."

"If we ever get there," Snape said morosely. "There ain't much water left. Morson, the bloody fool, wasted more than half of it when he tipped the barrel over this morning. And I don't see why we should share our supply with a murderer and his nigger. Let's hold a camp court, try 'em and shoot 'em. That's only fair."

"Fair as hell," Morson echoed.

"Just about!" agreed Van Eyck laconically.

They were silent then, watching each other furtively.

The Major's babblings grew louder and, if possible, more incoherent.

Something of the blackness of the night invaded the hut, enveloping the yellow flame of the stinking lamp.

Unclean insects manifested themselves; flying horrors pinged and bumped clumsily about the hut. Moths clouded about the lamp glass. Occasionally, as one fell into the flames, the hut was filled with the acrid, pungent odor of its burning.

The sky seen through the cracks in the wall of the hut, glared redly. Graves's beacon fire was well alight.

The heat was stifling.

"Open the door," Van Eyck said.

MORSON OBEYED. He and Snape sat down in the opening. But save that the air was cleaner, sweeter, the open door brought them no relief for the light breeze which blew was desert born and carried into the narrow confines of the hut the desert's furnace heat.

The men sweated profusely and although their bodies relaxed their eyes kept vigil. The atmosphere of mutual distrust created that feeling of stillness which is not peace but like to the high tension which precedes an electrical storm.

Monotonously the Major raved on. His voice seemed, at last, to act as a soporific. Morson slept, mouth agape, snoring loudly. Snape's eyes lost somewhat of their glitter. His head dropped on his chest, his eyes closed.

But only for a moment.

Almost instantly he opened them again and was in that artificial state of wakefulness which one experiences when awakening from a forbidden nap, when the mind seems unusually alert but is really slow and lethargic. He kicked Morson, rousing that man to a state of protesting wakefulness.

Minutes lengthened into an hour.

Van Eyck felt drowsy, but his uncomfortable posture helped him to avert sleep and the hand holding the revolver never relaxed. He sensed that Snape's thoughts were murderous ones; that, should he, Van Eyck, relax his watch and sleep, he would awake to find that death had visited his prisoner. For the matter of that, if he slept, he might himself never wake again.

He smiled grimly at that. He wondered if he would be justified in taking the offensive. Decided against it. Apart from the fact that he was one against two, he was inclined to sympathize with their attitude, The Major had killed their partner. But had he?

He had almost forgotten the Major's return to consciousness—so clever was that man's affectation of delirium—and started when, presently, the Major's groping hand reached out and came to a rest on his knee, the long fingers beating a slow tattoo.

He concentrated on the rhythm. The Major was trying to convey a message to him. He turned and looked at the Major.

"Morse!" the word was formed by the Major's lips in an interval between incoherent ravings.

Van Eyck shook his head slowly and whistled tunelessly, relaxing at the look of warning which came into the Major's eyes.

Snape moved away from the door. He was sitting now where the shadows were darkest. The Major's ravings recommenced.

Then again the beating of fingers on Van Eyck's knee. Again he bent over the Major and saw the lips form the words very slowly: "Snape and Morson killed Bland. Body buried in dune—"

"What the hell are you two whispering about?" Snape yelled, crouching in the corner of the hut, revolver in hand.

He laughed as the Major resumed his babblings; sneered at Van Eyck's lame denial.

MORSON JOINED Snape, and the two menaced the policeman with their guns. Van Eyck had been too intently watching the Major's lips and was taken off his guard. He rose slowly to his feet, his hands hanging loosely by his side, his revolver held in a listless grip.

"Carve the fool's liver out, Morson," Snape snarled, and Morson, chuckling ghoulishly, crept stealthily forward.

Van Eyck became galvanized into action.

"Hands up, both of you," he yelled, firing swiftly at the yellow spurt of flame which came from the corner where Snape crouched.

Both men's shot missed and before they could fire again the Major had leaped from the bunk, and, grappling with Morson, fell to the ground with him, rolling over and over.

They barged into the table, upsetting it. The lamp crashed to the floor and went out. The hut was plunged into a darkness with sneeze provoking powder fumes as revolvers spat yellow flames. And in that darkness four men struggled desperately.

Then, suddenly, the door banged violently and only two men were left in the darkness, breathing heavily; one groaning with pain.

"They've got me," Van Eyck gasped. "You all right, Major?"

"Yes." He struck a match, shielding its flame between cupped fingers, and crawled over to where Van Eyck sprawled. The match went out before he reached him and he went forward in the darkness.

"Morson struck me with his knife—between the ribs," Van Eyck said.

The Major felt for the wound with his long, capable fingers and located it without difficulty: In the darkness it seemed a mere trifle: Just an inch long indentation in the skin. Hardly any blood flowed from it.

The Major whistled softly. The wound might prove very slight or, supposing Van Eyck was bleeding internally, very serious.

And there was nothing he could do!

"Why don't you light the lamp?" Van Eyck asked.

"Not safe," the Major replied. "They may be waiting for us to do that; we'd be easy targets then."

HE STOOPED over Van Eyck and lifting him up and, wincing at the pain of his own wounded shoulder, put him in one of the bunks, making him as comfortable as possible.

"I'm going to free Jim," he said. "Where is he?"

"In the lean-to, back of the hut."

The Major moved cautiously to the door, opened it and crawled outside on hands and knees.

He heard nothing, save the roar of the surf, and the soft soughing of the wind.

On the high dune the beacon fire was blazing fiercely; sparks flew upward, losing their identity with the myriads of stars which made the sky glow phosphorescently, Anxiously, vowing a frightful vengeance on Snape and Morson should he find that they had harmed Jim, he rose to his feet and made his way swiftly to the back of the hut.

He almost fell over a soft inert form.

"Jim!" he exclaimed fearfully. Then "Jim!" in relief as he heard gurgling sounds. He bent over, took the gag out of the Hottentot's mouth and cut the rope which bound him.

"*Au-a,* Baas!" Jim exclaimed thickly. "I have known fear. I heard shots and the noise of firing. But I was helpless. I could not come. The Baas understands?"

"Truly, Jim."

"And you are not hurt, Baas?"

"The wound in my shoulder is no more than a pin prick, Jim. But come, and softly now. Evil men walk in the darkness."

"*Wo-we,* Baas. They run, not walk. I heard them. My limbs were bound, my mouth closed, darkness covered my eyes, but my ears were open. And I heard those two men running swiftly away from the place."

"Ah!" The Major commented softly in English. "The wicked flee—and none pursue." Adding in the vernacular, "Just the same, Jim, we will take no risks."

They went back to the hut, had hardly entered it, when they heard the sound of a man running.

"It is the Red Head, Baas," Jim said quietly.

As he spoke, Graves stumbled into the hut, roaring, "What the hell's all this shooting about? Light the lamp, damn it!"

THERE WAS a scratching sound, then the tiny flicker of a match flared and invaded the darkness.

"What the hell?" Graves said again as he let the match fall from his fingers. In that brief moment of light he had seen the Major, sitting beside Van Eyck's bunk; and the Major was covering him with a revolver.

The door closed with a *bang.*

"The Hottentot closed the door," the Major's voice said. "And he is standing behind you with a long sharp knife in his hand. So sit down and we will talk."

There was a moment's silence. Then a loud grunt and a shuffling noise.

"He has obeyed, Baas," Jim said. The point of his knife was resting very gently against Graves's neck.

"What's it all about?" the big man demanded savagely. "And why are you sitting in the dark like kids playing ghosts."

"Because we are afraid that Snape and Morson might be tempted to take a pot shot at us if we lighted up. Now will you be good whilst I explain?"

"I'll listen," Graves growled. "But if I find you're making a fool of me—"

He left the threat unfinished.

The Major laughed softly.

"I'm not making a fool of you. Listen."

Very briefly he related the story of the greed inspired murder, of the diamond strewn beach, and of the fight which had been waged in the darkness of the hut.

Occasionally Van Eyck's weak voice confirmed or amplified a statement.

Graves heard the story in silence and when it was ended exclaimed wrathfully, "And we sit here, doing nothing!" He had accepted the Major's story without question.

"What can we do?" the Major asked softly. "We can't track them in the dark."

"That's true!" Graves admitted. "Poor old Bland. Best chum a man ever had. But why didn't they kill you, too, Major?"

"They would have, I think, only Snape was afraid of Morson. Morson's a little mad, you know. So Snape was glad of my company until you returned. Besides, he felt safe. He didn't know I had seen."

Graves grunted understanding.

"What do you think made him suspect you, finally?"

"Who knows. An uneasy conscience, maybe. And then Van Eyck told him I knew all about diamonds and wasn't such a soft ass as I look."

"God, no! At least I can swear you are not soft. That was a good scrap we had this morning. Hell! And you were trying to put me wise, then. I've only just tumbled to it. You were trying to tell me things when we clinched. Hell! I'm a fool, if you like."

WHEN THE first light of another day dispelled the gloom of the hut, the Major, Graves and the Hottentot crept outside.

Their faces were grave and haggard looking, for they had discovered, during the course of the night, that Snape and Morson had decamped with the little that remained of the food and water supply.

They conversed in low tones so as not to disturb Van Eyck who, after a restless night had at length fallen into an easy, health-restoring sleep.

"I'm going after them," the Major announced grimly.

"You can't; you're wounded. Besides, it's my place to go. They killed my partner."

"You don't know the desert, do you?" the Major asked sharply. "No, I thought not. So what good of you going? Jim will go with me. We'll soon catch them up. They can't have got far unless they traveled all night. And I doubt that. No, you stay here with Van Eyck. You might be able to get a little water from the night dew if you spread out a tarpaulin. And there's fish in the sea!

"Keep your beacon going. Some ship's bound to see it.

"Now listen: Bland's body is buried in that dune. The diamonds you'll find on that beach where we fought this morning. I'm trusting to you to see that Bland's relatives get their share. And Van Eyck, he's entitled to some. There's plenty."

"How about you, Major?"

"Me?" The Major waved his hand. "I'll consider," he said grimly, "that all the stones I find on Snape and Morson belong to me."

"I still think it's my place to go after them," Graves grumblingly objected.

"Oh, forget yourself," the Major replied. "Remember Van Eyck's after me for murder. I didn't commit it, and I can prove I didn't. But I don't want to go up for trial. I detest publicity, don't you know. Going after Snape and Morson gives me a chance to get out of Van Eyck's clutches. Any more objections?"

Graves's answer was an outstretched hand.

"Good luck, Major."

The two men's hands met in a strong, firm grip.

Then, "Hell!" muttered Graves self consciously.

"Toodle-oo, old fellow!" smiled the Major, and a few minutes later, with Jim, he was rapidly following the spoor of Snape and Morson.

IT WAS an easy trail to follow leading southward along the coast. Evidently the fugitives were heading for Swarkobond, the nearest German settlement; and they had made no attempt to hide their trail, sacrificing caution for speed.

Shortly before sunset they caught up with Morson. He was sprawled in an ungainly heap on the yellow sands.

The sand beneath him was discolored with his blood; his face was distorted. Morson had died hard. His hands still gripped his rifle, its butt rested against his shoulder. Several empty cartridge shells were on the ground near him. An empty shell was in the chamber.

All about were signs of a struggle. Jim picked up Morson's knife; it was blood-stained.

The Major and Jim went on, following Snape's trail.

"He was running, Baas!" Jim exclaimed once.

Four hundred yards they went and again they checked.

Here the tracks showed Snape had pitched forward on his face, scattering food stuffs from his pack. He had rolled over and over, then had for a while lain still. The sand was discolored a rusty red in the depression which told Jim that!

Then Snape had apparently recovered a little: The trail showed that he had crawled painfully forward on his belly, had then risen to hand and knees, scuffling along, finally passing behind the shelter of a pile of barnacle covered rocks.

And there they found him, sitting with his back against a rock. A bullet from Morson's rifle had brought death to him. Two food packs and water kegs were beside him and, on a dirty white handkerchief spread out on a flat topped stone, were a quantity of stones, neatly arranged according to size. One or two Jim picked up nearby. They had apparently been discarded contemptuously by Snape as of little value.

The Major pocketed the stones which were on Snape's handkerchief.

"He had been grading them, Jim," he said slowly. "The ones you have there he had discarded because they did not measure up to any true value." He sighed, adding, "The desert works that way, too, with men, Jim."

IT WAS sunrise the following day when the Major and Jim reached the crest of a dune from which they could see the sealers' hut. They had returned to share with Graves and the wounded policeman the water and food recovered from Snape.

They saw a good sized cutter anchored off-shore. On the beach a number of men—Graves and Van Eyck amongst them—crawled along on their bellies digging frantically. Occasionally merry shouts were carried by a sea breeze to the two who watched from the top of the dune.

In the level space to the right of the hut was a small mound. A crude cross stood at its head.

"Wait here, Jim," said the Major. "I'm going to the hut."

"The Baas will be careful."

"Very careful, Jim. But there is no danger. They will not see me. Their eyes are fixed downward."

Ten minutes later he had joined Jim, his water kegs filled from a supply landed by the cutter, and a package of food.

"Where now, Baas?" Jim asked.

"What matter, Jim? We have food, water, rifle, revolvers, and ammunition. We have enough stones to buy anything we may desire. So let us go north. There we should find good hunting."

Jim grinned happily. He had feared that his Baas would wish to join the diamond hunters below.

"We could find again that Boer farmer, Baas, and buy pack mules and a horse from him."

"Happy thought, Jim," the Major drawled. "So let's go."

They slid down the other side of the dune.

WHEN GRAVES, Van Eyck and the crew of the sealing cutter, now happy diamond diggers, returned to the hut for a mid-day meal and siesta, they found a note, addressed to Van Eyck, nailed to the door. It read:

"Dear old horse: Snape and Morson are dead. They killed each other. I have taken to myself their provisions and what-not as payment, as it were, for services rendered. (I buried them far better than they deserved.)

And now, with Jim, I vanish into the so-called 'Blue,' for, you understand, I cannot be tried for that bally murder.

Toodle-oo!

Wish I had a new monocle.

Yours,

The Major.

"Damn!" Van Eyck exclaimed, thinking of the account in the Cape Town paper brought by the sealers which absolutely cleared the Major of the charge of murder.

It was an account which told of the deathbed confession of a woman; she had shot a man, a blackmailer, and in order to save her from the consequences of the crime the Major had concocted evidence which made himself appear to be the guilty party. "That's just the sort of Quixotic thing he would do. And of course he couldn't go to trial. It would mean exposure of the woman.

"Well, I'm going after him to tell him there's no need to hide up any longer."

Graves nodded, spat thoughtfully and then, because the desert and sea grades men as well as diamonds, said, "You ain't fit to go alone, Captain. I'll go with you."